MEN OF INKED, BOOK FOUR

UNCOVER ME

www.chellebliss.com

CHELLE BLISS
USA TODAY BESTSELLING AUTHOR

THE MEN OF INKED SERIES

Throttle Me - Book One
Hook Me - Book Two
Resist Me - Book Three
Uncover Me - Book Four
Without Me - Book Five
Honor Me - Book Six
Worship Me - Book Seven
Inked Novellas

Published by Chelle Bliss January 12th 2015
Editors Mickey Reed & Editing 720
Proofread by Fiona Wilson
Cover Design © Okay Creations

This book is dedicated to the bloggers, readers, and my fellow indie authors. Your friendship, support, and love will never be forgotten.

It drives me forward.

CHAPTER ONE

THOMAS

CONSUMED.

When I'd joined the MC and immersed myself into "the life," everything started to spin out of control. My world had been controlled. Every decision I used to make was methodical until I entered the lifestyle.

I had a mission, a true course, and a clear goal when I became a prospect. I'd get patched in, learn the ins and outs of the Sun Devil MC, find enough proof of their illegal activity, and then bring them down.

No one thought I'd climb the ranks, becoming sergeant-at-arms and one of the deciding members of the club.

I had my hands in everything.

When did the line blur? Was there a point where I became just as guilty as those I was trying to ruin?

At what point does a good guy become one of the bad?

I felt lost.

The person keeping tabs on me was James, my handler and best friend. We'd joined the DEA years ago and quickly became friends, leaning on each other in times of need and helping each other stay focused on the future—one without the Sun Devils.

He assured me I was the same man he'd met in training, but I feared he was wrong.

Being away from my friends and family for so long had an effect on me. They were my rock, my world, until I left them all behind.

How could I lead a life filled with violence, crime, and deceit, and still be the same man?

I hadn't realized how far I'd fallen down the rabbit hole until Bike Week. Sitting around the table with the guys, drinking our beer, watching the ladies, and shootin' the shit—and then she walked in the door.

When I heard her voice, my heart skipped a beat. Looking into her eyes, I felt the weight of my actions hit me square in the chest. Seeing Izzy was like being hit by a semi at sixty miles an hour and watching it happen in slow motion.

Unable to stop the collision, I tried to contain the damage the best I could. A sledgehammer to the head would have hurt less than seeing my sister, and knowing the danger she was in.

Everything could come tumbling down like a house of cards.

She played along, pretending she didn't know who I was, and it seemed to work. No one thought anything of it. Rebel was a little too interested in her, eye-fucking her at the table, but I kept my cool and waited for the right time to get her alone.

I'd spent my teen years trying to protect my sister. Seeing men looking at her like she was a piece of ass drove me fucking insane. The jealousy and protective nature were ingrained in me—all Gallo men were born with it. From the time we were little, we protected each other and would give our lives for one another, if necessary.

My only goal when I saw her was getting her the fuck away from the MC and Rebel. Having her near fucked with my head.

It's hard to describe through words, but she made me ache for something I didn't have.

My family.

I called the one man I knew would keep my sister safe —James Caldo. He had my back, and I knew he would protect my sister with his life. When she was safely whisked away, I decided I had enough.

It was time.

No more waiting for the perfect moment.

Perfection is one of those bullshit words people use.

There would be no right time to do it.

Only the now.

The motherfuckers were going down.

3

CHAPTER
TWO

THOMAS

AFTER I PULLED into the parking lot, Izzy still on my mind, I turned off the bike and sat there for a moment.

"Yo!" Rebel yelled, pulling me from my thoughts and slamming me back into reality. "Where the fuck's the girl?"

I shook my head, clenching my fists to control my anxiety. "We were stopped and she had blow on her," I said, climbing off my bike and cracking my neck.

"What the fuck?" he asked with a clipped tone as he stood outside the clubhouse of the Vipers.

The Vipers weren't a rival, but shit had been tense for months. Rebel had been working to secure a business arrangement with them, a deal that would bring a lot of money to the club and dig his grave deeper. With the new venture, his time in the federal penitentiary would exceed more years than he had left on this Earth.

"Fuck if I know, man. Dickhead cop searched her and found it in her pocket. Carted her ass off to jail." I shrugged, praying that he would buy the line of shit.

I never thought of myself as a liar or an amazing actor. But my time with the Sun Devils had taught me that I had that ability. People bought my lies, ate it with a spoon, and didn't question me. Maybe it was my demeanor or my "who the fuck cares" attitude, but they believed the horse-shit I shoveled.

"Better her than you, brother," Rebel said, slapping me on the back as I walked by him.

I wanted to punch him in the face. Tamping down my anger, I closed and opened my fists at my sides before reaching for the door.

"Was she worth it?" he asked before I could walk inside.

"What?"

"Was her pussy as good as I imagined?" He licked his lips and stared me in the eye.

I didn't flinch, a snarl barely hidden by my words. "Shit wasn't as fuckin' great as you'd think. She's used. Worn out from too much cock. Not worth the trouble with the cops, either. That shit is for sure."

"Hmm," he said as he rubbed his chin. "Such a shame. Maybe we'll find you a little something to make up for tonight's disappointment."

"Yeah," I muttered, opening the door and leaving Rebel behind.

The party was in full swing. The people inside were from different MCs from around the country with Bike Week festivities only a few miles away. Deals were to be discussed after a couple of drinks and greetings. Business took precedence. Money was the driving force and the great equalizer, removing hatred—if only for the short term.

I stood there for a minute, taking in the scene. Club whores were everywhere. On their knees, sitting in laps, and serving drinks. Men with various patches were scattered around the clubhouse, drinking and talking. Drugs, booze, and women were the norm.

I was over it.

The life was wearing on me. I'd had enough, but this wasn't something I could just walk away from without a thought. I had put years into taking the Sun Devils down. I had to find a way to stick it out just a bit longer.

Failure was not an option.

"Hey," a voice called from across the room. The man was waving his hands, motioning for us to approach.

"Who the fuck is that?" I asked Rebel, keeping my eyes trained on the stranger.

"Vipers VP, Greaser. He's a total asshole. Don't trust a fucking thing he says," Rebel muttered quietly behind me as we walked toward Greaser.

That shit was the pot calling the kettle black. I had witnessed Rebel backstabbing more people than I could count. He was a double-talker who could look you dead in the eye, swear on the life of his kids, and break his word without giving it another thought.

Where I came from, your word meant everything. A man was only as good as it, but in this world, it didn't mean a goddamn thing.

"Hey, man," Greaser drawled as we approached. "Good to see your ugly mug again." He held out his hand, waiting for Rebel to shake it. Then Greaser turned to me, eyeing me with suspicion as he shook Rebel's hand. "Who's this?" he asked as he ended the handshake.

"This is Blue, my sergeant-at-arms."

I didn't speak as I waited for Greaser to look me up and down and form a judgment. Not being an in-your-face type of guy, I let him have his fill. I didn't give a fuck if people liked me or not. I wasn't here to make friends.

"What happened to Rabbit?" Greaser asked as he leaned back in his chair, keeping his eyes glued to me.

I didn't back down from his stare. He didn't scare me. The corner of my lip ticked, though. The look he was giving me had started to piss me off. I could only assume he'd received his nickname from his hairstyle. His hair was slicked back like a classic fifties greaser from the movies. He had become lost in the time of James Dean. In his day, he probably was handsome, but the road, as it often did, had worn on him and aged him substantially.

"Fucker got popped a while back."

"Too bad. I liked him," Greaser replied.

Rebel slapped me on the back, jarring me. "Blue here has been a major asset to the club. I trust no one more than him."

Greaser's glare didn't disappear as a small smile crept across his lips. "If Rebel vouches for you, then I know you're trustworthy."

"If you base your judgment on anything that comes out of Rebel's mouth, then clearly, your thinking isn't fucking right," I said as I slipped my hand into his and squeezed.

His body began to quake, a laugh bubbling out of him as my words sank in. "Ha!" he yelled, roughly squeezing my hand. "That shit is the truth. Rebel wouldn't know the truth if it bit him on his dick." His face softened as he laughed. "Take a seat, gentlemen," Greaser said as his grip eased.

"Is it safe to talk here?" Rebel asked as he looked

around the room. "Or should we go somewhere more private?"

Greaser waved his hand around before picking up his beer. "We're safe here. If someone is listening, it'll be hard for them to hear with all the noise."

"Gotcha. I need a fuckin' beer after this night."

"What happened?" Greaser asked, bringing the beer to his lips.

"Fuckin' fine piece of ass was right in front of me and I gave it to Blue."

Greaser shook his head. "Never give away pussy."

"She was a druggie and was arrested on the way here."

"Fuck," Greaser muttered. "No pussy is worth bringing the eyes of the law down upon the club."

"Blue was with her. They let him go, but they got her."

"What's her name?" Greaser asked.

The last thing I wanted was Greaser or anyone else looking into Izzy. My insides were twisting at the thought of them finding her.

"The pig said she had a rap sheet a mile long. She's just a junky and nothing more."

"What?" Rebel asked, staring at me.

"She's inconsequential, man. She was a lousy fuck and not worth another thought."

I'd put a bullet in anyone who could harm my sister. Maintaining my cover wasn't as important as my family.

"As long as you think there'll be no blowback."

"Fucker, the only thing she knows is the size of my dick," I replied, looking around the room. "Anyone serving drinks in this shithole?"

"Bunny!" Greaser yelled across the room as a small female jumped and turned before heading right toward us.

Her tiny feet moved quickly, her long legs almost shaking at the knees as she came to a stop in front of us, standing next to Rebel.

"Y-y-yesss," she stammered with her eyes wide and glued to Greaser.

"Beer?" he asked.

"Tequila and a beer please," I said, smiling at Bunny.

"Beer and a kiss, darlin'," Rebel teased. Then he puckered his lips as he slid his arm behind her legs.

She tried to plaster a smile on her face as she leaned over and gave him a quick peck on the lips. Before she could back away, he grabbed her face and forced his tongue in her mouth. I turned to Greaser, who was watching in amusement, laughing and slapping the table.

When Rebel released her, she turned around and started to walk away, but not before he could land a quick slap to her ass. She squeaked, picking up the pace to get out of arm's reach before another assault by Rebel.

"She's a fine specimen, Greaser," he growled as he wiped his lips.

"Yeah. She didn't look into your old ass, motherfucker," I replied as I pulled the cigarette pack from my sleeve. Once I'd grabbed a smoke, I tapped it against the box before placing it between my lips.

"With age comes experience," Rebel hissed.

"Your shit's going to fall off soon. It's overused and needs to be condemned," I teased before lighting the tip. After taking a drag, I let the smoke sit in my throat, the slow burn soothing my nerves.

I couldn't remember what it meant to relax. I knew in essence what the word described, but while I was on the job, undercover with the MC, it wasn't a verb I could identify any longer. I was constantly on edge, looking over my shoulder, and waiting for the shit to hit the proverbial fan at any moment.

I had to have aged at least twenty years since I had found my way inside the Sun Devils MC. I didn't know if I'd ever be the same.

Could I go back home and be the Thomas Gallo I had been in my youth? The carefree ball buster amongst my family? Or had I been forever altered and perpetually changed by this mission?

At times, I second-guessed my decision to join the DEA. I should've stuck it out at the tattoo shop and been happy with a life with my family.

But I craved something more.

I'd wanted the rush, and knowing that I was doing something worthy made me feel good.

Once inside, I'd gotten a reality check. No matter how many men we brought down, how many drug dealers we threw in jail, or how many MCs we were able to rip apart, there would be another one to take their place before the judge could pass sentence.

The sound of the bottle scraping against the wooden table pulled me from my thoughts as Bunny slid the beer in front of me, brushing my fingers with the backs of her knuckles. I looked up at her and smiled.

"Where the fuck did you go there?" Rebel asked as he grabbed my beer.

"Zoned out for a minute." I wished I was anywhere but here.

"Here's your shot, baby," Bunny cooed as she replaced the beer Rebel stole from me.

"Thanks, Bunny," I said as I plucked a ten-dollar bill from my pocket and placed it on her tray.

"Get lost, Bunny. We have shit to talk about," Greaser growled when she lingered for a moment, staring at me.

She scurried off into the crowd without a reply.

"Did Rebel fill you in on the details of the deal?" Greaser asked me before taking another sip of his beer.

"Yes." I brought the shot glass to my mouth and downed the cool amber liquid.

"What are your thoughts?" Greaser asked, turning the beer bottle in his hand.

"The logistics are a concern, but it's doable. Can the players be trusted?" I asked, still feeling the burn of the tequila in my belly.

Rebel had been tossing around the idea for some time, but when Greaser had said that he was all in, he'd jumped on it and run full steam ahead. Instead of controlling the drugs and guns, Rebel and Greaser had decided that the two clubs would go into money laundering. They felt that the risk was lower and the monetary gain higher. I looked at it as another thing to add to the long list of offenses I was able to track and prove when it was time to bring the club down.

"Yes," Greaser stated without going into detail.

"I'm sure we can make it successful for everyone. What's the cut?" Taking another drag of my cigarette, I stared at Greaser, waiting for his reply.

"Ten percent." He motioned with his fingers, calling over someone across the room.

"Fuckin' ay," Rebel bellowed as he slammed his beer down on the table. "We got this shit."

As he spoke, a beautiful brunette came up next to

Greaser. He wrapped his arm around her waist, stroking her exposed stomach with his thumb.

"We'll head down next week to discuss it further as long as your club is on board," Greaser said as he climbed to his feet.

"Sounds good, my old friend," Rebel replied. "I need to find some pussy. My balls are aching."

Once they'd shaken hands, Greaser wandered off with the brunette. Then Rebel sat back down, taking a gulp of his beer.

"I'm going to get some head."

"I'm going to get the fuck out of here. I've had my fill of pussy tonight," I said, finishing off my beer and sticking the pack of cigarettes back under my sleeve. Standing, I looked around the room and turned to Rebel. "Have a fun night, brother." Then I squeezed his shoulder, walked away, and headed for the door.

I stepped outside into the cool air of a March evening and peered up at the sky. I wanted to be home, back in Tampa with my family. Tomorrow would be Sunday dinner and everyone would be gathered around my parents' table.

I wanted that life back. My life.

As I climbed on my bike and headed back to the motel, I wanted to call James and see how things had gone with Izzy. I needed to know that he had been able to get as far away from here as possible and that there were no problems.

The spring air chilled my skin as I drove the back roads of Daytona toward the fleabag motel and my bed for the night. I was ready to ditch this damn town and head back to HQ.

The life might be fucked up, but I had a new normal, a new rhythm I had grown accustomed to. Any change in the routine made me antsy.

I didn't trust any of the motherfuckers in this town. Each club was out for themselves. I didn't give a fuck about their clubs or their wrongdoings. My main goal was bringing down the Sun Devils and, by association, the Vipers, and getting home in one piece.

Staying alive was the name of the game.

CHAPTER
THREE
THOMAS

WEEKS HAD PASSED SINCE DAYTONA. The time was drawing near for me to leave this town and her behind. Sitting at the back of the club, I kept my eyes fixed on Roxy. She didn't belong in a place like this. In her mid-twenties, she was stuck in a dead-end life with no escape. Her face was sad, the sparkle long evaporated from her eyes. Her long, dark auburn hair grazed her waist as she danced on stage, swaying against her skin, drawing me in, and putting me in a trance. My heart ached as I watched her.

She was beautiful—stunning, actually—but I knew she was capable of so much more. I'd spent many nights with her. When she was wrapped in my arms, lulled into tranquility, she shared her dreams with me as her eyes filled with tears. She wanted to be mine, but I couldn't do it. Asking her to be my old lady didn't feel fair. I wasn't a lifer.

She had been born into this life and given no other option. She would be a club whore or old lady and dance at the club. College was out of the picture after finishing high school. She knew her role, and like a good girl, she lived up to their expectations.

She was the one person I could be myself around. When we were tucked away in my room, tangled in my sheets, I could let my guard down, show my sweeter side. It was the only time in my miserable club existence where I felt whole. Roxy would wrap me in her goodness and make the day seem a little bit better.

Sometimes, guilt would creep in when I would think about the future—hers and mine. What would happen to her after the bust? The MC would be in chaos and I would be gone. The strippers depended on the support and protection of the MC, and the business would be in disarray. She was the type of girl who would land on her feet, but where would she even begin on that journey without the club to fall back on?

I pushed the thoughts of the future away, focusing instead on the present. Her long legs hugged the pole as "Beg for It" by Iggy Azalea blared through the sound system. I sucked on my cigarette, letting the haze of smoke cloud my view and give it a dreamlike quality.

She was of average build, not strung out and thin like most of the cokehead whores in the club—a rare good girl trapped in a life she didn't want. Her hips were lush, meeting the curve of her waist.

I had to block the voices of the men who were screaming obscene words in her direction and wanting to lay their hands on what was rightfully mine. It turned my stomach, making me feel the need to rescue her from the stage and hide her away from the world—but it wasn't my place.

She wasn't mine. No matter how badly I wanted her to be, I couldn't be a prick and ruin her life with my lies.

As her set ended, she bent down to gather the money that had been thrown on stage. Men began to whistle, hurling curse words like they were compliments as she scurried off, clutching the bills to her chest.

She knew I was here—I'd caught her eye halfway through her routine. I knew she'd be out to find me once she had a few minutes to collect herself.

Tonight, I needed her in my bed. The last couple of days had been shitty, so I needed to feel her to remind me why I was here. Feeling the good helped spur me forward and give me purpose when dealing with the bad.

I turned around, not wanting to watch the next girl on stage, concentrated on my beer, and took another drag of my cigarette. Minutes later, small fingers tangled in my hair, sending shivers down my spine.

Turning, I took in the sight of Roxy. "Hey, beautiful." I groaned, her fingers on my skin driving me close to the edge. Once I'd stubbed out my smoke, I swiveled around on the stool.

"Hey yourself, handsome. Nice to see you're back in town." She smiled, her teeth shining as the corners of her mouth almost kissed her eyes. But it quickly evaporated as she looked over my shoulder.

"What's wrong, Rox?" I gripped the back of her neck as I cupped her cheek.

She grimaced, averting her eyes from whatever had made her smile disappear. "Just a bad night, but it's better now that you're here." Slowly, her eyes rose, meeting mine as a small grin spread across her face. "I want to get lost in you. Please say I can be yours, even if only for a night." Her blinking eyes dropped to my mouth.

Digging my fingers into the nape of her neck, I brought her lips to mine. "I can make you forget." Then I nipped at her mouth, dragging my tongue along her soft flesh.

Tiny moans escaped her as she melted into me, standing between my legs as she wrapped her arms around my neck. "Blue," she whispered, with pleading eyes. "I want to run away and leave this place behind."

Releasing her lips, I searched her face, trying to read her sincerity. "Angel, what's got you so down today?"

She sighed, placing her forehead against mine.

"Tell me what happened."

"I don't want you to get mad," she whispered, closing her eyes.

"Out with it, sweetheart," I replied, grabbing her by the waist and easing her off me. "You know I always have your back."

Swallowing hard, she stared at the floor and clasped her fingers together. "Well," she started, and shook her head. "There's this one creep that comes in here. He's not with the MC, but he won't leave me alone."

I could feel my blood begin to pump faster before my heart followed suit. Through gritted teeth, I asked, "What. Did. He. Do?" I punctuated each word, trying to keep my voice low.

"He's always in here when I work. I don't know, Blue. I keep thinking I see him other places. I swear I saw him outside my apartment the other day." She slowly brought her eyes to mine.

"What else?" So help me God, I wanted to kill the motherfucker.

17

Roxy might take her clothes off, but she wasn't a bad girl. She was the sweetest person I knew.

"He's sent me flowers. They were unsigned, but I knew it was him. When I see him, I get the fucking willies." She gripped my shoulder, squeezing it tightly in her hands. "He scares me," she confessed, blowing out a quick breath.

"Do you have his name?" My breathing was harsh, as I was ready to lose my shit.

I shouldn't have been bothered with shit that happened at the club, especially to a woman associated with the MC. This wasn't my real life. It was a façade and would soon be in the past, but I couldn't be a complete prick. I liked Roxy too much to not protect her.

"What are you going to do, Blue?" Her grasp tightened on my shoulder as her eyes stared behind me.

"Is he here?" I asked, pushing her away before I climbed to my feet and looked down at her.

She nodded, her frown growing severe as she fidgeted with her fingers. "Just make him leave me alone. Don't hurt him, though."

Most women—and I use that term loosely—who worked here would want me to get rid of him, but not Roxy. I don't mean she was a pushover or a weak woman —not by any means. She was tough as nails and could handle her own in most cases. Working in a sleazy strip club made that a necessity. If you were shy or weak, it could be spotted a mile away, and everything with a dick would exploit it to their advantage.

"Roxy," I growled, peering into her eyes. "I'll do what-ever I need to if it keeps you safe." Then I placed a light kiss on her forehead, letting the small strands of red hair tickle my nose. She didn't speak as she leaned into my kiss. "Just point him out and I'll take care of him."

She pulled back, looking around me toward the bar. "He's sitting over there, staring at us. He's wearing the baseball hat."

He didn't take his eyes off us. Prick had balls, I'd give him that much.

"Go finish getting ready to leave while I *talk* with him." I winked at her. "Go." I turned her around, smacked her ass, and then watched her walk away.

After she disappeared behind the curtain, I stalked toward him.

"Listen, motherfucker," I snarled as I approached.

A small smile crept across his face as he folded his arms in front of his chest. "I'd watch how you speak to me," he warned, showing no fear.

"I don't give a rat's ass how I speak to you. You need to leave Roxy the fuck alone." I puffed out my chest, feeling territorial.

"Or what?" he asked, tilting his head.

"I'll fuckin' bury you."

"Who the fuck do you think you are?" he asked as he rose from the barstool, standing toe to toe with me.

"She's mine. You keep your eyes off her. You stay the fuck away from her. You don't look at her or breathe the same air as her. Am I fucking clear?" My arm felt like a windup toy. Some invisible force was holding it back, but if the right button were pressed, it would propel forward, breaking the cocksucker's jaw.

"I don't see your name on her." His smile turned into a cocky-ass grin, and he appeared ready to go to battle.

"Clearly you aren't from these parts and don't understand how shit works. Let me help you out," I said in a calm, even tone before my clenched fist hurled forward, slamming into his face. My knuckles stung as the sound of crunching bone filled the room. Even as the song "Crazy Bitch" by Buckcherry blared throughout the strip club, I could hear my hand connect with his jaw.

His head snapped to the side as he stumbled, but he stayed on his feet. Then he righted himself, rubbing his jaw with his fingers. "Not bad for an old bastard," he stated, spitting blood near my boots.

My fist flew through the air and collided with the other side of his face. As soon as his body jerked to the right, I smashed him with my right fist, stunning him.

As I laid into him, hurling punches one after another, landing each blow with a little more force, he laughed. *What type of crazy ass laughs as he's getting his ass kicked?*

As his body wobbled, swaying as he tried to find his footing, I yelled, "Stay the fuck away from her, or the next time, you'll be taken out in a body bag!" Crouching down, I hit him with an uppercut, watching his head snap back before his body crumpled to the floor.

He didn't move.

His laughter had disappeared, and his eyes were closed.

I'd knocked his ass out.

"Need me to take the trash out?" John, the bouncer, asked over my shoulder.

"John," I said as I faced him, trying to stop myself from flipping the fuck out on him. I needed someone to keep an eye on Roxy from here on out when I wasn't around, and I thought I could count on him. "Do not let him back in here. Ever. Got me?"

"Yeah, man. Sorry. I didn't know he was a problem."

I could see remorse in his eyes. John wasn't a good person, but he never wanted to disappoint a member of the MC, especially me.

"He's been bothering Roxy." I shook my hand, the pain from slamming it into the little prick's face over and over again finally seeped into my bones. "If he tries to come in here again, you need to let me know. Do not let him through those doors. Walk Roxy to her car each night to make sure she gets out of here safely. Understand?"

"Yeah, Blue. I got it. I'll tell the other guys," he huffed out as he grabbed the guy by the feet and began pulling him toward the door. As John dragged the motionless body, small trickles of blood dotted the floor.

I was worried about her safety. I'd have one of the prospects keep tabs on her, watching for a bit to make sure he left her alone. Everyone loved Roxy. I knew I wouldn't get any slack for looking out for her.

Roxy's mom was an old lady. She rode on the back of Tiger's bike back in the day. She'd had Roxy when she was twenty-one and didn't give a fuck about her. Tiger died before Roxy was in elementary school, when he was out on a run doing club business. The problem was that only Tiger truly cared about their daughter. I wasn't around when it happened—it had been over twenty years—but people still talked about Tiger in the clubhouse.

Roxy's mom was a real piece of work. She tried hard to find a new victim to latch on to. The only thing she cared about was status. The prize she sought was becoming an old

21

lady again, but there was a problem. Everyone knew she was a cunt. No one would claim her as his. She'd spent the last twenty years hopping from bed to bed and acting like a club whore, ignoring her daughter. She didn't have the respect of any man who called the Sun Devils MC their brothers.

Roxy had been doomed from the beginning; this had been her destiny before she'd been able to dream. Her mother was absent in her life, preferring to open her legs rather than care for her only child. For what she'd lived through, having been raised by babysitters and the men of the MC, Roxy had turned out relatively well.

I'd never look down at her for taking her clothes off for a living. Everyone had to eat and survive. She hadn't let the lifestyle become her. She owned her role, but unlike her mother, she wasn't an easy fuck. She didn't jump on any hard dick, looking for an angle.

I watched the fucker's skull hit the doorjamb as John pulled him outside, the door closing as soon as his head cleared the entrance. A small smile of satisfaction spread across my face from knowing he'd feel that shit in the morning.

"Where'd he go?"

I turned to see Roxy looking around the room, searching for her stalker. "He's been taken care of." I held my hand out to her with a lopsided grin.

Her eyes grew wide as she reached for my hand, noticing the redness and swelling. "You didn't."

"He's still breathing, Rox. Don't worry. You tell me if you see him again, okay?" After bringing her hand toward my mouth, I placed a light kiss on her wrist.

She closed her eyes and took a deep breath. "Yes." Her body swayed as I kissed her skin.

22

"Let's get the fuck out of here."

She nodded, her eyes still sealed shut, keeping her hand clasped in mine.

Usually, we went to my place, staying close enough to the club that I could be there within a few minutes, but tonight, I wanted to be alone and away from prying eyes. Being with Roxy helped me relax, and with things heating up at the club, I needed to chill the fuck out before my damn head exploded.

***

"Angel, are you okay?" I asked as she settled in my lap and I wrapped an arm around her.

While I tangled one hand in her hair, we sat on her apartment patio, listening to the sound of the bugs chirping in the distance. The peace and tranquility in the country was a juxtaposition to my daily life.

Leaning her head against my shoulder, she pulled her legs into my lap. "I think so." Her voice was quiet as she sagged into me.

"He won't bother you anymore. I'll keep someone on you for a little while to make sure he doesn't come back." I gripped her hair in my hand, forcing her eyes to meet mine.

"Thank you." A small smile spread across her lips.

"I'm sorry I haven't been around much. The club has been busy with *things*." It's hard to be with someone when you are unable to share your life entirely with her.

That was the one thing I missed the most.

I felt like no one knew me anymore.

"It's been lonely, but I kept myself busy." She stroked

my chest through my shirt, sending tiny shock waves through my system.

The warmth of her touch and the coolness of the air sent a chill through my body.

"I'm sure you do."

"What would I do without you, Blue?" Her tiny fingers traced my collarbone before making a path to my jaw, catching on each coarse hair in her wake.

Her words flooded me with guilt.

What would she do without me?

Roxy was my true north in this fucked-up life. She was the good in all the bad, fucked-up bullshit of MC life. I never spent much time thinking about what I was to her or how much I meant to her—not until recently, at least.

The days were drawing shorter; my time in this life would soon be ending. And then what? What would happen to her? My stomach twisted into knots as I took a deep breath and tried to push down the feelings of regret and responsibility from having allowed myself to get close to someone.

I'd vowed I wouldn't let anyone into my life, but my need and craving for human companionship had overshadowed the promise I'd made to my work and myself.

"You're tough, Rox. You don't need me or any man to live." I pulled her tighter against me, resting my cheek on the top of her head.

Closing my eyes, I tried to picture my life without ever seeing Roxy again. Pain bloomed across my chest, the dull ache more than I'd thought I'd ever feel for another person outside my family.

"I'm not. I like to pretend I'm one tough bitch, Blue.

It's all lies. I'm a survivor, nothing more. There's a different type of living. Before you got here, I was wandering through each day like a zombie. Going through the motions to survive. Eat, work, and sleep. But when you first touched me…I felt alive for the first time in my life." She snuggled her face into my neck, caressing my skin with her lips.

I could feel my pulse beat against her lips, keeping my voice soft as I said, "You do the same for me. You're the only good in my life." Sadness flooded me at the thought of walking away.

"I love you, Blue," she whispered so quietly that I barely heard her.

I felt dirty. *Everything is so fucked up. How did I let it get this far?*

"Rox, you know I love you too, baby. I just can't." I wanted to punch something. Curse the universe for the cruelty of the situation.

"I know," she said, her voice a little stronger as she sat up and faced me. Then she leaned her forehead against mine. "I live in the now, and right now, I'm yours and you're mine."

"I am." *Fucking shit.* I was, and I couldn't deny it.

The sadness became overwhelming. Wanting to drown in her, get lost in the feel of her body, I crushed my lips against hers.

Our quick breaths mingled as our mouths fused. Searching for comfort, we kissed with such fervor that my lips ached. I lifted her off my lap and carried her into the house with her legs wrapped around my waist.

The warmth of her pussy through my jeans made my already rock-hard dick throb to be inside her. Tonight, I'd take it slow. Shutting out the real world, I would let myself drown in the feel of her.

I'd allow myself to dream. Feeding myself the lie that we were back in my home, my real home, with her beneath me in my bed.

She wasn't a stripper and I wasn't a liar.

We were a couple making love, cherishing each other. The fairytale wasn't in the cards for either of us, but for right then, I'd live in the delusion I'd painted in my mind.

CHAPTER
FOUR
ANGEL

EVEN AS HE UNDRESSED ME, I could see that something inside him had shifted. Blue was always intense. Closed off like a vault, hiding his true feelings away.

He'd changed since he'd come back from Daytona. He didn't have to tell me—I could read his emotions as easy as I could read my own.

Tonight felt different. I felt his love pouring out through his kiss. I sensed him losing himself in me…in this moment and us. Rarely did I see sadness in his eyes, but tonight, it was etched across his face.

Is he in danger?

The thought of losing him, having him ripped from my life, had me in a panic.

What if he vanishes?

No one had shown me love until Blue had entered my world. I had been drawn to him; unable to stop the silent pull he had over me. I'd given in and opened my heart to him.

Tears began to sting my eyes as he removed my clothing. I blinked a couple of times, pushing my sadness away.

This isn't the end, is it?

Blue wouldn't just abandon me. He wasn't that type of guy.

Who the fuck was I kidding? I'd spent my life inside the MC. I wasn't a club whore or old lady, but I had been brought into the fold at an early age. I knew how women were treated, their value minimal at best. Blue seemed different, though, and that was the reason I had given him my body—and, ultimately, my heart.

Standing before him naked, I removed his clothing bit by bit and savored the feel of his skin, taking mental pictures of his body and locked the memories away. Even if it were the last night I'd spend with him, I'd look back on our time together with nothing but happiness.

He'd shown me that love was possible—and that I was worthy of it. I wasn't a piece of trash to be ogled by anything with a prick.

It's easy to forget your value when you're paid to take your clothes off. I'd become an object to men, and I'd started to believe it.

That was until he'd made me feel more.

I deserved a happily-ever-after. I wanted the fairytale I'd been sold as a child.

Blue carried me to the bed, gently laying me down against the mattress. Sliding his hands down my skin, he nestled between my legs, staring down at me as if soaking in the memory just as much as I was.

Crouching over me, he rubbed the tip of his cock against my wetness, sliding in easily. Air escaped me as he seated himself inside me, filling me with a delicious stretch only he could deliver. Without thinking, I wrapped my legs around his torso, drawing him deeper inside. Burrowing my face into his neck, I held tightly to him, holding my body against his.

His hands drifted down my back, leaving a trail of heat as he slipped them under my ass. Cupping my cheeks, he shifted my bottom, giving him better access. I moaned, digging my face deeper into his neck, feeling my body shake in his arms.

"Blue," I whispered against his neck, feeling his pulse beat rapidly beneath my lips.

"Roxy," he moaned, thrusting into me in a slow rhythm, stroking my depths.

I wanted to profess my love, beg him to be mine, and ask for him to never leave me, but I didn't. If he didn't say the words back, I'd be crushed.

Cradling his face in my hands, I watched him come undone. As his weight collapsed on top of me, I snaked my arms around him, feeling the heaviness against me.

He'd forever changed me. There was no looking back. Even if he walked out of my life right then, I'd have to figure out how to dust myself off and move forward without him.

It was easier said than done. I knew it even as I thought it.

We usually laughed, teased, and the conversation was easy. Tonight, however, there was a silence that was more deafening than I could bear.

Rolling onto his back, he slid his arm underneath me and pulled me to his side. I propped myself up on my elbow, resting my head in my hand, and stared down at him.

"Sleep, baby," I whispered, tickling his chest with my nails as I traced the contours of his pecs.

The sheet was draped around his waist, small peeks of hair sticking out above the white cotton. He closed his eyes, but I didn't dare. I didn't want to waste a moment of tonight sleeping. I ran my fingers over every inch of his body, memorizing every line and ridge of his torso as his breathing grew heavy and he slipped into a deep slumber.

My eyes began to burn as they filled with tears. I couldn't shake the feeling that something bad was about to happen.

Moonlight drifted through the window of my tiny bedroom, illuminating his body. His chest rose and fell with each breath, whispers escaping his lips as the minutes passed.

Planting soft kisses against his velvety skin, I let the tears fall.

I'm not this weak girl. Fucking shit.

I never let myself dream of a forever. I had known that this wasn't that when it had begun, but over time, it had grown into more than I'd ever dreamed.

He was my rock. The one person I could count on. My everything.

Laying my cheek against his chest, I listened to his heart beat in a steady rhythm. There was a comfort in the sound, listening to him breathe and knowing he was there. Closing my eyes, I allowed myself to dream of our future —a house full of blue-eyed children with their father's rugged looks and my red hair.

I wanted a family. Something I'd never had growing up. My mother had been absent most of my life. Being an only child, I knew I wanted a large family. I wouldn't do that to my children. It was either none or a house full. No in-between and no singles. I wanted bulk.

I could see it—his face lighting up as he laid eyes on our first baby, kissing my head and thanking me for bringing his son into the world. The idea was sweet, and thus...just a dream. Falling further into the fantasy, I let myself get lost in his warmth, enveloped by the only man to have ever stolen my heart.

**

The bed shifted, waking me. Throughout the night, I'd woken and checked that he was still by my side before drifting off again.

After slowly opening my eyes, I found Blue sitting on the edge of the bed, half dressed and staring at me.

"Hey, baby." I stretched, rolling to my side to face him.

"Morning, angel." Reaching out, he ran the backs of his knuckles down my arm before settling his hand against mine. "Thanks for last night."

Is he really thanking me? "What's wrong, Blue?" There was something he wasn't telling me, and it gnawed at me like a disease.

"Nothing for you to worry about." He flashed me a quick smile that didn't reach his eyes.

"Why don't you stay with me today?" I wasn't ready to let him go. Squeezing his hand, I gave him a sweet, lopsided smile, patting the empty spot next to me.

"Can't, babe. I have shit to do, but there's nowhere else I'd rather be." He leaned forward and kissed me on the lips.

"Will you come back tonight after I get off work?"

Please say yes. Please say yes.

"I'll be here if I can."

Denied. That wasn't the answer I had been hoping for. It wasn't a yes or a no—it was a way to appease me, and I knew it.

"Okay," I said as I sat up and pressed my front to his back, relishing the feel of his skin.

He gripped my hands as I squeezed him. Turning to me, he said, "Hey. Stop that."

My eyebrows shot up. "What?"

"I can see your wheels turning. I'm here, babe. I'll be back."

I sighed, peppering his shoulder with kisses. "Is this the end?" I asked against his flesh. "Just be honest with me."

He shook his head and placed a kiss on my nose. "No. I'll be back. I'm not done with you yet."

Warmth bloomed inside me and happiness filled me. Maybe I'd read the signs wrong.

"I just can't promise tonight. Shit has been getting heavy at the club. Be patient with me, Rox." He ran his nose against my hairline, taking in my smell.

Tiny goose bumps dotted my flesh and the wisps of hairs on my body rose. "I'd wait a lifetime for you, Blue." I climbed into his lap, resting my body against his.

"I'll text ya later. I'll let you know either way. Okay?"

"Yes. As long as I know you're coming back."

"Angel," he said, grabbing my chin, forcing my eyes to his. "I'll be back. I give you my word."

Nodding, I wrapped my arms around him and hugged him quickly. After releasing him, I crawled to my feet and stretched. The worry I'd felt vanished.

Looking at the clock, I noticed that we'd slept later than we normally did. "You better get your fine ass out of here before the guys wonder where you are and come looking."

He grabbed his shirt off the floor, where I'd dropped it the night before. "Eh, those assholes can wait for me," he muttered as he pulled it on, adjusted himself, and rose to his feet.

"We all wait for you, Blue." I gave him one last quick kiss on the lips before I opened my closet to slip on a robe.

"Talk later?" he asked, yanking on his boots.

"Yeah. Now go."

He nodded with a smile and headed for my bedroom door. Before he disappeared, I slapped him on the ass. His loud laughter echoed as he closed the door and walked down the hallway.

Collapsing onto the bed, I let myself finally breathe. I felt like I'd been holding the air in my lungs since we'd sat on my patio last night. Then I closed my eyes, said a little prayer, thanked God, and fell back to sleep.

***

Before I went on stage, I checked my phone, but there was still no message from Blue. I wanted nothing more than to text him, but I didn't want to be *that* girl. Being needy was outside my comfort zone, but he had my head all fucked up and twisted.

After analyzing my makeup, I plastered on a fake smile before I headed for the door. No guy wants to throw money at a stripper with a sad face. I didn't want to seduce the men, but I wanted to captivate them enough that they'd feel inclined to offer up some of their hard-earned cash.

"Hey, Foxy," I said, stepping toward the stage.

She counted her last bill and looked up with a smile. "Hey, Roxy. You're looking—"

I held up my hand. "Don't say it. I know I look like shit."

"Get it together, mama. It's a good crowd tonight. Best tips I've had in a long time."

I sighed, knowing she was right. Keeping my work and personal life separate was a must. The men came here to feel like I wanted them. They were here for a show, and come hell or high water, I'd give it to them.

"Game face." I giggled as I tried to give her a sexy I-want-to-fuck-you look.

"Close enough." She laughed as she shook her head. "Go get 'em, tiger."

"Catch ya when my set is done." I waved as she walked away and I headed toward the stage.

I stood behind the curtain, listening to my introduction. Pushing back my shoulders, I gave myself a pep talk.

I can do this shit. They are here to see me. Pretend you're giving a show only to Blue. Every man in the audience is him—no one else.

Once I heard my name, I stepped past the curtain. Then I took the stage, commanded their attention, and let myself think of only him. Clearing my mind, I gave the number my all, climbing the pole, twirling in the air, and bending myself in ways that weren't natural.

Catcalls and whistles were easy to block out over the sound of "Buttons" by The Pussycat Dolls. The three minutes and forty-six seconds seemed to pass quicker than normal as I thought about Blue. When the number ended and the men clapped, I bowed and quickly grabbed the bills scattered about the stage before heading to the dressing room.

I didn't care about counting my tips. The only thing I wanted to do was check my phone. But the screen was blank as I pressed the "on" button. Sighing to myself, I tossed the phone on my station.

"Hot date?" Foxy asked, fixing her lip gloss in the mirror.

"I was hoping for a call." I plopped my ass in the chair, kicking off my heels to rub my feet.

"They always say they'll call." She smacked her lips together and hoisted her tits higher in her red cutout bra.

"He's different."

He is, damn it. He wasn't like the other pricks and perverts sitting in the club tonight. He was a gentleman. Treating me with respect, he showed me softness and made me feel important.

I stared at myself in the mirror, trying to determine if I was full of shit.

"Don't fool yourself, babe. You'll have a lot of disappointment if you do."

"I'm aware of how most men are. He's not like that, Fox."

She walked behind me, looking at me in the mirror. "If you say so, kid." Then she squeezed my shoulder, a sad smile on her face.

"Foxy, I know how *most* men are, but Blue is different."

"Ahhh," she said as she clicked her tongue against the

roof of her mouth. "Blue." She hung on his name like she knew him intimately.

My stomach turned at the thought of him with another woman. I wasn't a fool. I knew he probably had a handful of girls he'd spent his nights with in the last month. Hell, it could be in the double digits.

He wasn't mine.

I had no claim on him.

"Have you—" I started to say before she held up her hand.

"With Blue? Never."

"But you know him?"

"Every girl does, Roxy."

"They do?" I asked, shocked by her admission. "Are people talkin' shit?"

She laughed, shaking her head. "Who's dumb enough to talk shit about Blue?"

"You tell me. You're the one who made the statement."

"Girls talk, babe. Trust me—every girl in here has tried with him."

"What?" My mouth gaped open.

"They've all hit on him. All asked to go home with him. But the answer is always the same."

"Which is?"

I mean, what the fuck? Why couldn't she just spill it? I swear she got off on driving other women crazy.

"He always tells them no." She grabbed my hair, playing with it in her hands as she kept her eyes locked on mine.

My cheeks felt flushed, heat rushing to my face. "He does?" I asked. Then I swallowed hard as relief flooded me.

"He always tells them he's not interested and that he's only here for one girl."

Closing my eyes, I tried to hide my emotion. *He turned them all down.* I wanted to collapse and cry happy tears, but I couldn't. I wouldn't let her know how much her words meant to me. Then I heard her footsteps as she moved away from my station, but I didn't dare look.

The one thing I'd learned since being here was to never show fear...or sadness. This was a cutthroat business. When one girl made huge tips, it lessened the income of the others. Some of them would use any angle possible to bring you down and end the competition—even Foxy.

"You and him a thing?" she asked as she slipped on a different pair of shoes.

"I don't know if I'd call it that."

"He fuck you?" she asked.

Opening my eyes, I turned toward her and tilted my head. I'd always felt she was the one person I could trust in this place. She was more of a girlfriend than a frenemy.

"Yes."

"Does he stay the night?"

"Sometimes."

"You fuckin' anyone else?"

"No."

"Well, I know he isn't fucking any other strippers."

"I don't know what the hell we are, Foxy. Honestly, it's complicated."

"Babe, all relationships are complicated. They're fucked up and glorious. Life without complication is boring as hell. You know when shit isn't complicated?"

Part of what she said was right. Life was fucked up. "When?"

"When you're old and pissing yourself in the nursing home. We die the same way we came into this life. Alone. That shit ain't complicated."

"Thanks for being a buzzkill. Jesus, that's some depressing shit."

"It's the truth. Enjoy whatever you and Mr. Complicated have going on. Someday, you'll wish you could have the fucked-up, complicated life to do again."

I didn't know if I wanted to laugh or cry. Time passes by in a blink of an eye, and there's nothing we can do to stop it. Someday, I would be old, Blue would be old, and this would be all in the past. The only thing I knew for sure was that I didn't want to die alone.

"Thanks for the pep talk, Foxy. Ever think of changing professions?" I asked, trying to keep the mood light.

"As what?"

"An inspirational speaker." I giggled, throwing my head back and holding my stomach.

"Oh, fuck off. I speak the truth. It isn't pretty, but I'm right."

I didn't want to sit here another moment and wonder about "what if." Instead, I grabbed my phone and typed a message to Blue.

Me: I hope to see you tonight. I'll be in my bed waiting for you, handsome.

After dimming the screen, I put the phone in my locker and readied myself for another set. The ball was in his court now.

CHAPTER
FIVE
THOMAS

JUST AS I was about to send a message to Roxy, my phone rang. It was Flash. Cocksucker Flash. He'd put my sister in danger. Even though he grew up in my hometown, I didn't think he knew me, but then again, he was a dumb motherfucker. Maybe he was too young and too focused on my sister to make the connection.

"What?" I barked, ready to head to Roxy's.

"Thomas, you have to find Izzy!" he yelled, his breath harsh as he spoke.

"What the fuck are you talking about, Flash?" If something had happened because of Flash, I'd slit his throat.

"It's Rebel. He figured out who *she* is…who *you* are! You're both in danger, man. Find her!"

It took everything in me not to drop the phone and run. "Where are you?" I walked on silent feet toward the door, checking if someone was eavesdropping. After opening the door, I looked in both directions, making sure no one was nearby.

"Other end of the clubhouse. I'll meet you out back. We need to find her, Thomas."

"On my way!" I yelled, hitting end before I grabbed my keys.

Trying to play it cool, I walked through the clubhouse, leaving word with one of the prospects that I'd be out for the night. I'd done it many times, so it wouldn't seem out of place.

My chest felt heavy as my heart beat wildly against my insides. Panic grew with each step I made toward Flash.

What if we are too late? Rebel wasn't a kind man.

He'd take no pity on my sister. He'd rape her and kill her just to get back at me.

I kicked open the back door and saw Flash pacing near his car. When he looked up at me, relief flooded his face as he realized I wasn't another member of the club.

"Ready?" His voice cracked.

"Yeah, but we're taking my car." I fished my keys out of my pocket. "Get your ass moving!" I yelled when I saw him strolling over nonchalantly as I unlocked the door.

"Thomas—" Flash started as he climbed in, sliding across the black leather before he closed the door.

"How long have you known who I was?" I gripped the steering wheel in one hand and started the car with the other, trying to control the urge to punch him in the face.

"Since the beginning," he responded, finally turning to face me.

"You're a dumb fucker. You knew who I was and yet you brought my baby sister near the club," I seethed, bile rising in my throat as I pulled out of the parking lot.

"I wasn't thinking." He looked down, fidgeting with his hands as I laid into him.

"Dumb fucking shit. I can't believe you'd do that shit."

"Listen, that shit's in the past. We need to find Izzy." He stared straight ahead, pulling his phone from his pocket.

"I could call James. Maybe he can track her." I took my phone out my jeans.

"He would know where she was." His tone was clipped and shitty.

I glared at him. "What the fuck does that mean?"

"Just call him. Or you want me to?" Flash didn't meet my gaze.

As I dialed James's number and waited for him to answer, I felt like the veins in my head were about to burst.

"What the fuck?" he hissed as the call connected.

"Where the fuck is Izzy?" I asked, breathing heavily, both pissed off and worried.

"I'm on my way to see her now. What the hell is going on, Thomas?"

"Flash just called me. He said Izzy was in danger. Somehow, Rebel found out who she was. He knows who I am too. Find her, James, and do it now!" I roared, slamming my fist against the steering wheel as I held the wheel and phone in my other hand.

"I'm pulling on her street now," he growled, the sound of his tires screeching very audible.

"I don't know who knows what at this point, brother. Find my goddamn sister."

"On it," he replied, his voice unsteady and panicked.

"Call me back. I'm headed that way with Flash in tow."

"Give me five," he responded before the call went dead.

Wait a motherfucking minute. Did he say he was on her street?

Clearly, there was something everyone had failed to mention to me. James didn't know about her disappearance, and he wasn't near the MC compound, where I'd assumed he was tonight. He had already been on his way to see my sister.

James was going to see my sister.

I'd kill Rebel and then I'd have to end James's life for having even thought about Izzy.

All hell was breaking loose. Roxy messaged me as I hung up with James, but too much shit was happening to respond. She'd have to wait. My sister was my highest priority.

The streets were barren as I drove as fast as humanly possible toward Izzy. Flash made calls, trying to find out who knew what. The information was sparse and Rebel too tight-lipped.

As I debated about whom I wanted to kill first, James or Rebel, my phone rang. When I tapped the speaker button, he spoke before I could say hello.

"She's gone," he bit out, sounding slightly winded as I heard his car start in the background.

"Gone or missing?" I asked, anger oozing from my voice.

"One shoe on the floor and her phone on the coffee table. She's missing."

"Fucking Rebel," I muttered. "Flash and I are an hour out. We need to figure this shit out and what our next move should be."

"Fuck," he hissed, the roar of his engine drowning out his voice.

"Stay the fuck there and make calls. Do not leave in case she shows up. We'll be there in sixty."

"Hurry the fuck up!" he yelled before disconnecting the call.

"Tell me everything you know, Flash, and do it now."

"I'm FBI, Thomas. I know you are undercover, and so am I. I was sent in as backup and an extra set of eyes."

"That's bullshit. The FBI doesn't feel that the DEA can do it alone. I had this shit handled. It's your fault this is all going down."

"My fault?" He slammed his fist against the dashboard.

"If you hadn't brought her to Daytona, Rebel would never have known about her and started sniffing around. It's your damn fault. If he kills my sister…I. Will. End. You."

My left leg shook as I kept my eyes focused on the road. I couldn't stand to even look at him. He was a traitor in my eyes—a disgrace to the badge.

Flash spilled his guts for the rest of the trip in between making phone calls and trying to get a beat on Rebel and Izzy. My heart never stopped pounding, picking up pace as we pulled on Izzy's street. We wasted little time at Izzy's, jumping in James's car and heading out to find her. As we barreled down the highway, James received a call with details and a location where my sister was being held.

Silence descended in the car as we drove toward the motel. Honestly, the lack of talking was out of fear. There were three men in this car that loved Izzy. We were all scared of what we'd find when we burst through the motel door.

As we pulled off the highway, I said, "This is how this

shit is going to happen. I'll get the information from the desk clerk while you and Flash make sure no one leaves."

"Okay," Flash said, pulling himself forward.

"Then, when I get the room number, you'll wait outside"—I turned to face Flash—"and James and I will go inside and deal with whatever clusterfuck we find."

"But I want to go inside, too," Flash whined.

"Man the fuck up. We need someone to keep an eye out in case others show up."

"Fine," he snapped, slapping the front seat before he slumped back.

"Fucking pussy," James mumbled, glaring at him in the rearview mirror. "Who's getting Rebel?"

"Let me deal with Rebel. You get Izzy out of there," I said, turning to look out the window.

When the car stopped, I surveyed the parking lot, surprised when it came up clean. It was a run-down, shitty-ass motel in the middle of Florida.

After smooth-talking the registration girl, I motioned toward Flash, pointing to my eyes and then around the exterior of the building. Then I lifted my chin, standing off to the side as James reared up, using his legs to kick in the door.

Before I could enter, James was through the door. As I walked in, I saw Izzy unconscious on the bed. As if in slow motion, James ran toward her and a bang echoed through the room. His body jerked to the side as he reached for her, but he stayed on task.

Without thinking, I charged Rebel as he sat in a chair with a smug look on his face. Before I could reach him, he climbed to his feet and held up the gun. Acting on instinct, I slapped the gun from his hand, and it flew across the room before falling to the floor. Out of the corner of my eye, I saw James carrying Izzy outside and to safety. Rebel and I were the only ones left.

Giving him a quick uppercut, I connected my knuckles with his jaw. The crunching of my bones against his sent pain shooting through my arm. As if on autopilot, I began to beat the living shit out of him. Rebel wiped the blood dripping down his chin, glaring at me as he knelt before me.

"You're a fucking rat, Blue. I would've never pegged you for a cop."

"Fuck you, Rebel. You deserve everything you're going to get. Before your body even begins to rot, I'll be taking the entire club down and putting an end to filth like you."

The blood was rushing through my body so fast that I could hear it as it pumped through my ears. I put the gun against Rebel's forehead, watching his eyes cross as he stared at it.

"You don't have the balls to pull that trigger," he seethed, returning his eyes to mine.

"You know nothing about me, Rebel." As I spoke, the door slammed and James walked in. "I want to know how you found out about me," I roared, my hand almost shaking as I held the gun against his head.

"Go fuck yourself," Rebel sneered, spit and blood flying from his mouth.

James stepped forward, but I put my hand up. I wanted Rebel. I wanted to be the one to put the bullet between his eyes and end any danger Izzy was in. It was the only way to ensure she'd be safe. Rebel knew information that could end her life—and mine.

I smacked Rebel with the butt of the gun. "You want to get out of this room alive? You better start talking."

"You're a traitor and a fucking rat. You might as well kill me, because I'll put your ass in the ground otherwise. I'm dead either way," Rebel bit out, wincing from the pain. "I brought you in and helped you move up the ranks. Fucking shoot me, you pussy."

"If you don't do it, Thomas, I will," James hissed, pulling his gun from his pants.

"Who. The. Fuck. Knows?" I repeated, positioning myself in front of Rebel and blocking James's view. He paced around the room, his body tense as he glared at Rebel.

"Fucking sucks not knowing something, doesn't it, *Blue*?" Rebel growled.

I pointed the gun at Rebel's shoulder and pulled the trigger.

"Fuck!" James yelled, glaring at me.

Rebel's body swayed backward before he righted himself. "First chance I get, I'm going to taste the pussy on your beautiful sister." He laughed.

Swallowing hard and gripping the gun in my palm, I fought the urge to kill him. I wanted information before I put an end to him. He was making it harder than I'd thought possible. My sister was off limits.

"I bet she tastes as fucking sweet as she looks." Rebel smiled, bringing his hand to his face and licking.

James lunged forward, pushing me out of the way as Rebel's eyes grew wide. Then he pulled the trigger and Rebel's body fell back in a heap on the shaggy green carpet. Leaning over his bloodied body, James spat in his face.

"Rot in hell, motherfucker!" he shouted, a growl coming from his mouth.

"What the fuck?" I asked, hitting his arm.

I was happy he was dead, but fuck. I'd wanted to be the one to kill him, and I'd wanted to know who else knew about Izzy. I had been all about torturing the bastard to get the information if need be. The DEA could go fuck itself when it came to my family. Above all else, my family sat at the top, my number-one priority, even above my own safety.

James looked at me and shook his head. "You two would never be safe with him around. He deserved to die. He *needed* to die."

"I didn't get the information out of him," I groaned as I sat on the bed, relaxing and letting the gun rest against my leg.

"No one knew. If they did, he would've had backup here with him. He had to know we were going to come after him."

I sighed, tossing the gun next to me on the bed. "You're right. This complicates shit with the club. Damn it."

"Only thing it does is move you up higher in the ranks, brother," James said, sitting next to me and staring at Rebel's body as the blood almost reached his boots. "What do you want to do with the body?" he asked, motioning toward the corpse.

"You take Izzy home, and Flash and I will handle it," I replied, standing and sticking the gun in my waistband. "Is she okay, James?"

"Yeah. She's just passed out. Hopefully she won't remember a damn thing."

"Fuck. No one can know about Rebel's death. Got me? No one besides the few people we called. Especially not Izzy. Do not tell her." I walked out the door, leaving James behind.

Anxiety raked my body as I walked toward the car. I needed to see Izzy with my own eyes. Flash stood outside as Izzy lay slumped over in the back. Opening the door, I could hear her small snores.

"I checked her. She's fine," James said, pushing me away and scooping her into his arms. "I'll get her home. Shh, doll. Sleep," James whispered in her ear as he held her body tight.

"Flash!" I barked, causing Flash to jump.

"What?"

"Get your ass in the room. Let's get Rebel and get the fuck out of here. James is taking Izzy home."

Flash looked at Izzy and James then nodded to me before disappearing into the room.

James laid Izzy in the front seat. "You be careful, Thomas," he said as he gently closed the car door, trying not to wake her.

I stepped closer, standing toe to toe with him. "I'll text you when it's done. Keep her safe."

"You're okay with this?"

"Fuck no. I'm still going to kick your ass when every-thing is said and done, but for now, you make sure she's okay—and clean your arm."

"I'll wait until she wakes up and then I'll head back up to make sure shit doesn't go down in the MC."

"No, you stay with her until you get the all-clear from me. Do not come back. Do you understand me?"

"I can't leave you without backup," James said, shaking his head.

"I'll be fine, James."

No one knew where we were. Those dumb fucks were too busy getting drunk and stoned, on top of drowning in pussy, to realize that Rebel and I were missing.

"I can't bear the thought of losing you, Thomas. You're like a brother to me."

"I don't have time to stand here and argue with your stubborn ass. Let me ask you this: Do you love her?" I lifted my chin, motioning toward my sister.

"Yes."

"Then keep her safe, James. I can handle the club, and Bobby will be around for help. Flash too. Now get the fuck out of here and take her home. Make sure she's sleeping."

"Not a problem," James said, smiling as he started to turn his back.

But I couldn't let him off the hook that fucking easily, so I did a total asshole move. I cold-cocked him when he wasn't looking, landing one flat against his jaw.

"What the fuck was that for?" he howled, rubbing his chin.

"Keep your dick in your pants," I replied before leaving him standing outside with a stupid-ass grin on his face.

Then I watched as Izzy and James pulled away, leaving us behind to clean up the mess.

CHAPTER
SIX

THOMAS

TELEVISION MAKES it seem easy to dispose of a body and cover up a crime, but it sure as fuck isn't. Florida does have some advantages, though: the state is riddled with alligators, vultures, and dense forests where humans rarely travel. But finding the right location and doing the task is harder than it looks. I racked my brain, trying to decide the best course of action to get rid of Rebel.

Flash and I cleaned up the motel, spending a couple of hours scrubbing the blood and shit from the carpet, to no avail. Why did the asshole have to bleed so damn much? The room was a fuckin' bloody mess.

"What the fuck are we going to do now?" Flash's voice was high-pitched as he looked around the room.

"First, calm the fuck down. Jesus. Shit like this happens." I slapped him on the back of the head as I put some bloodied towels into a garbage bag.

He reached for his phone. "I should call this in."

I knocked his hand down, making the phone fall to the floor. "Don't be a dumbass."

"What else can we do? We have to call it in and go through the proper channels." He raked his fingers through his hair, staring at the giant stain in the shag carpet.

"We're going to cut out the carpet and pay off the desk girl to keep her mouth shut."

"But that's... But..." he stuttered as he shook his head.

I kneeled down, looking him in the eyes as I tried to keep my anger in check. "Listen, Flash, and listen very carefully. This is the only way we *can* do it. I'll handle it if you're too chickenshit."

"I didn't say I was scared, Thomas. I just worry about what will happen when they find out."

"They?" I asked, cocking an eyebrow at him as I climbed to my feet.

"Yeah. You know, our real jobs. Or have you forgotten about them?" He rose to his feet, placing his hands on his hips and glaring at me.

"Motherfucker, *they* are on my mind every minute of every goddamn day. *They* will never know about this. Do you get me?"

His mouth hung open as his eyes grew wide. "But that's wrong."

"Jesus." I threw up my hands, trying to do anything but wring his neck and add him to the pile of bodies that had accumulated during my time in the Sun Devils MC. "It was self-defense, but there would be backlash. Do you want to lose your job? If they find out about Izzy and how you mixed your personal life with your undercover work, what will they say?"

His mouth snapped shut as he began to rub his face. "Fine. You're right. We all fucked up on this one."

I pulled my knife from my boot. His eyes widened as he backed up.

I swear to shit my patience for this man is hanging on by a thread. "I'm not going to kill you. This is for the carpet."

"Oh, okay." His face softened as his shoulders visibly relaxed.

What type of requirements did they have to get into the FBI? Either his IQ was off the charts but he was lacking in common sense or something wasn't right. I'd like to believe he was a clueless genius. What a goddamn oxymoron.

We didn't speak as I cut the bloodied carpet then rolled Rebel's body inside to carry it out. It basically screamed, *We're hiding a body*! But at this point, I didn't give a fuck. The motel was deserted and I just wanted to get the fuck out of there.

After cleaning the room, we carried out the evidence and wiped it down, ridding it of prints. Luckily, I found Rebel's keys on the table near the door, since we were now carless. I hadn't thought the entire plan through. We were winging it. Clueless geniuses weren't cut out for winging shit, but I, on the other hand, had grown used to it.

After tossing his body in the trunk, I headed to the reception desk to handle the front desk girl. With a smile and a couple hundred dollars, I explained how the woman inside the room had turned into a tiger in the sack, trashing the room. Sliding the bills across the desk, I asked for her discretion, and she reassured me that privacy was of great importance to her.

"In the passenger's seat. I'm driving, Flash," I said, reaching for the driver's-side door handle.

He nodded, not putting up a fight as I climbed in and turned on the engine. After he sat down, closing the door behind him, I took off, not wasting another moment.

"Where are we going?" he asked, buckling his seatbelt and taking a deep breath.

"To a place they'll never find him." I had the perfect spot picked out. There was a forest nearby, and I knew there was plenty of wildlife there that would take care of his body. I had left out the part of how exactly we were going to place his body.

We couldn't leave him whole. He needed to be broken down into smaller bits and scattered throughout the forest. It was a necessary evil, and one I didn't want to think about, but fuck it. Sometimes, shit needed to get done.

In all my life, I'd never thought I'd be a part of covering up a murder, but it had been self-defense. If one of us hadn't killed Rebel, he'd have come after us or at least gotten his hands on Izzy again. That wasn't something I could have let happen. He'd needed to be taken out, and James had done it before I'd been able to pull the trigger.

Twenty minutes south of the motel was the Withlacoochee National Forest. Covering miles upon miles, it was desolate and expansive. Parts of him would be placed by the lake and in the dense underbrush, waiting for scavengers such as vultures to eat the remains and dispose of the evidence. At least enough of it that it wouldn't lead the authorities straight back to us.

Bikers turned up dead all the time. It wasn't anything out of the ordinary. Hopefully, it would be chalked up to gang violence and quickly forgotten, thrown on the bottom of countless unsolved cases sitting on a desk.

"Are we dumping him in a lake?" Flash asked as we turned down a dark road.

"Part of him," I replied, glancing at him before returning my eyes to the road.

"What the fuck do you mean, *part of him*?" His voice cracked on the last three words.

I laughed, shaking my head. "We can't leave him in one piece. We're going to scatter him around."

"How the fuck are we going to do that?"

"Easy. A few simple cuts and it's done." I knew it was a crock of shit. There was nothing easy about cutting up a body. I'd seen it done during my time with the Sun Devils.

"What are we going to do it with—your pocket knife? This should be fun to watch."

I shook my head again, laughter bursting out of me. There really wasn't much funny about the situation, but his stupidity was priceless.

"Rebel has a bunch of shit in the trunk that we can use. I said *we*. You're taking part in this shit too. You're going to be just as culpable as I am if you decide to open your fat mouth someday." Finding the spot that offered some cover, I pulled into the brush and turned off the car, including the lights.

"You're a fucker, Thomas."

"I've always been one. I'll do anything to protect my family, Flash. *Anything*. Don't ever forget it. Now, get your ass out of the car and help me finish this."

"Fucking bastard," he mumbled as he climbed out, slamming the door behind him.

I smiled, happy that he realized I'd easily kill him to protect my sister. Flash didn't want to tangle with me. I'd end him in a hot fuckin' second. At this point I was pretty sure James would gladly take up the task for me.

Rebel's head clunked against the trunk as we pulled his body out and let it fall to the ground. Using my phone for light, we searched the trunk to find the tools needed for the job. Inside, he had a hacksaw, a hammer, an axe, and a couple of other small hand tools that would make the job easier.

It took us thirty minutes of sawing, hacking, and chopping until I was satisfied with the size of the pieces. The entire time, I wanted to vomit, but I kept telling myself that there was no other way.

We took a couple of handfuls each trip, wandering apart and throwing pieces of Rebel in the forest. I instructed Flash to place brush and debris on top. The animals would easily find them from the smell.

We met back at the car when the deed was done. The laws we'd broken tonight were very clear, but sometimes the law was meant to be broken. No one could say that they'd never do it, especially when it came to protecting family.

After throwing the tools in the trunk, we headed back toward Izzy's in relative silence to get my car. As we got closer, Flash finally piped up and interrupted my thoughts.

"Now what?" he asked, fidgeting with the radio.

"I'll hide the car and keep it under wraps. Take my car back and leave it a block from the compound. I'll grab it after I store Rebel's car. See if anyone is talking about Izzy or me. I'll head to my friend's to spend the night. Call me if you hear anything."

"Okay," he said, his voice still shaky and unsure.

"It'll be okay, Flash."

"What if they know about you, Thomas?"

"You let me handle it if they do. I can bring an end to the club tonight if needed. I want to try to get them on record for a few more things before I end the operation, but it can end at any time. I have enough to put most of them away for their natural lives." Coming to a stop in front of Izzy's house, I felt like I could breathe, seeing James's car in the driveway and knowing Izzy was home safely.

"I'll call if I hear anything," Flash said as he opened the door. Stopping before he climbed out, he turned to me. "I'm sorry, Thomas."

"For what?" I asked, caught off guard by his statement.

He didn't look me in the eye when he said, "For involving Izzy and putting your entire family at risk."

"Flash," I said as I jumped out of the car. "What's done is done. It's in the past. The only thing to focus on now is keeping them all safe from this point forward."

Staring at me with soft eyes, a small smile on his face, he replied, "There's nothing more important. I have your back, brother."

"Then no apology necessary. Let's get changed and get the fuck out of here before someone sees us. I have extra clothes and some shit to wash up with in the trunk of my car."

"Always prepared, aren't you?" He followed me to the trunk.

"I've learned to be." I nodded, popping the trunk and rifling through the contents.

After grabbing two fresh T-shirts, I tossed one to him and set mine down. Once I'd removed the one I was wearing, which was covered in blood and dirt, I reached for a rag and a jug of water. I wet the rag, wiping away the traces of Rebel left on my flesh before slipping on the new shirt. Then I repeated the process with my pants before I washed my face and hands.

I tossed the water and a new rag to Flash, waiting for him to get cleaned up. After gathering our clothes, I put them in the trunk, covering them with the other contents inside. I didn't want blood-soaked clothes to be visible. Then Flash caught the keys I threw at him and still looked unsure about the entire situation.

"You got this. Just go back and rest. I'll call you tomorrow. Remember, leave the car a couple of blocks away and I'll find it."

"Okay, man. Follow me back toward the compound, though?" he asked, twirling the keys in his hand.

"Fine. Let's go." I motioned for him to get in as I slammed the trunk and headed toward Rebel's car.

I'd hide the car in the storage unit I'd rented months ago just in case I needed to hide out or hide something in a pinch. Never in my life had I thought I'd have to hide evidence of a murder.

I wasn't worried about the cops finding his car, but I was concerned that the club would start searching for Rebel. And I needed time.

I followed Flash back toward the clubhouse, breaking off once he parked my car and handed over the keys. After hiding the car, I knew exactly where I needed to spend the night. There was only one person I trusted. I'd head to Roxy, get cleaned up, spend the night, and have her as an alibi. I wouldn't ask her to lie for me outright, but she'd say anything to save my life, and I knew it.

I had a lot of thinking to do on the mile-long walk to

Roxy's. Hiding my face, keeping my head down, I walked with quick steps, the future on my mind. There were so many variables, so much unknown, that I couldn't quite wrap my head around it all—Roxy, the club, my family. Where did I fit in anymore?

I wasn't the same man I'd been when I joined the DEA. If you had asked me then if I'd kill a man and hide his body, I would've looked at you like you had three heads. But I had done it. That was the new Thomas Gallo. I was just as guilty as every club member, but my motives were different. They cared about money and hate. I only wanted to keep my family safe—and Roxy too. My sole purpose was bringing down the MC and getting the fuck out and back to where I belonged.

Where did Roxy fit in? What would I do about her? She and I had met a couple of months after I'd been patched. We weren't a couple and I sure as hell wasn't exclusive. I couldn't be. Fuck the shit about leaving someday. It was more about keeping up appearances. All the guys in the club fucked around if they had an old lady or not. The bonus to it was the ladies liked to talk. The girls in the club knew some deep, dark secrets. Stupid fuckers would get shitfaced and spill their secrets when their cocks were buried deep in pussy and they were out of their fucking minds.

I'd spend my time with them, getting them hammered, having some fun, and pulling information from them. I hadn't been careless in how I'd gleaned the details, but I'd made them feel comfortable enough to tell me. I knew more shit about every bastard inside the MC.

Could I leave this town and Roxy behind? The thought of it made my stomach constrict. She was too good to be thrown out like a piece of trash. When she found out the truth about me, would she be willing to forgive me? I had to think about that too. There were more than just my thoughts to take into consideration. Maybe she wouldn't want me. I wasn't a total cocksucker. The thought had crossed my mind a time or two.

The other issue was my family. The Gallos are a clan. It wasn't hard to get membership, but would she fit in? I knew they'd welcome her with open arms. If I loved her, they'd sure as fuck love her too. The real question was if Roxy would like them. Would she feel adequate enough to be around them?

They could be overwhelming. Smothering people with love and affection was something they had perfected over the years. Roxy was a lot like Izzy. Headstrong, a ball buster, didn't take shit from anyone, and could bring a man, specifically me, to his knees. They'd hit it off and be nothing but fucking trouble.

My family had always been close. We were a tight-knit group. A moment of silence was just a fairytale, as we were always up each other's asses. "Loud," "obnoxious," and "rowdy" were words that could be used to describe my family. But Roxy had grown up alone, surrounded by the club, with no real parental guidance. The Gallos could be overwhelming for her.

I didn't know what the future held. Was she just someone I'd smile about as I looked back on my time with her? A faint memory lost in the past?

CHAPTER
SEVEN

ANGEL

I COULDN'T SLEEP. Blue always returned my messages. Always. Even if it was a quick message to say, "Not tonight," he never forgot. I didn't like being ignored, and unlike most people in my life, Blue was always mindful and acknowledged me. I knew he usually had more important things to do, but damn it, it still hurt.

Tossing and turning, I punched my pillow, trying to find a position comfortable enough to lull me to sleep. Staring at the ceiling, I wondered where he was. It's dangerous for a woman in a… whatever this relationship was, to think of where the man she loved might be.

I did love him, and for that, I could be a fool, but you can't turn your heart off and tell it to shut the fuck up. No matter how hard I tried, it never listened.

Every time I thought about him with someone else, my chest ached. I felt weak each time I allowed myself to think about how he wasn't mine and never would be.

The room was hot, and the humidity felt heavier tonight. Giving up on sleep, I climbed to my feet and headed toward the living room. I didn't see a point in lying there, staring at the ceiling, and thinking of stuff that I couldn't change.

As I rounded the corner to the living room, I heard my back door open. Stopping dead in my tracks, I held my breath and listened. A scratching noise, as if the person were trying to jimmy the lock, made my heart start again, slamming into my sternum and beating in a rapid rhythm.

Gripping the wall, I flattened my back against the cool, smooth surface and debated my next move. Should I make a run for the front door or try and hide?

Fuck. Why didn't I grab a robe or some shit?

A loud creak as the door opened made me jump, and a small whimper escaped my lips. I was frozen with fear, rooted in the spot, and unable to move.

"Roxy," a voice called out in the darkness.

The sound of my blood whooshing through my ears muffled the voice. Closing my eyes, I said a prayer that they weren't here to hurt me.

"Yes," I replied, keeping myself glued to the wall.

"Angel, it's me."

It took me a moment to register the voice. *Blue.*

Sucking in a breath, I began to shake. As my knees gave out, my body started to slide down the wall until strong hands grabbed me around my ribs and propped me up.

"Roxy?" Blue asked, his forehead crinkling as he stared at me. "What's wrong?"

"What's wrong?" I asked, my legs feeling strong with his help. "What's wrong?" I repeated, raising my voice at the stupidity of his question.

"Yeah." He squeezed my ribs, keeping his eyes locked on mine.

"You basically break in to my house and give me a goddamn heart attack and you're asking *me* what's wrong? Seriously."

He started to laugh. Glaring at him, I reached up and slapped his face. His laughter died immediately, his smile disappearing as his face snapped back to mine.

"What the fuck?" he seethed, releasing my body before wiping the corner of his mouth.

"You're an asshole, Blue. I thought someone was here to murder me."

"Aww, baby. Come on. Don't get upset with me," he whispered, sliding his hand up my thigh.

His snarky, carefree attitude for once had become too much. I didn't know if it was the adrenaline still coursing through my veins, but I reached up and smacked his face again. This time, he didn't budge.

"You wanna play rough tonight, Rox?" The corner of his mouth turned up as his jaw ticked. "Come on, baby. Hit me harder."

His cockiness and smug bullshit were just the ticket. Reaching up, I moved my hand toward his face one more time, but he grabbed it, stopping it from connecting.

"I knew you were in there, tiger. It's been a while," he said, grabbing my nightie.

"Don't fuckin' touch me, Blue. I'm so pissed at you I can't see straight." My body was on high alert. My heart was still pounding from being scared, and my mind was reeling at the bad shit that could've really happened if it hadn't been him breaking in.

Sliding his hand farther up my thigh, he watched my

face. Sucking in a breath, I tried to hide the small moan that wanted to slip from my lips. As he cupped my pussy, rubbing his palm against my clit, I snapped. My opposite hand, the one free from his grip, flew through the air and connected with his cheek.

Whoops. He wasn't expecting that one.

His eyes flashed before he released my hand and slapped me back. Shock filled me; my breath was lost, and a slice of pain radiated through my cheek.

Fuck, the man knew how to press my buttons.

I liked it rough.

I'd never shied away from it. Blue never hit me hard enough to cause damage, but he did set my body on fire.

Before I could react, his hold on my pussy grew rougher and he crashed his lips to mine, sucking out what air was left inside, leaving me breathless.

Clawing at his shoulder, I wrapped my legs around him, rubbing my core against his rock-hard dick. Gripping my hair, he pulled on it, causing a burn against my scalp. Then he cupped my ass as he pushed me against the wall, leaving no space between us. When our lips locked, we used each other for air and fed off each other as I scratched his skin through his shirt. I wanted to dig my nails into his flesh, leave my mark, and let every whore out there know where I'd been.

Reaching between us, my body on fire and my need growing greater by the moment, I pulled at his shirt, having to feel his skin. Breaking our kiss for a moment, I yanked it above his head and dropped it to the floor.

Wasting no time, I unbuttoned and unzipped his jeans, using my feet to free his ass and cock from the coarse material. As I locked lips with him again, without waiting, he thrust inside me, slamming my back into the wall.

Unsheathed, his rigid cock filled me. Calling out, "Blue!" I ripped at his back with my nails, tearing the skin as I scratched.

He hissed against my lips, a sound of pleasure and warning. I knew he was as turned on as I was. Pushing back, fucking him as hard as he was fucking me, I bounced on his dick, letting my tits jiggle against his muscular chest.

Holding my hips, he used his hands to slam me down on his hard length, causing me to moan louder than I had before. He fucked me with so much ferocity that I thought I'd pass out. I didn't, thank fucking God. I relished it, soaked in the feeling of him inside me, ramming his body against me. His grip on my hips was so hard that I knew I'd have bruises there tomorrow—ones I'd cherish until they faded and disappeared.

"Touch yourself," he growled, causing me to open my eyes and look into his stare. "Pinch your nipples."

I wouldn't argue with that. Reaching up, I tweaked my nipples with my fingertips, turning them slightly in my grasp.

"Harder," he commanded, as he watched my fingers toy with my stiff peaks.

I pinched them harder; it radiated down my abdomen and shot straight to my clit. Crying out, my body so close to the edge, I threw my head back and smacked it against the wall.

His lips found my pulse as his teeth dug into my flesh, sending another dose of pain-slash-pleasure through my system. Everything in my body was on fire. My body became so tight. The orgasm that felt miles away was ready to break free, but I needed something. I was chasing it, bucking against his body, pinching my nipples—and nothing.

Staring at me, he could see my frustration mounting. Blue always knew. He had this sixth sense when it came to fucking. He was like the Amazing Kreskin of orgasms.

Without asking, he wrapped one hand around my neck, putting pressure on my veins but not cutting off my breathing. My face began to feel tingly as the blood flow was cut off. When he pinched harder, I felt lightheaded and sucked in air, barely able to squeak out a sound. His grip became tighter, the pressure intensified, and my body snapped, releasing the pent-up energy that had collected all evening.

As I bucked wildly, my vision blurred, my eyes rolled back in my head, and I gasped for air. As he thrust into me, his speed increased and he held me in place. And when the colors exploded behind my eyelids, I felt faint. Edging closer to passing out, I reached up, placing my hand against his. His grip on my throat was a little too much, so I tapped his fingers for a reprieve.

Releasing my neck, he grunted, pumping into me before crushing my body against the wall. When he wailed through his release, his body shaking, I watched in wonder as he felt the same ecstasy I had only moments before. His lips parted and he made a few swipes of his tongue across his lip as his eyes were squeezed shut and he rode the crest of the orgasm that gripped his body.

Watching a man come, especially Blue, was one of the most beautiful sights I'd ever experienced in my life. Knowing I'd done that to him, gave him a reprieve from his life and brought him total pleasure, made me happy. I knew how silly it sounded, but in all honesty, it was being connected and feeling needed that brought me the most happiness.

And Blue made me feel that way. He brought me more joy than anyone else ever had in my life. Human connection on an emotional level was something I'd lacked in my life, but with him, I had it in spades. Even if I wasn't his, I felt it.

"Fuck," he mumbled, resting his forehead against mine and breathing raggedly.

"What's wrong, baby?" I whispered, touching his face and cradling his cheeks in my hands.

"Just not how I wanted tonight to go. I didn't think I'd take you in the hallway."

"Blue," I responded, lifting his face to look into my eyes. "It was perfect. I like when you're not soft with me."

"I know."

"Sometimes, I need the intensity to remind me I'm alive. Reminds me that it isn't a dream. I love your soft side too. Tonight was perfect. I'm just happy you came."

As soon as the words left my mouth, he burst into laughter, shaking my body, which was still in his grip. "I'm happy I came too," he echoed, laughing between words.

I couldn't help it. With the seriousness between us broken, I started to laugh uncontrollably. Blue had that ability—no one else. He could go from dead serious to playful in a heartbeat. It kept me on my toes, always wondering what he'd say or do next. Behind it all, I knew there was love and understanding. Moods didn't bother me. Shit, I had a million of them, and he always took them in stride.

"Let's get you back in bed, angel," he whispered against my lips, his hot breath skidding across my face.

Smiling, I nodded and hooked my feet against his ass.

Shuffling his feet because his pants were still halfway down his legs, he carried me to the bedroom and then placed me on the bed. Without saying a word, he kissed my forehead before slowly backing away.

Enthralled, I stared at him as he began to strip off his jeans. The bedroom was dark, just the moonlight streaming through the room, illumining his body and showing his ridges with even greater distinction. With his chest bare, I could see every ripple in his stomach moving together as they constricted. The dragon on his ribs danced as he shifted, bending to remove his pants. Leaning back, I drank him in and enjoyed the view.

"Keep looking at me like that and we'll never get to sleep." He laughed, folding his jeans and tossing them on the chair in the corner. "First, I need a shower." He sniffed his skin, wrinkling his nose as his scent registered.

I never cared how he smelled. He was the only man whose sweat was a turn-on.

"Go ahead. I'll be waiting. Don't be too long, Blue." I scooted up the bed, shooing him with my hands.

His lips split into a smile as he nodded, turning his back to me before he disappeared into the bathroom.

Because he left the door cracked, the sound of the water splattering against the tile filled the room as I lay there waiting for him. The pitter-patter changed as the water splashed from his body, hitting the wall in different spots.

Grabbing my phone, I climbed from the bed, tiptoeing toward the door to catch a glimpse. His back was to me as water cascaded down his flesh. Water droplets collected and fell from the glass shower enclosure as he washed his hair. I snapped a photo with my phone and smiled to myself—the image would be forever mine.

God, his ass was amazing. Tight, high, and round, with a small smattering of hair, more like peach fuzz, hanging above and fizzling out as it crawled down his cheeks. As he began to turn, I rushed away, leaving him to finish showering.

After crawling back in bed, I turned off my phone, wanting to shut the world out for tonight. Nothing else mattered besides Blue. I just wanted to be with him. I'd pretend that our life wasn't reality for tonight. I'd face the cold, hard truth tomorrow. Why face it today when you can put it off until tomorrow? That was my motto.

The pipes squeaked as he turned off the water, and then the room grew quiet. My heartbeat sped up as I heard the shower door open and close. Waiting wasn't something I was particularly good at, but it was part of the package when I spent time with Blue. Waiting for him to call. Waiting for him to arrive. Waiting for him to text me. Waiting for him to ask me to be his. Everything involved waiting, and somehow, over time, I'd made peace with it.

Turning my body to face the bathroom, I waited for him. As I tucked my hand under my face, his body filled the doorway, backlit by the light. Resting against the frame, he crossed his arms. I couldn't see his eyes, but I assumed he was looking at me. Watching me.

"Rox, I have to ask you a favor." He pushed himself from the door with his shoulder before moving toward the bed.

"Anything you need, Blue. Anything." There wasn't

anything in the world I wouldn't do for him. I wasn't a fool; I knew he'd do the same for me.

Sitting down on the edge of the bed, he ran his fingertips across my cheekbone. From the contact, tiny sparks of electricity danced across my skin, which was still tender from where he'd struck me.

"I need you to vouch for me if anyone asks any questions."

Biting my lip, I looked at him and blinked a couple of times. He'd never asked me to cover for him. I could see something lurking in his eyes—a seriousness I hadn't seen before.

Without putting much thought into it, I replied, "I will."

"All you need to say is that I was with you tonight. You can do that for me?" He stroked my face.

Moving my cheek against his touch, I smiled. "Always."

His hand left my face as he pulled back the sheet, giving my hip a quick slap. "Glad we have that settled. Move over, babe."

Doing as I'd been told, I shimmied across the cotton sheets, making a spot for him on the bed. He climbed in, held his arm up for me to nestle against his side, and rested his other hand across his chest. Then he sighed deeply, letting out a breath before pulling me against him.

Making small circles across his skin, I watched my fingers as they moved. Within minutes, his breathing deepened and his body filled with tiny twitches. As I began to drift off, my body felt light and my mind began to clear.

But just as I felt the blackness taking me, I heard him whisper, "Izzy."

I sucked in a breath, feeling like someone had punched me in the gut. I was lying in his arms, I'd just had sex with him, and I'd vowed to be his alibi, but he'd just said the name of another woman.

It wasn't my place to ask questions, but that shit hurt. My nose tingled as water began to fill my eyes. Unable to see clearly, I blinked, letting the tears stream down my cheek and fall onto his chest.

I cried myself to sleep as exhaustion and tears carried me off to my dreams. Someplace where mine was the only name he called out and he only belonged to me.

CHAPTER
EIGHT
THOMAS

WATCHING over my shoulder and studying every member in the club had become exhausting. It wasn't that I hadn't kept my eyes peeled before, but now that Rebel was dead and he'd found out my real identity, the need to be extra cautious and mindful of those around me had increased.

It had been two months since Rebel died, and for sixty grueling days I'd waited to be exposed. The plan with the Vipers moved forward even in Rebel's absence, causing the list of charges to grow.

Rebel's disappearance had people on pins and needles. His car was still safely tucked away in my storage unit, and his remains had yet to be discovered. Wild accusations had flown around the clubhouse for weeks. Cowboy had become the new president, calling the shots in place of Rebel. The mysterious disappearance had been pinned on a rival club, the Death Angels. They'd started some shit in Daytona and were the obvious scapegoat. All members of that club had been executed during a late-night raid on their compound. There was no one left in that club to deny the murder of Rebel.

After things died down, the death of Rebel behind us and a new president at the helm, James and I finally had time to talk face to face. There was no way in hell that the conversation would be pretty. I didn't have all the facts, but I was pretty sure he was fuckin' my sister. I considered him my best friend, my lifeline to the real world away from this club. He was the man who kept me grounded and focused even when I thought of giving up.

Our friendship had blossomed over drinks while in training—way too many most nights—and late-night talks about family and our values. It sounded a little funny, but I meant it in the manliest way possible. We'd talk about putting away the bad guys, feeling a need to keep the world safe, and we both wanted the rush that came from this type of work. There's a danger in undercover work that can't be found anywhere else in life. Jumping out of a plane, swimming with sharks, and all other types of adrenaline-junkie activities didn't even come close to living undercover.

James and I had a kinship. We were cut from the same cloth. We didn't take shit from people or give a fuck what anyone thought of us. We were both deep-seated in family. Mine was still fully intact, but his had been ripped apart by drugs. That was his driving motivation. Mine was the need to feel like I was doing something good. I could've sat at home with the rest of my siblings and worked in the tattoo shop, but it lacked the thrill I wanted, the need I felt.

With each day that passed while being in the Sun Devils MC, I realized how badly I missed my life before the DEA. Drugs, sex, violence, death, and general asshole behaviors were part of everyday life, and they weighed heavily on the soul. It was part of this MC, and I knew I wasn't cut out for it.

I missed my family. Life had become boring for me, so I'd decided to try my hand at something else—something dangerous. Looking back, I knew it hadn't been worth the risk.

I didn't know how I could've ever thought that my family wouldn't be at risk in this line of work. I should've known that something could go wrong and someone would find a way to get to me, especially through my family. Even if Flash hadn't brought Izzy to Daytona, she and the rest of the Gallos would have been at risk.

I had a hard choice to make when this assignment was over. Stay in and work for the greater good of society or quit and go back to my old life. No matter how boring life seemed, at least everyone would be safe from something that had been caused by my actions. My family was every-thing to me.

Which brings me back to Izzy. She was my little sister. I spent my teen years chasing away boys, teaching her to be badass and not to put up with shit from assholes like my brothers and me. I knew that Izzy wasn't being used. The girl was just too damn smart to let that shit happen.

I wasn't even pissed that she was with James—if that were the case. I was more worried about the fallout that would occur when they ended. I assumed this because Izzy didn't have the best track record, and James was a fuck-stick on legs.

James was like my brother from another mother. He and I were alike, and that was why we got along so well. What really fuckin' stung was that he hadn't told me anything was going on. That shit just isn't cool. You can't fuck your best friend's sister and forget to mention that shit.

I needed to make him squirm. Have him worry a little bit about how I felt about the entire situation.

Izzy had to be with someone, but no one could ever live up to my high standards. But James was the closest thing I had to a brother who wasn't blood. If he truly loved my sister—would give his life for her—then I'd give my blessing.

After knocking on his apartment door, I looked over my shoulder, surveying the surroundings just to be sure I hadn't been followed. The coast was clear, and from this vantage point, I could see the street in both directions. "Hold on," a grumpy voice called from inside.

"Let go of your dick for five seconds and open the fucking door." I pounded on the door, not wanting to stand out here any longer than I had to and risk being seen. I was sure I could've given an excuse about getting some pussy, but any secret from the club would have thrown up a flag of suspicion.

"Fucker," James said as the door opened.

I laughed, punching him in the shoulder as I walked inside. The place was dark and a fucking mess. James was always a clean freak, but the inside of his apartment looked like chaos had ensued.

"What the fuck, dude? This shit isn't like you." I threw some papers that had been sitting on the chair to the floor and sat down before grabbing my smokes and setting them on the table.

"I've been busy." He pulled out a chair, sat across from me, and cracked his knuckles.

"I guess so, by the looks of this shithole. Been doing a lot of traveling?" I smirked.

"Thomas," he said, holding up his hand. "I'm sorry." He sighed, shaking his head.

I had known him long enough that I could read his emotions. I wasn't dumb enough to say that I could read *him*, because I'd fuckin' missed he was screwing my little sister.

"I thought we were better friends than that, James. Why wouldn't you be straight up and tell me?"

"It's complicated." Hanging his head, he fidgeted with his hands, balling them into fists and then releasing them.

"Fucking someone isn't all that complicated."

"It was more than that and it was nothing at all."

"You better rephrase that shit."

"I didn't mean for it to happen, Thomas," he said, lifting his head to meet my gaze. "You gotta understand that."

"I do," I responded, knowing the type of man James was. "When did it happen?"

"At your brother's wedding." He reached for my cigarettes, but I quickly pulled them out of his reach.

"Keep going."

"It just happened. We drank a lot and talked most of the reception. One thing led to another and—"

"And you fucked my sister," I deadpanned, feeling my blood start to course through my veins faster than normal.

"It's not like *that*."

"Tell me what it was *like*."

He cleared his throat, running his fingers through his hair. I could see the vein in his neck pulsing as his blood pressure rose. "I listened to you talk about Izzy forever.

75

You built her up and told me how amazing she was, and I listened to every word. I felt like I'd known her forever when I met her. Thomas, how you described her didn't do her justice. I've never met anyone like her."

"So, it's my fault you stuck your dick in my *little sister*?" I growled, pulling a cigarette from the pack and lighting it.

"No!" he yelled, shaking his head vigorously. "I hung on your stories when you'd talk about her, and when I met her, it came full circle. I never believed in love at first sight, but I knew I wanted to be with her, and not in that fucking way, you prick. I wanted Izzy in my life. She has this zest for life." He paused and hung his head again. "Jesus, I'm sounding all soft and shit. I love her. I fucking love her!" He drew in a quick breath as he finished his confession.

Letting the smoke escape through my nose, I asked, "Have you been seeing her since the wedding?" I still needed details, but the thought of James being in love with my sister didn't piss me off—it was the lies. It was better to know the type of man she was with than the unknown and uncertainty of her being with a stranger. I knew James would never intentionally hurt her.

"No. Dude, she fucking vanished. She'd left me without even saying goodbye." His mouth hung open. "I mean, what other woman does that shit?"

I laughed, throwing back my head and thinking of James finding that Izzy had ditched his ass in the middle of the night. There's nothing that hurts pride more than shit like that. James was a cocky motherfucker, so it must've wrecked him, even if it was only for a short time.

"That sounds like Izzy."

"I know. I've never met a woman and felt connected to her immediately. She's my kryptonite, man." He laughed, and I joined him.

"God, you're such a pussy, James. I thought you were tougher than this shit."

"I was, but Izzy fuckin' ruined me."

"Don't mention Izzy and fuckin' in the same sentence."

"Oh, sorry," he said, his face growing sober as he bit his lip to stop the laughter.

"I'm serious, fucker."

"So am I." He smiled, the tension between us easing as the air felt lighter.

Jesus, maybe his pansy ass had rubbed off on me, or maybe it was spending time with Roxy. I was as pussy-whipped as he was, but the big difference was I had no future with her, unlike James with my sister—if she stuck around long enough for there to be a future.

"So, you saw her at the wedding and then when did you see her again?"

Upon standing, he walked to the counter and grabbed a pack of smokes. I never knew James to smoke unless he was drinking, but I was sure the severity of the entire situation had started to wear on him as much as it had on me.

"I didn't see her again until you called from Daytona."

It all started to click in my brain. Izzy had freaked out when she'd heard that I was calling James. I hadn't been able to figure out why and had assumed she was just being her usual headstrong self. Man, I had been so fucking wrong.

The air was so fucking thick when James and Izzy had seen each other again. She had been panicked and not herself. I'd thought maybe it was because of the situation she'd been in, but now, I realized she'd been acting like she'd gotten caught. No one wanted to have to face the person they'd ditched without a word, but she hadn't had a choice.

"Are you seeing her now?" I stubbed out my cigarette after having let most of it burn down without taking but a couple of drags.

"Not right this fuckin' minute," he teased, a slow smile spreading across his face.

"Asshole. I mean have you been seeing her *since* Daytona?"

"Yeah, man."

"Expand on that answer." I wasn't in the mood for short and sweet.

"Every chance I get, I go see her."

"That shit is risky, James," I hissed, wondering what would happen if someone followed him.

"It's not. I'm always careful. I make sure you have backup and that I'm not followed." He smashed his cigarette in the ashtray, having barely smoked any of it.

"Spend time with my family?"

"Yes." He tried to hide his smile, but to no avail.

I felt a pang of jealously that he had probably spent more time with them in the last couple of months than I had in years. "Tell me what's going on with them."

"City and Suzy are expecting in a couple of months—"

I interrupted, jealousy growing inside me. "I still haven't met my sister-in-law. There's so much I've missed out on because of this job."

"You have an amazing family, Thomas. I don't know how you can be apart from them."

"I'm starting to question it myself. Keep talking," I responded, needing to hear more.

"Suzy's great. She's so sweet, and I can see the love she has for your brother all over her face. She doesn't hide her feelings. You're going to love her."

"I'm sure I will. If Joe loves her, she has to be amazing. What about Mike?"

"He's seeing Mia."

"Wait. Who's Mia?"

"His girlfriend. They've been exclusive for a long time. He quit fighting and works with her and at the shop."

My head started to spin from thinking about everything I had missed. All the holidays, birthdays, and now, Joe's wedding—it was almost too much to bear. A woman had finally snared Mike and I hadn't been there to see it.

"What does she do?" I asked, wondering what had caused my brother to give up his dreams of being a championship fighter.

"She's a doctor, and they have a clinic together."

"Huh." Mike and a doctor weren't a pair I'd match up ever in my life. He was into inflicting injuries, not patching them up.

"I know, right?" He laughed, understanding what I meant after having spent time with Mike. "He's totally pussy-whipped and in love with her. He hasn't asked her to marry him yet."

"Surprising. The bastard is a hopeless romantic. That much I know about my brother. As passionate as he is about fighting, he has to be in love with her to have given it all up."

"Yeah." He paused, his forehead crinkling above his eyes.

"It's okay, man," I said.

"I just feel shitty. I know you have to miss them."

"I do. This assignment should be over any day now. Just waiting for the paperwork to come through and make the arrests."

"They said it would be in the next week."

"It can't come fast enough." I sighed, rubbing my hands against my jeans. "How are my parents, James?"

"They're fine, Thomas. Your mom is fucking amazing. She can cook her ass off and is the sweetest little thing."

"Don't be blinded by her charm. She's a viper underneath." I laughed.

Everyone thought my mother was a sweet, innocent lady, but she'd kick any of our asses if we got out of line. Even my father was scared of the woman, though he would never admit it.

"I'm sure Izzy learned her skills from somewhere." He snorted.

I blanched, still letting the thought of him *being* with my sister sink in and trying to not picture them fucking. "What about Anthony?"

"He's not with anyone. Just playing some gigs and working at the shop. He's a ball buster, that one."

"We're all ball busters," I replied, cracking my neck. I was so fucking tense. Between the shit with the club and dealing with James and Izzy now, everything in body was wound tight. "It's in the genes."

"I'm leaving tonight to spend some more time with Izzy. Just so you know."

I closed my eyes, thinking about how badly I wanted to go home. It had been ages since I'd hugged my mother or laughed with my dad about how shitty the Cubs were doing. There would be nothing better than to sit around the table and sink my teeth into anything my mother whipped up.

I wanted to go home.

"Give everyone my love, James. I'm jealous as fuck right now. I want this shit to end. I want to be there too."

"You'll be home soon, man. I won't tell everyone that because I don't want them to get too excited, but it's going to happen before you know it." He smiled, patting my hand to placate me.

"Yeah, sure," I responded before pushing the chair back and climbing to my feet. "I better get out of here and get back to the club."

"Are you okay, man? You aren't looking so good," James said, concern etched on his face.

"I'm just done with this shit. It weighs on me."

I didn't know if I'd ever feel like myself again. The only way for that to happen was to be around the people who knew me best. If anyone could bring me back to center, it would be my family.

I walked toward the door, a feeling of dread filling my belly. I didn't want to go back, but I knew there wasn't another option.

"Want to hit me? Maybe you'll feel better," he said behind me as he followed me to the door.

I turned, a smile on my face at the thought, but I just couldn't. "Nah. I don't want to hurt you, man."

He pointed to his chin. "Free shot. Sure you don't want it?"

I held out my hand to him, sick of fighting in general. "I'm good. All I ask is that you say hello to everyone for me."

He placed his hand in mine, squeezing hard and shaking it. "Will do, Thomas. Call me if anything goes down. I'll have my phone by my side all weekend." He released me, holding the door open for me to go.

"Yeah. Always." I pulled down my shades, placed them over my eyes, and descended the steps to my bike.

Climbing on, I cursed myself for the time wasted. Don't get me fucking wrong. I knew I was doing good work, but the time lost with my family could never be recovered. The end was near.

CHAPTER NINE

THOMAS

FORTY-EIGHT HOURS after talking with James, word came down through the channels that the bust was about to go down. My world, along with all the members of the club, would forever be changed. Everything I'd worked so hard for was finally coming to fruition.

Flash texted me as I walked around the club, taking in the people who were sitting around. It would be the last time they'd be together without being behind bars.

Flash: *Three hours and it's happening.*

Walking into my room, I typed a reply to him.

Me: *Gotcha. I'll be ready. Get your shit together.*

I dialed Bobby immediately. He was the king shit in the operation. James and I both reported to him, and he called the shots. Often, we left him out of some decisions, but in general, we followed his direction and kept him in the loop.

The call connected as I heard static coming through the earpiece. "Talk to me." Bobby wasn't into small talk and he never said hello.

"I just got word that shit's going down tonight. Is it true?" Silently, I was praying to God that it wasn't a cruel joke.

"Yeah. Be ready. James is on his way back and will be with the group during the raid."

"What's my exit strategy?" I asked, pushing the thought of James being with my family when word came down out of my mind.

How would we explain away that I wasn't going to be in the clink with the rest of the guys? It wouldn't be hard for them to figure out that I was either a rat or an undercover cop. The worry and frustration I had put out of my mind came flooding back. Fuck. This could be only the beginning of watching over my fucking shoulder.

"I worked that shit out with the FBI."

The man didn't have many words. Great. We were finally communicating, but a little information would be nice. It was like pulling fucking teeth when it was my goddamn ass on the line.

"And?"

"Since it's a federal case, everyone will be split up while awaiting trial. We have men being shipped all around the country. They won't be able to track who is where, and that should ensure your safety—and Samuel's too, of course."

I breathed a sigh of relief. Maybe their plan could work. I didn't see any other option but to pray to Christ that splitting up the group would make it almost impossible to track each member's whereabouts.

"So that's it?"

"That's it. You'll be booked to keep your cover, but once everyone is split up, you'll be released."

Thank fuck for small miracles. I'd have to spend some time in the very place I'd been working to send every member of the MC. Thankfully, it wouldn't be for long.

"How long?" I asked, checking the clock on the wall. This shit would be like watching water boil. Time would tick by slower than ever.

"Three hours maximum. Be on your toes. Are all the members there?" The sound of paperwork being shuffled around on the other end of the line broke my trance with the clock.

"Yeah, they're here. We're having a party tonight."

"Good. Talk to you soon."

When the call disconnected, I turned the phone over in my hand, trying to decide what to do next. As I looked around the room, taking in the place I'd called home for more months than I cared to remember, it hit me. I'd never see Roxy again. I couldn't touch her again and say goodbye. I'd vanish like the rest of the guys. She'd assume I was in jail, hopefully forget about me, and move on.

As soon as I thought the words, I knew it was bullshit. I didn't want her to move on. I didn't want to be forgotten. I was a selfish prick, because I hadn't put much thought into how my presence in her life would impact her when I left.

When I should have felt a sense of joy and total relief, the only thing I felt was crushing sadness. I'd lied to myself. One lie had led to another and then snowballed. I loved Roxanne. I don't mean I just loved fucking her or I liked her. Fuck no. I loved her with my entire being. Her sweetness and kind nature had captured my attention and eventually my heart. My head said, *No...just use her*, but my heart was a complete asshole.

Resting my chin against my shoulder, I inhaled deeply, the smell of her perfume still lingering on my shirt. As I closed my eyes, I thought of her face filled with laughter and the feel of her skin against mine. Falling backward, I let my body bounce on the edge of the bed before placing my elbows on my knees. Then I sat there like a dumbass and stared at the wall.

A loud pounding at the door drew me out of my self-imposed Roxy funk. "What?" I yelled, pushing myself off the bed and moving toward the door.

"Are you coming out for a drink?" the prospect asked me. I couldn't remember his name, and I didn't try.

"Move," I growled as I pushed past him, stalking toward the common area.

Glancing at the clock as I leaned against the bar, I realized I had sat in my room in a total haze for an hour. Two hours or less and this shit would be over.

"Tequila." I held up two fingers, needing the one-two punch that could only be delivered by such quantities of Patrón.

The prospect placed two glasses on the bar and quickly filled them. Before he could walk away, I slammed one back and said, "Another."

Why do this shit sober? I could have a nice buzz by the time everything went down. Since they were sending me to jail with everyone else, I wouldn't have to handle a gun or read anyone their Miranda rights. The members of the club had been partying for hours, so I didn't see any reason why I should be the only sober one.

The minutes slowly ticked by as I thought about Roxanne and how my life was about to change. Sitting with the boys, drinking, and laughing were just a façade for the violent storm of emotions that were battling inside me.

I downed another shot of tequila before sipping a beer, feeling a sense of guilt for the children who would become fatherless. It wasn't my actions but theirs that would cause the eventual separation. When someone leads a life of crime, they take that risk. The women who loved them and had borne their children had known the eventuality of their incarceration when they had become their old ladies. The only people who didn't have a choice in the situation were the kids. They hadn't asked to be born into this life—they were the innocent victims.

I drank shot after shot, chasing each with the beer I nursed as I tried not to watch the clock. Time escaped me as my mind became fuzzy, my thoughts scattering as the liquor coursed through my veins.

I jumped from my chair as the doors slammed open. Screams erupted, women went scrambling, and chairs fell over as men stood and reached for their guns. Following their actions, I went through the motions to keep my cover.

James burst through the door, holding up his badge and a search warrant. "Put your weapons down and get on your knees."

The men stilled, looking to each other to decide what to do next. I could see it in their eyes. They wanted to fight back, make this shit a blaze of glory, but we were outnumbered. Slowly lowering my gun, deciding to be the leader, I kneeled on the floor and tossed my weapon.

The law enforcement agents, which included DEA, FBI, US Marshals, and local law enforcement, waited with their weapons drawn, pointing at every member of the club.

"Give it up, gentlemen. We have an arrest warrant for each of you and a search warrant for the property," James declared, shaking a piece of paper in his hand.

"Fuck," Cowboy hissed as he followed my lead.

Murmurs and growls filled the space as each member laid down their guns as they dropped to their knees.

"Don't worry, brothers." Cowboy looked cocky and calm, not realizing the severity of the situation.

Even the best lawyer in the world wouldn't be able to get the guys out on bail. Federal courts and crimes weren't easy to deal with, and it was harder to buy off the judges. The case would be too big—on every major news channel —for it to be swept under the rug. People would scream foul if judges sided with the MC, with all the evidence we had been able to accumulate over the months.

James stalked toward me, placing his gun in his holster and grabbing his handcuffs. "John Lansing," he stated, opening the handcuffs and attaching the first to my left wrist, "you have the right to remain silent…"

I blanched, always having hated that name. It wasn't me and never would be.

He gripped my hands, sticking them behind my back. As he attached the second one to my right wrist, he finished reading my rights.

When I climbed to my feet, James marched me out past the other members. As I walked by, I found that each man was going through the process. I nodded to them, pretending it was going to be okay.

James stopped close to his car, far enough away from the building, and turned me to face him. "Shit is finally over." He sighed, rubbing his forehead. "I thought there would be some gunshots. Thank fuck for that."

"If Rebel had been the head, there may have been. I'm just happy I'm one step closer to home."

"They can't wait to see you, Thomas."

"Yeah," I whispered, turning my back to him as I saw the door open.

"Get your ass moving," he barked, pushing me toward one of the vans to carry us to the station.

Smiling, I dragged my feet, being a total asshole and making him push me in the direction.

"Move your feet!" he yelled, shoving me harder.

"Fuck off," I replied, coming to a complete stop.

"You're a dick," he whispered before nudging me again.

Slowly moving my feet, I took step after step toward my ride to freedom. After climbing in, I sat in the back and watched as they loaded the rest of the guys in the three vans parked on the property. As soon as the doors slammed, they started to bitch and question each other.

"What the fuck?" Rooster adjusted his body, trying to find a comfortable position.

We all felt the same way, but some of us dealt with it better than others. Rooster was still nursing a shoulder wound he'd received during the shootout with the rival group that had *killed* Rebel.

"We'll be out in no time," I lied, and I didn't feel an ounce of guilt.

"We fuckin' better. Cowboy better have some shit lined up."

"I'm sure he does." I smiled, knowing that the fucker hadn't even thought about something as big as this.

With the issues with Rebel's disappearance and getting the club in order, it hadn't even entered his mind.

The guys joked on the way to our final destination without a care in the world. It was a pervasive issue in the MC—smugness. They thought they were invincible, that everyone could be bought. On the local level, I would have to agree, but on the federal level it wasn't that simple. They'd find that out soon enough.

Once unloaded, we were each booked and placed in separate parts of the jail. No more than two club members were allowed in the same area. Splitting us up was smart, especially to keep my cover.

Staring at the ceiling as I waited, I listened to the prospect complain about being in jail. At my breaking point, I yelled, "Dude, shut the fuck up already!"

His face drained of all blood. "I'm sorry," he said as he sat on the edge of his cot and stared at me. "I've never been in jail."

"Get used to it. It's part of this life. If you can't handle the shit, you better get the fuck out now."

"Yeah." He adjusted himself, lying back and remaining silent.

As I drifted to sleep, I thought of Roxy, allowing myself to linger on the memory of her touch and smell while I waited for my freedom.

***

"Lansing," a deep voice called out, interrupting my sweet dreams.

Why couldn't they just shut the fuck up and let a man get an ounce of sleep?

"Lansing!" the voiced yelled again, fully breaking me away from the happy place I'd allowed myself to go.

"What?" I said, not bothering to open my eyes.

"Get up. Let's go."

I looked over at the kid in the next bunk and sighed. "Good luck, kid." Then I cracked my neck, stretching the soreness from my muscles. Turning, I saw that James was the one waiting for me. "Can I piss first?"

"No. Stop stalling and get your ass moving."

"Motherfucker," I muttered, adjusting my morning wood and fighting the urge to cold-cock him when the barrier between us was removed.

"Put your hands through the bars." He dangled the handcuffs in his hands, shaking them for effect.

Grumbling, I did as I'd been told and then glared at him as he snapped them shut. Pulling them back through the bars, I waited for him to unlock the door without breaking eye contact.

We didn't speak as he walked behind me. Through the windows I could see the other club members encased in their cells—exactly where they deserved to be. A few others were being handcuffed and would probably take the same walk, but with a very different outcome.

"Last room on the left."

Settling into the chair, I placed my cuffed hands on the table and waited for him to close the door. As soon as I heard the click, I couldn't hold it in any longer.

"It took you fucking long enough." I shook my hands, bringing his attention to them.

"You're such a sissy." He laughed, grabbing the key from his pocket as he approached the table.

"Want to switch places and see who can last longer without complaining?"

"Shut up," he teased, unlocking the cuffs before taking a seat across from me.

"What's the plan?" I scratched my longer-than-normal facial hair that had grown overnight. I wanted a shower more than anything. I barely felt human. The stench of old liquor and jail clung to me.

"They're all being sent to different federal holding facilities to await their hearings and eventual trials. Keeping track of each other will be almost impossible. You're going to have to go to headquarters and be debriefed for a couple of weeks to be safe. After that, you should be able to go home."

I blinked, staring at him and processing the words. Home. Would it still feel that way to me after being absent for so long? I had never been away this long. Even after training and returning home for a visit, I had felt like I hadn't quite belonged anymore. After a week, I'd fallen into the smooth, easy routine and felt like a Gallo again. Could I do that now?

"When do I get to leave?" I leaned back in my chair, crossing my legs at my ankles, and stretched.

"Bobby is on his way to get you, and you'll be on a flight to D.C. tomorrow."

"Good. I can't go back to that cell. Sorry again you got pulled away from the family."

"To get you out of this bullshit life it was worth it." He smiled, running his fingers through his hair.

"I just want it all to be over." I tried to smile, but nothing came.

His own faded as he scrubbed his hands over his face. "What's wrong?"

"Where do you want me to begin?" I laughed without

cracking a grin and shook my head. I could sit here all day and bitch about shit, but then I'd be playing into the crack he'd made earlier.

"You were in too long. They should've never let the case drag on the way it did. It was meant to be short term, but you got in too deep for them to end it. They saw the big fish dangling before them and didn't care how it would affect you."

"I can deal with the shit. I can shake the life I'm leaving behind. There are a few casualties that I hadn't put much thought into until now."

"Roxy?" he asked, resting his hands on the table.

"Yeah. What happens to her now?"

"Probably what happens to all the women tied to the club. They get by somehow."

"I'm going to vanish, James, into thin fucking air. It won't sit well with her. She loves me."

"Do you love her enough to risk everything?" He tilted his head, studying my face. "She'd hold your life in her hands."

"I don't know. I do love her, but what if she looks at me as a traitor?"

"It's something you're going to have to decide and talk to headquarters about. They'd have to sign off on that shit."

"I know, and they're going to be cocksuckers about it. That shit I know."

A knock on the door broke the silence that had developed as we both thought about the repercussions of this mission. When you're inside, it's hard to see the end. I'd lived day to day and hadn't thought about the future. After a while, it'd felt like it would never get here, so I'd allowed myself to become one with my new persona. I'd thrown caution to the wind, and now, my heart would be the casualty.

"Time to go," James said, nodding toward the door and standing.

I followed suit, sighing as I felt my shoulders slump from relief. "When will I see you again?"

"I'll meet you up in D.C. in a couple of days. I'll be with you the whole time. We were both neck deep in this, and since I was your contact person, I need to be there. It'll be soon."

"You're coming straight there?" I asked as I moved toward the door, quirking an eyebrow at him. I wondered if he'd take a side trip to see Izzy before he met me.

"Yes."

I grabbed the doorknob and turned slightly. "When you call Izzy, can you tell her I'm okay and to let everyone know I'll be home soon?"

"I'll tell her. She'll be relieved."

"Yeah, I'm sure they all will be."

CHAPTER
TEN

THOMAS

AT TIMES, I felt like a criminal as I was debriefed at DEA headquarters. I'd been grilled hour upon hour, day after day, and it was becoming annoying. I was ready to go home. I'd given the agency enough of my time.

James had arrived a few days after I did and had been put through the wringer too. We were outsiders within the agency. Everything that had occurred while I'd been undercover was called into question, and we were both being asked to explain the actions. We had been interviewed about the evidence, our behavior, and everything in between. Finally, after fourteen days, we were told we could leave, but had to be ready to come back when called.

Before I went back to the hotel to pack up my shit, I headed to the deputy administrator's office to have a heart-to-heart. I hadn't seen Roxy or spoken to her in two weeks, and I had done a shit-ton of soul searching during that time.

I was ready to fight for her and us. If she loved me the way she'd professed, how I knew she did deep down in my bones, then it would all work out in the end. I didn't worry that she'd out me. By now, some of the people had to have talked if she'd started looking for me. I needed to see what she knew and if the cat was out of the bag.

I knocked on the door, cracking my neck, turning it from side to side, and readying myself for a fight.

"Come in," a voice called from the other side of the door.

Opening the door, I saw the Deputy Administrator sitting behind his desk, riffling through papers. "Sir, I need to speak with you for a moment."

He stopped moving, looked up, and stared at me. Slowly, a smile spread across his face as he stood. Then he walked toward me with his hand held out.

"Thomas, good to finally see you again."

There was no way in hell this paper-pushing fucker remembered me. I was sure he'd been briefed on the entire situation and knew about the case.

Shaking his hand, I said, "You too, sir." I was lying my ass off, but by now, it had become second nature. "I needed to speak with you about something important."

He backed away, motioning toward the chair in front of his desk. As I sat, I took a moment to look him over. He was wearing an expensive suit, and he had perfectly combed and gelled hair, a clean-shaven face, and probably not a day out in the field under his belt. He was just a suit. He'd never put his life on the line, living a lie each day and trying to pretend to be someone he wasn't. He didn't understand how the lines blur and the small pieces of you get muddled to the point where you're not the same person anymore.

"I've dedicated over a year of my life to this mission—"

"We owe you a debt of gratitude for all your hard work."

"Please let me finish, sir." I held up my hand and his mouth snapped shut. I was pissed off that he'd interrupted me. Sitting forward, I rested my elbows on my knees before I spoke again. "I've given more to this agency than most people do. I've put my life in danger as well as my family. Without my work, the Sun Devils would still be on the street with no inroad to bring them down. Without me, you're nowhere." I paused, letting him absorb my words.

He nodded, placing his hands together and resting his index fingers against his lips. He was studying me much the same way I had him when I'd sat down.

"There's someone I can't just leave behind from my time working undercover with the MC. I'm here asking permission to contact her." I leaned back in the chair and crossed my arms over my chest.

"Absolutely not." He didn't move or blink as he uttered the words from behind his fingers.

"Sir," I started, not willing to just accept that and walk out. I'd fight for her. "I respectfully ask you to please consider me in this equation. I've already suffered and sacrificed enough for this job."

"I'm respectfully declining your request, Agent Gallo. It's too risky. As a member of the DEA, you are not to have contact with any person who was part of your under-cover work." He looked at me with his lips set in a firm line. "No. I'm sorry and I wish I could help you in some way." Unfuckingbelievable. Just a flat-out denial of my request without even putting thought into it.

"I'll have my resignation on your desk before I leave today," I replied without thinking. "I've given enough, most likely too much, to this agency. I'm no longer willing to put my life or those I hold dearest in jeopardy. I only have one life to live and I've sacrificed enough." I stood, glaring at him. "I respectfully quit, sir."

He shot out of his seat, rounding the desk to stand toe to toe with me. "That's unacceptable, Agent Gallo."

"Sir, I'm done. The months I spent undercover kicked my ass. I can't do it anymore. I'll be here to help with the investigation when called upon, but I no longer wish to be a DEA agent. It's time I reconnect with my family and find another path in life. A course where I don't have to give up so much of myself to do good in this world."

His face came closer to mine. I almost wanted to laugh. Did he think he scared me? Honestly, I could puff out some air and the man would fall over. He wouldn't know how to handle my fist connecting with his face.

"If you obstruct this investigation in any way, Agent Gallo, you'll be arrested for conspiracy. Watch your step very carefully from here on out."

"Yes, sir. I didn't give up these months just to watch it all get washed down the drain. I'll be at your service when needed, but I have more important shit to do than stand here and talk to you." Without shaking his hand or saying goodbye, I turned on my heel and marched out of his office.

Stopping at his receptionist's desk, I grabbed a piece of paper and a pen, scribbled a letter declaring my resignation, effective immediately, and signed my name. Then I left it on her desk and asked her to deliver it to the Deputy

Administrator immediately before I made my way to the elevators.

Freedom is a funny feeling. I'd thought I'd spend my life serving the people of this great country as part of the DEA, but after one undercover stint that had lasted longer than expected, I was done. No longer the man I was before, I wanted to find myself again, decide who the real Thomas Gallo was, and find a way to put all the bad shit I'd done behind me. Whatever the fuck that was at this point—I had no fucking clue.

When the elevator doors opened, James was standing inside, smiling. "How'd it go?" he asked as I joined him.

"I quit." I didn't dare look him in the eyes. He'd be pissed that I'd thrown in the towel over some pussy.

"So did I," he stated calmly.

My head jerked to the side. "What?"

"I quit too. Fuck them."

"I can't believe you did that."

"Thomas, did you ever think you'd quit?" he asked, tilting his head as he stared at me.

"No, but I'm stunned you'd throw it all away." I leaned against the wall, glancing at the display to see how many floors we had left. Twelve.

"I didn't throw shit away. I'm done with all the bull-shit. I want to spend time with your sister."

Another victim. I prayed Izzy felt the same about him, or else he'd just made the biggest mistake of his life.

"I wish you well with that, James." I tried to hide my smile, but I knew the man was batshit crazy about my crazy sister.

"We quit for the same reason. Sometimes, the heart takes control and we can't deny what we want most."

"When did we become such goddamn pussies?" I laughed, hitting my head against the wall.

"I don't think we are. We've just evolved."

"Yeah, we'll go with that. I need your help, James." I looked up at the ceiling. "Cover for me a few days with the family while I go see Roxy." I closed my eyes, waiting to be yelled at for my carelessness.

"Be careful, man. It's dangerous for you to go back there. Why don't you let me go get her and bring her to you?"

I shook my head, clenching my teeth. "No. I have to be the one to do it. She needs to understand how I feel and why I did what I did. She needs to feel me and remember the love we have. I can't send anyone in my place. Only I can convince her to leave and trust me."

"You're taking a huge risk. Let me come with you at least."

Just then, the elevator dinged and the doors opened. After walking out, I stopped and waited for him to turn to me. "I have to go alone. I know she'll listen. I pray that she loves me enough to understand all the lies."

"Call me, Thomas. Keep in contact and tell me what's happening."

"I will. Let's go get our shit and get the fuck out of D.C.," I said, pulling him into my arms for a bro hug.

Slapping me on the back, he said, "I never thought I'd hear those words."

We were on a flight by nightfall, landing in Florida before heading our separate ways. After we wished each other luck and made plans to meet up, I headed toward Roxy.

CHAPTER
ELEVEN

ANGEL

IT HAD BEEN weeks since Blue and the rest of the club disappeared in federal custody. Wild rumors had started shortly after their arrest. There were murmurs that Rebel had been placed in witness protection and was feeding information to the Feds about the club. The timing made sense, so many of the old ladies and the left-behind prospects believed that shit as gospel.

I was exhausted, barely able to stay awake as I drove home from my shift. Business at the club had plummeted after the arrests. Either the clientele was behind bars or people were too scared to come around, thinking they were being watched or that the club was bugged. It didn't seem worth showing up for fifty dollars in tips after dancing my ass off and letting men paw me like I was a sex toy. I was sick of it, ready to leave the life behind, but that would require relocating. What if Blue came looking for me, though, and I wasn't here? I couldn't leave until I knew where he was or how to contact him.

Walking into my kitchen, I tossed my purse on the

table, not bothering to look at my phone. What was the point? My phone had been silent since he'd vanished. It didn't stop me from keeping it within hearing distance. I'd hurl myself off a bridge if I missed his call.

As I sauntered through the living room, a hand suddenly grabbed my wrist. I screamed bloody murder, flailing my hands as I tried to hit whoever was holding me in their grip. My heart was pounding so quickly that I thought it would explode. The blood coursed through my body, causing my temples to throb and my body to shake.

"Stop!" he snapped, grabbing my other wrist and holding me captive.

I couldn't see his face as I shrieked, hoping someone would hear me. Then my instincts kicked in and I fell to the floor, deciding I wouldn't make it easy. I'd use any means necessary to survive and not be raped by the slimeball.

"Fuck you!" I yelled, now using my feet as weapons.

"Stop," he said again, trying to capture my legs with no success.

I kept kicking, pushing myself backward and toward the coffee table in the living room, as I searched for something to strike the intruder with.

"Roxy, stop fighting me!" the man hollered as he captured my ankle.

Instantly, I froze. I knew that voice. Maybe my brain was processing it wrong, the blood flowing through my ears helping mask the voice and making my fantasy come to life. I was likely hearing shit.

"Get off me, fucker!" I screamed, kicking him in the balls.

As he bent over, cupping himself, I took the opportunity to reach back and open the drawer. As my fingers felt the cold steel of my gun, he pulled my feet, yanking me away.

"No!" I cried out, tears flooding my eyes.

"Roxy, it's me, Blue," he said, his voice strangled from pain. His hand released my leg before the light in the living room switched on, illuminating his face and giving me a view of my Blue.

I covered my mouth, shocked and a little horrified that I could have killed him. "How?" I mumbled from behind my fingers. My eyes were wide, slowly filling with tears as I drank him in.

"Rox," he whispered, kneeling down on the floor and wrapping me in his arms.

"How?" I asked again, unable to form any other words. I could barely process that he was inside my house after not having heard from him in two weeks.

"I had to come for you." He cradled my cheeks in his hands, placing kisses across my forehead before capturing my mouth.

"How?" I repeated in a garbled voice, his lips impairing my ability to speak.

He drifted backward and stared at me. "It's a long story, baby. I had to see you."

Before I could respond, he kissed me again, pulling me into his arms. At this point, I didn't give a fuck how he was here. All that mattered was that he was here in front of me and I was in his arms. His words, *I had to come for you*, echoed in my head as our tongues danced together, the longing we both felt clearly conveyed without words.

Had he escaped from jail? My heart was still pounding roughly in my chest, but now I felt paranoid as I thought about the cops busting through the door. Fuck. I couldn't have him ripped from my life again.

Breaking the kiss, he sat down on the floor and hauled me into his lap. "We have to talk, angel."

"Talk. You have my full attention after once again making me think someone was here to murder me." I laughed, rubbing my nose against his. "Wait," I said, backing up enough to see his entire face. "Did you break out of jail? Are they looking for you, Blue?"

He laughed, shaking his head. "No one is looking for me."

"But how?" I asked, my jaw dropping in shock.

Touching my chin, he pushed my jaw closed, kissing my lips as he gripped my ass.

"Rox, do you love me?" he asked, staring at me.

"You're kind of scaring me, Blue." I chewed my bottom lip, my eyebrows turning downward as I tried to figure out what the hell was going on.

"Don't be scared. It's simple. Do. You. Love. Me?" His ice-blue eyes cut me deeply. I could see behind them the same war I had seen in him the last time we were together.

My voice was shaky as I spoke. "Yes."

My stomach started to hurt, the adrenaline from being scared to death wearing off. Blue looked so damn serious that I knew something heavy was about to happen.

"You need to listen to me and understand everything I'm saying. Can you do that?" His voice was strong and stern. There was no smile playing on his lips and no smug smirk—only a serious look, his lips set in a thin line.

"I'm listening." I reached up, stroking his cheek and still not believing that he was really here, that I was sitting in his lap.

"Do you love me enough to leave this life?" he asked, motioning around my apartment with his hand. "To leave all this behind?"

I started to giggle. He had to be joking. I didn't live in a palace with servants. I was a stripper, living in an apartment with mediocre furniture at best. I didn't have a family to worry about. No parents to keep me here. Blue was my constant, and he had grown into my beacon of happiness over the last couple of months.

"I'm serious, Roxanne."

"Ooh, you're breaking out my proper name. You must be serious." I tried to stifle my laughter, but it was hopeless.

"Rox," he barked, shaking me slightly in his grip. "I mean it. Can you walk away from this town and your life and never look back? There's no turning back once you walk out that door." His eyes darted around my face as he stared at me.

"Are you in witness protection or something?" I blurted out as soon as the thought popped in my mind.

"No, angel. I'm not in witness protection."

"Then why can't I come back?"

"It's too dangerous. Too risky for me, and it will be for you too if you come with me."

My mouth hung open again. Had I heard him right? I shook my head, trying to rid myself of my mental fog.

"You want me to come with you?"

"Roxanne. I love you. I've loved you for a long time. There's no one but you in my heart. I couldn't move on without you." He nestled his face against my neck, inhaling my perfume. Moaning lightly, licking my flesh. "I wanted to run away with you for a long time, but I couldn't. My duty held me back. It stopped me from making you mine. I knew I couldn't have you. I had to wait to claim you for myself."

Reaching up, I grabbed his hair, fisting it between my fingers. "Blue, it's always been you."

"I tried to walk away. I spent days trying to tell myself to leave you alone, but I couldn't. You're *it* for me, Roxy. Please say you'll come with me and never look back."

My heart sped up, hammering in my chest as his words sank in. "You want me to be your old lady?" I asked as my chest nudged his with each rapid breath.

Moving his face from my neck, he grabbed my face and brought my eyes to his, capturing my full attention. "I'm not a biker. I just want you to be mine and only mine."

My heart felt like it would burst. My nose tingled as tears filled my eyes, blurring my vision.

"Do you mean that?"

"Roxy, I mean it. I was nothing before you came into my life. You kept me sane during the most trying time in my life. I wouldn't have survived if it weren't for your love."

I silently took in everything he'd just professed. It was everything I'd wanted to hear, yet it scared me to death. He was talking some heavy shit, and I tried to process it all. Maybe he'd skipped bail and he wanted to leave the country before his court date.

"Are we moving to a new country?"

"No." He shook his head, the corner of his mouth twitching as he fought a smile.

"Then how? I just don't understand how you're here and want me to leave with you. Will we have to be on the run our entire life?" I paused and placed my hand over his mouth. "Even if you say we have to move for the rest of our lives, I'll follow you. I told you that I loved you, and I don't love easily, Blue."

A giant smile spread across his face, so massive that it almost kissed his eyes. "Roxy, we won't have to be on the run. It's not like that."

"Um, okay. I need a minute, baby." I covered my eyes, slowly rubbing them and trying to wrap my head around his words. I was more confused than ever. Then something he'd said in the beginning came crashing into my thoughts.

"Wait. You said you're not a biker?"

He shook his head as his eyes briefly looked away before returning to mine. "No. I never have been."

My eyebrows drew together again as I crinkled my nose. "But—"

"I can't tell you everything. You'll need to trust me. Do you trust and love me enough to come with me blindly? I promise to tell you the whole story."

"That's some scary shit, baby."

With that, his entire body shook as he burst into laughter.

"Rox, you loved me when you thought I was a biker. They're bad news. Criminals, drug dealers, and murderers. But you still loved me. What could be worse?"

"Hmm," I muttered, pursing my lips as if in deep thought. "You have a point there." I joined in his laughter before quickly sobering. "I'll come with you. I told you I'd follow you anywhere. Life has been torture here without you. Work is slow and I'm sick of taking my clothes off for strangers. I'm getting too old for this shit anyway. I want to start over and become something else—someone else."

He wrapped his arms around me, pulling me tight against his chest. "I promise to spend every day of my life making you happy, Roxy. You won't regret it. I promise you that."

I felt all warm and gushy inside. Finally, when I'd thought all hope had been lost, I heard the words I had been waiting for since the day I'd realized I loved him.

"I know you will, Blue." I peppered his face with kisses. The possibilities were endless, and I felt truly joyful for the first time in my life. Seeing the world through new eyes and dreams, I knew I could make myself over and start fresh.

"Why are you still sitting here, then? Pack up what you can in a few suitcases and let's get the fuck out of here. I'll explain the rest to you later."

Here was the point where most women would say no and ask a million questions, but in all honesty, what the hell did I have to lose? Nothing was holding me here. I had no roots in the area. I was just another lost soul making my way through life with no tether. I'd follow him to the gates of hell if it meant a possible chance at happiness.

Hopping to my feet, I held out my hand and helped lift him from the floor. He drew me into his arms, placing his lips against mine and kissing me with passion and adoration. I felt it down to my toes. Tingles racked my body as his hands wandered my exposed flesh.

Blue was back and I couldn't be happier.

***

We passed road signs signaling our distance to Tampa and he kept saying, "We're almost there." But I could barely keep my eyes open as we drove down the dark roads headed for the west coast of Florida. I fought a valiant battle, forcing my eyes to stay open.

"Where are we going, exactly, Blue?" I asked, and his name came out in a yawn.

"To my home," he replied, not taking his eyes off the road.

"Hometown or home?" I tried to shake myself awake as I pushed myself up in the seat.

"My home. This is where I'm from and where I really live."

My head started to spin as I realized there was very little I knew about the man. "You have a *home* home?"

"Yes, and I'm taking you there. Are you sure about this, Roxy? There's no going back. I don't mean I'll take you prisoner or hold you captive, but if you go back, you'll be in danger."

Swallowing hard, I nodded. "I'm sure," I said before letting out a giant breath. "Tell me where."

"I live in a town called Palm Harbor. It's about twenty minutes north of Clearwater. My parents and siblings live nearby."

My eyes grew wide. *Oh my God.* What if they hated me? I mean, who says, "Hey, Ma. This is my girlfriend and she's a stripper," and have his mother embrace the person? *Fuck.* My stomach began to knot and my palms grew sweaty.

"Parents?" I said, rubbing my hands against my jeans.

"Don't worry. They're going to love you."

I felt overwhelmed. He'd said "siblings." As in plural.

109

I'd never spent much time meeting other people's family. I was the girl who lurked in the shadows, not the type you brought home to Mom.

"I don't know, Blue." I slumped down in the seat and stared out the window as we exited the freeway and headed toward the coast.

"Stop worrying. If I love you, they'll love you."

"What are you going to say? 'Hey, Mom. This is Roxy and she's a stripper'? I mean, come on. No one can welcome that into their son's life."

"You don't know my parents. Besides, you can be anyone you want. You're starting fresh."

"True," I said, turning to look at his profile, which was lit by the streetlights as we passed them and they flickered off and on.

"I don't have to meet them just yet, do I?" I whispered.

"You can meet them when you're ready."

"Who are you, Blue?" It was a good question, and I didn't have the answer. I hadn't even known he had a brother or sister, let alone many.

"As soon as we get home and crawl in bed, I'll tell you everything."

"Promise?" I squeaked out, closing my eyes as embarrassment flooded me. I sounded like a fifteen-year-old girl asking her boyfriend to promise her the world before losing her virginity to him.

"I swear. I need to hold you when I tell you everything."

"Okay," I whispered, staring into the darkness.

I closed my eyes, trying to think of happy things to drive the panic I felt inside away. I had to remember that Blue made me happier than anyone else ever had. He was still the same man. Sure, there were plenty of things I didn't know about him, but I knew I loved him. I knew how he felt about me and that he never treated me like a piece of trash. He was it for me.

Suddenly, my body jerked, waking me from my dream as the car came to a stop. When I opened my eyes, I stretched in my seat and took in the house in front of me. It was big. Not just big, but grand. This wasn't a shitty apartment complex or a small bungalow from my old neighborhood.

There was a high archway with a chandelier dangling down and lighting the front door. A three-car garage sat to the left of the house and had two large, dark wooden doors. The roof was tiled, but I couldn't see the shade in the darkness. The house was a light color, but it was too hard to tell which shade of pastel lined the exterior walls. The front door had to be ten feet tall, with a large metal knocker for guests. It was a stunning two-story structure.

"This is where you live?" I asked.

Turning off the car, he said, "Yes, this is home sweet home. I know it's too much."

"No, it's amazing. How in the fuck did you live in that shitty-ass room for so long when you had this waiting for you?"

"I didn't have a choice."

"Why would you shop at Kmart when you could have shopped at Nordstrom? Jesus."

"It's more complicated than that. Let's go inside. I haven't been home in over a year."

"What the fuck? Men are so damn strange," I mumbled as he climbed out of the car and closed the door. I sat there for a moment as he jogged in front of the car. As he opened my door, I couldn't help myself as I asked, "Do your parents own this house?"

He burst into laughter. "No, Roxy. This is all mine. Come on. Let me show you your new home."

My new home. I hadn't thought of it like that. Sliding my hand in his, I placed my legs outside and stood. As I straightened my back, I winced as my muscles ached from the long drive.

"Stiff?" he asked, wrapping his arm around my shoulder and closing the car door.

"Yeah. Just a little." I tucked myself in the crook of his arm and looked into his brilliant azure eyes.

As we walked toward the door, he tried to find the key with one hand. "How about I'll run us a bath and tell you everything?" After unlocking the door, he pushed it open and held his hand out for me to enter first.

"Sounds divine." I stepped inside and felt the air leave me in one fell swoop.

The interior was more beautiful than the exterior. It had a Mediterranean feel, with dark hardwood floors and stucco walls. In the foyer there was a grand staircase with wrought-iron railings that tangled together, creating an intricate pattern. An oversized modern chandelier hung from the ceiling, giving the space a warm glow. It was breathtaking. An urge to twirl around like a princess with my arms outstretched overcame me, but I fought it, not wanting to act like a lunatic.

I might have lived in a shithole, but I'd studied magazines, dreaming of a better life. This fit the bill.

"Do you want to look around or take a bath and sleep?" he asked, tossing his keys on the side table I'd missed when I walked in.

"Bath. You can show me around in the morning. I feel like shit and probably don't smell much better." I laughed, feeling way out of place in a lavish home like this.

He held my hand, walking up the steps by my side as we made our way to his bathroom. The nerves I'd felt changed and molded into something different. No longer were my jitters from fear. Instead, they filled me with excitement over all the possibilities that lay before me.

CHAPTER
TWELVE
THOMAS

THE ENTIRE NIGHT had been exhausting. Fortunately, without much hesitation, she'd left with me, believing in me enough to follow me on blind faith. But after the long drive, the only thing I wanted to do was hold her in my arms and wash away the grime from the day.

"Are you going to tell me your story now, Blue?" Roxy asked, looking at me over her shoulder as I scrubbed her skin with some plastic thing I'd run some soap over. Izzy had told me years ago that they were good for skin, and bought me one for Christmas. I'd thought it was dumb as fuck back then, but it came in handy tonight.

"Yeah, angel. I'm just trying to figure out where to start." I dipped the scrubber in the water before lifting it and scrunching it to get more bubbles. "First, my name isn't Blue."

She laughed, bringing her knees up and hugging them. "Sweetie, I figured that much. What is it?"

"It's Thomas." I pulled her body toward me, dragging her ass against the bottom of the tub.

"That sounds so formal," she teased as she rested her chin on her knees.

"My family calls me Tommy."

"I like Thomas better. How big is your family?"

I touched her back with my free hand, watching the water trickle down her skin and follow the path of her spine. The whiteness of her skin was a stark contrast to my olive complexion, and I was always mesmerized when I touched her.

"Well, my parents live nearby, and I have three brothers and a sister who are in the area. They all work at the family tattoo shop."

"No shit. Wow. That must've been great growing up." She peeked over her shoulder again and smiled. "I would've given anything to have a sister. Or a pain-in-the-ass brother, for that matter. I'm jealous."

"Looking back now, it was fun. We were always together and causing trouble. Sometimes, it became over-whelming, especially when my little sister came along, but we all looked out for each other." I ran the scrubber over her back, watching the bubbles cascade and pop as they trickled down her skin.

"Are your parents still together?" She turned back around and ran her fingers over my legs, which were caging her in.

"Yeah."

"You guys sound like the Brady Bunch without the divorce. You're so lucky, Bl—Thomas."

"We were the Brady Bunch on crack. Fistfights were common, teasing was merciless, and the noise was constant in my house when I was growing up. You're going to love them, Rox. I just know you will."

"I think so too." She rested her head on my shoulder. "So, if you're not a biker, who are you? What the fuck don't I know? Are you a cop?"

"Such a saucy mouth." I tapped her on the nose and laughed. "I don't know where to start. I love riding, so in that way, I am a biker. I was never really a member of the Sun Devils MC. You're right, Rox. I am in law enforcement. I was a member of the DEA, but I quit."

I laid it out, giving her the entire story. She held my life in her hands in this moment.

"Wow. Fuck. Who knew this entire time you were a cop. You were working undercover?"

"I was," I replied, tracing small circles on her skin with my fingers. "Do you hate me now?" I asked, brushing my lips against her cheek.

"Why would I? I wasn't in the MC. I know half of those guys looked out for me and raised me when I was a kid, but I have no allegiance to them. They never loved me. They put up with me and looked out for me because of my mom and my dead father. You're the only one who has ever truly cared about me. You're the first person in my life I've felt secure with. You're my home, baby."

"This is a whole new life here, Roxy. You can be anything and anyone you want to be. If you want to go to college, you can. If you want to get a job, you can do that too. You're in charge of your destiny from here on out. I'll never hold you back. I knew I needed you in my life when I couldn't imagine another day without you."

"I don't know what I want to be, but I know it will require clothing." She broke into laughter, snorting a little.

"I'm the only one who sees you naked," I growled in

her ear as my lips touched the edge. "I won't share your body ever again."

"Thank God," she whispered, moaning as I dragged my tongue against her skin.

"Do you want to change your name?" I asked, wondering if it would be better to have a new identity too.

"Well..." She paused and turned her body around in my arms. "Roxanne isn't really my name."

My eyebrows drew together, the confusion I felt inside likely written all over my face. How the fuck didn't I know that? I'd sent names to James, trying to gather information. I'd even sent him information on Roxanne since I'd been sleeping with her and growing more attached, but he never shared her full name with me.

To say I was shocked would be an understatement. "It's my turn to say, 'Wow.' What is it?"

She looked down for a moment before moving her eyes to mine. "Roxanne is my middle name, but my first name is Sarah."

"Sarah Roxanne Parker," I replied, whispering her real name back to her as I stared into her eyes. I smiled, liking the sound of it. "I still love Roxy too."

"You can call me anything you want." She laughed, rubbing her nose against mine. "No one really knows my legal name. My mom never used it. She hated it, but it was a family name that my dad wanted to use. So I'm a Sarah."

"You're mine and that's all I care about." I placed my mouth over hers, drawing her body closer to mine.

Wrapping her legs around my back, she moaned into my mouth as she felt my hardness against her body. I lifted her ass with my hands and deposited her in my lap, bringing her pussy flat against my length. Even though I was exhausted, the only thing I wanted to do was crawl inside her and claim her body.

Not bothering to use protection—I knew she was clean, and I sure as fuck was—I pushed inside her and felt instantly at peace. The water sloshed in the tub, spilling over the sides as her body collided with mine.

Our mouths never separated as we fucked each other. It wasn't lovemaking; it had been too long for that. This was purely animalistic pleasure and a need to feed the craving. Her tits bounced with each thrust, and her mouth fell open into a silent moan. Not wasting a moment, I pumped harder and faster as her fingers dug into my shoulder.

I felt like a kid in high school, ready to blow my load after two minutes of fucking. Maybe it was from finally telling the truth that an enormous weight had lifted. Or maybe it was that that I hadn't fucked her in more days than I cared to count.

Minutes later, I was spilling my seed as I sank my teeth into her shoulder. Crying out in a pain-pleasure mix, she followed me over the crest and rode the wave of ecstasy.

Even though I wanted it to last for hours, I was fucking exhausted. Tomorrow night, I'd make up for my lack of stamina. I had too much shit going on in my head to take my time. I'd wanted to come and leave my seed in her. I'd wanted to say, "Hey, world. I've been here. I own this shit."

Mission accomplished, I held her in my arms as my happy cock shrank before eventually sliding out. "I love you, Sarah Roxanne Parker," I whispered in her ear, grabbing her face and bringing her eyes to mine. Searching her face, I saw water collecting in the corners.

"I love you too, Thomas." She inhaled deeply, her

chest puffing out as her rock-hard nipples rubbed against my chest.

"Want to go to bed?" I asked, running my hands up and down her arms, trying to stave off the cold. The water was hot and the air conditioning had kicked on, causing a chill in the air I hadn't noticed while we'd been fucking.

"I'm exhausted and happy, and I want nothing more than to sleep in your arms." She pushed off my legs, using them as leverage to stand.

I held her thighs, steadying her from falling. Standing, I helped her from the tub before I got out and grabbed towels. Wrapping her up first, I slowly dried her skin, rubbing the soft cotton against her goose-bumped flesh. She smiled, watching me closely as I touched her. Looking at her, I saw the person underneath. Roxanne was her sex-kitten persona, but Angel was the real girl many people never saw. I knew her, though. She was the one I'd fallen in love with.

After I sheathed her body in a towel, tucking it near her breasts, she repeated the process on me. But before we walked out of the bathroom, I snatched her towel and threw it into the tub along with mine. I didn't want anything between us as we slept tonight.

She screamed before giggling. "Hey, it's cold!" Rubbing her arms, she danced back and forth, her lips chattering from the chill.

"I'll keep you warm. I need to feel you against me tonight—and every night forward."

"Baby, who knew you were so sweet?" She batted her eyelashes.

I smiled as her lips touched mine. This moment with

her was the happiest I'd felt in longer than I could remember.

"Come on, Roxy." I lifted her in my arms, trying to warm her with my body as I carried her into the bedroom. Then I set her on the edge before I undid the blankets.

"Babe?" she asked, looking up at me and grabbing my wrist.

"Yeah?" I stopped moving and stared at her.

"Can you not call me Roxy anymore? It just brings me back to the club and taking my clothes off. It was my stage name, and I'd prefer not to hear it again anytime soon."

I hadn't thought about that. "Hmmm," I said as I rubbed my chin. Staring at her, I took in her features. "I'm just going to call you Angel."

"Whatever floats your boat, Thomas." She drew out my name, laughing and clicking her tongue as she spoke. "As long as it isn't Roxy."

"I'm not saying I won't slip up from time to time." I bent down, kissing her lips and brushing her cheek with my knuckles.

"I'm going to come up with another nickname for you. Blue is so damn good, but I don't want to think about the past. Only our future," she whispered against my lips.

"Anything you want." Pulling back the covers, I captured her in my arms, taking her mouth, hard and wet, before releasing her.

She slid across the silky material, lying on her back and looking up at me. *Fuck.* I wanted her again. Before we closed our eyes, I fucked her one last time. This time, I lasted until the muscles in my legs gave out and exhaustion took us both.

CHAPTER
THIRTEEN
ANGEL

WHEN I WOKE close to noon, Thomas was still in a deep sleep. Tiny snores passed his lips as his chest rose and fell with his breathing. I took a moment, drinking him in, and thought of how fortunate I truly was. Living a dead-end life, with no one to call mine and no family, I'd felt like my existence was hopeless. He'd changed all that, though. My life had veered off course and changed direction without my consent, and I couldn't have been fucking happier.

After slowly inching out of bed as I tried not to wake him, I grabbed a fluffy black robe from the back of the door and went to explore the house. I stopped at each open door, peeking inside and not trying to be too nosy. There were three other bedrooms and a bathroom as I made my way to the stairway. The house seemed a little excessive for a single guy, but it was decorated with masculine finishes. The hardwood floors were a dark wood that showed my reflection in their glossy finish.

The place was spotless. Everything was put away, and

it all sparkled or shone from the cleanliness. It didn't look lived in and had that "maid" feel to it. Walking down the staircase, I ran my fingertips over the smooth railing, feeling the coldness of the wood. I took in the foyer as I descended the stairs. It was opulent, with marble floors that formed a circle and were surrounded by the same dark wood he had upstairs. The space was two stories, with windows above the door that let the sunlight cascade inside.

I wasn't sure where to start. The place was a mansion. My entire apartment building could have fit inside and there still would have been room for more. Turning to my left, I saw the family room and headed to check it out, but a group of photos on the wall caught my eye.

I walked straight toward the photos as if drawn to them. There was so much I needed to know about this man. There had to be ten photos on the wall with different people in them—including Thomas. They were laughing and hugging, and I could see the love practically jumping out of the frames. My heart ached as I wondered what it would've been like to grow up like him, surrounded by love.

Moving closer, I touched a picture with my fingers. I could see by the eyes and extreme facial features that, in it, he was a young boy, probably no older than four, cradled in the arms of a beautiful woman. She stared at him with love in her eyes as he smiled, facing the camera.

I wanted that. A mother like her—someone who looked at me like I was the only thing that mattered.

I hadn't known what that felt like until I'd met him. Even when he hadn't said the words, I had known. Some things can be felt without having to hear the words "I love you." He treasured me and never made me feel cheap.

Still staring at the photo, I jumped when I heard his raspy morning voice.

"Angel."

"Jesus," I said, flinching and putting my hand over my heart. "You scared the hell out of me."

I laughed at how silly I had been. Who else would have called me that but him? I hadn't heard him walk in, so I needed to learn the sounds of the house. Every place has them—the small squeaks and creaks that make you feel at home instead of on edge.

I stared back at the photo, feeling my cheeks heat from embarrassment. He wrapped his arms around me, the mint of the toothpaste tickling my nose as his warm breath skimmed my neck.

"Whatcha doin' down here alone?"

"I didn't want to wake you up. I just thought I'd make us some coffee," I lied. I was nosy. Wanting to see the house and get to know the man by seeing what he had surrounded himself with.

As he squeezed me, his soft laugh vibrated against my ear. "I'll make us some. I think Izzy stocked the pantry."

"Izzy is—" I remembered her name that he whispered in his sleep.

"She's my sister, babe. Don't worry. There's no one but you in my life. Unless you count my extremely nosy and pushy family."

I sagged against him, a feeling of relief washing over me. "Is this your mom?" I asked, pointing at the photo I had been admiring.

"Yeah. It's my favorite childhood photo with her. I can't wait to see her."

"I can see how much she loves you. She has to be excited to see you." I stroked his arm, feeling the hairs move under my fingertips.

"She doesn't know I'm here. I wanted to surprise her." He slid his hands to my waist, turning me in his grasp.

"Why would you do that to her? She's probably worried sick." I rested my cheek against his exposed chest, nestling my face between his pecs. I could hear his heart thumping inside.

"If she knew I was coming home, there would be a house full of people. I want to spend time with my parents and my siblings. The others can wait. My mom loves to throw a party. You'll see."

"She's going to have a heart attack when you walk through the door."

"Maybe. Want to come find out?"

I bit my lip, not wanting to hurt his feelings but not ready to do the entire family thing just yet. "Not today, baby. Give me a couple of days and I promise I'll go with you." I brushed his back with my fingertips, feeling his body quake in my arms.

"Okay," he said before kissing the top of my head.

"I want this day to be about you. There's plenty of time for them to get to know me." I hugged him, wanting to never let go.

"Will you be okay here today by yourself for a while?" he asked, holding me by the shoulders and looking down at me.

"I will," I said with a smile. "I'm going to snoop

through your shit while you're gone. I figure that will take a couple of hours, easy." I bit my lip to hide my laughter.

"Don't be too naughty. I'll have to spank you if you do."

"Thomas, you know I love when you're rough. I may be bad just so you give it to me good."

"Babe," he growled, his voice growing deeper. "I'm going to fuck you so hard later you won't be able to walk for a week."

"Promises, promises," I teased. "If I don't get coffee soon, I'm going to be real grumpy." I pouted, batting my eyelashes.

After he made a pot of coffee, he ran around the house, getting ready before saying goodbye and heading to see his family. I'd be lying if I said I wasn't a little jealous that someone missed him, but I told myself that Thomas missed me when we were apart. I wasn't alone anymore.

CHAPTER
FOURTEEN

THOMAS

I STOOD OUTSIDE THE DOOR. Cracking my neck, shaking my fingers at my side, I took a deep breath before I walked inside. My mom would lose her shit. Hell, the entire family was about to lose it when I came through the door. I had to ready myself for the ear-piercing screams and blood-curdling shrieks of happiness that only the Gallos could deliver.

The house looked the same. Life had marched on without me. Sunday dinners had gone on as planned since I had been a child, whether I'd been in my chair or not. Nothing had changed but me. I was the wild card, the different one. My life had been forever altered through my actions undercover. Didn't matter if the shit was justified or not—I was no longer normal. I had become a criminal like the others, just as guilty for my actions as they were. The only difference was I wore a badge and they wore a cut.

Without knocking, I opened the door and walked inside.

"Hello." I didn't see her, but I'd know my mother's voice anywhere. It haunted me in my dreams and comforted me in my times of self-doubt.

"Ma!" I yelled, moving toward the kitchen, where I heard her voice coming from.

"Tommy?" I could hear the shock in that single word.

She flew out of the kitchen, jumping into my arms and kissing my face. "Baby! Oh my God. You're home!" she yelled in my ear, squeezing me so tightly that I could barely breathe.

"Ma," I repeated, trying to pull in a breath.

She drew back and stared at me. "Is it really you?"

I chuckled, taking in the changes in her appearance. Time had passed, and my mother looked older than I remembered, with a few more lines around her eyes and cheeks. A majority of her stress had probably been caused by my absence. Then again, she had an entire family of people who would cause any normal woman to age early.

"It's me, Ma."

Releasing her legs from my body, she placed her feet on the floor but kept her arms wrapped around me. "You look different, Tommy." I smiled and didn't fucking dare say the same thing to her.

"Tommy!" my dad called out, walking into the foyer.

"Pop," I replied, holding out my hand, since my ma was still attached to my body, squeezing me.

"Maria, let the man go. You have to share him some-time," Pop said without moving from his spot.

"If I do, he may disappear." Her voice was muffled, since her lips were against my skin.

Pop walked behind her, removing her arms from my

body. Ma took a step back, blotting her eyes and wiping away the tears that had drifted down her cheeks.

"Son." Pop wrapped me into a giant bear hug.

My father, brothers, and James were the only men in my life I'd shown affection to. No one else ever got that from me. That shit didn't leave this house. It was grounds to get your ass kicked, and I didn't need an extra fight on my hands. Italian men didn't have an issue showing their love to one another.

"Hey, Pop," I whispered, holding on to him just as tightly.

The man had been my hero when I was growing up. He was larger than life and could make most men in the neighborhood quake. I'd wanted to be worthy of being his son when I grew up. I thought I'd accomplished that goal in his eyes, but inside, I knew the truth. I'd muddied the waters between good and evil.

Over his shoulder while still wrapped in his arms, I saw the entire Gallo crew as they filed into the foyer. Izzy popped out first, a giant smile forming on her face before James came up behind her and placed his arms around her waist. I guessed they were still going strong. Joey pushed James aside, knocking him and Izzy over a bit, and came straight for me. My brother didn't often show emotion, but I could see the happiness on his face.

"So fucking good to see you, brother," he said, tapping my pop on the shoulder. "Mind sharing?"

"Your mother often says I'm greedy," Pop said, laughing before releasing his grip on me.

Izzy gagged. "For shit's sake. You two give way too much information."

They laughed as my pop put his arm around her shoulder, and Joey held out his hand and smiled. When I placed my palm in his, he pulled me into a giant bear hug. Joey and I were most alike. We were so close in age that I swear my mother must have wasted no time in getting knocked up again.

"Joe, it's so fucking great to see you, man," I said, slapping him on the back.

Then a blonde walked into the foyer and leaned against the wall. A giant smile was plastered on her face as she stared at Joey and me. She was wearing a cute, flowery sundress that didn't do anything to hide her belly. She was definitely pregnant, and had to be Suzy, Joe's wife. He grabbed my arm, backing away, and turned to the blonde.

"Sugar, come here." He motioned to her to stand at his side, and she followed his command without protest. "This is Tommy."

She looked up at me, her large blue eyes twinkling. "Tommy," she repeated. "I've heard a lot about you."

"Don't believe a word of the bullshit he fed you about me." I laughed, winking at her.

She blushed as her smile widened, and she winked back. "You're prettier than I thought you'd be."

Looking at my brother, I saw his stare go to Suzy and his hawk eyes bore into her, but she didn't care. "You're prettier than I thought you'd be too. Who knew Joe could get such a killer babe?"

She chuckled, bringing her hand up to cover her mouth.

"You two done?" Joe barked, and glanced between us.

"Just fuckin' with ya, man."

She turned to him, stood on her tiptoes, and kissed him. "Oh, Joey, you know you're the most beautiful man in the world. He's your brother, and Gallos don't do ugly. I'm yours and yours alone. I have a mini-you growing inside my belly. Duh."

His face instantly softened and his body visibly relaxed. This girl was good. She knew exactly how to handle my brother. I didn't think I'd see the day when he would become pussy-whipped, but there she was in flowers, blonde hair, and blue eyes. She was the boss, just like my mother.

"Fucker, get your ass over here and kiss me!" Mike yelled out, pushing Suzy and Joey aside. He puckered his lips and held out his arms, and I couldn't stop myself from laughing. Motherfucker was still a goofball.

"Only if you give me tongue," I teased, sticking out my tongue and wiggling it.

He gagged, holding up his hands and waving them. "I'm tapping out."

"Come here, ya big pansy ass. I've missed you," I said, moving closer to him and wrapping my arms around him.

This was more man love than I had experienced in a long time. This was my family—all gushy and overemotional—and I'd missed every moment of it while I'd been away.

Mike hadn't changed much, except that he looked happier and more relaxed. Maybe he wasn't spending his life in a gym, taking out his aggression and bullshit on a punching bag or Rob.

"It's good to see you, Tommy," he said, holding my neck in one hand and slapping me on the back with the other.

"You too, Mikey. You too. Where's the little lady?" I asked, looking around the room as Mike let go of me.

"Mia!" Mike yelled, and glanced around the room. "She picked the worst time to use the restroom. I swear women are—"

"Women are what?" she hissed as she walked into the foyer.

She was stunning. Her long brown waves trickled down her shoulder and framed her breasts. She was tall and voluptuous, and I was impressed with my brother's catch. Who knew a beefhead could bag a doctor who looked like her?

"Mia," I said, holding out my hand to her.

"Damn," she said, placing her hand in mine. "Another sexy Gallo man." She laughed, tossing her head back as her hair followed suit.

"What?" I asked, crinkling my eye and shaking my head.

"Devilishly good looks. Are you as cocky as the others?" she asked, smirking.

"Nah. They're the pricks. I'm a complete gentleman," I said as I brought her hand to my mouth, kissing her soft skin.

"Mia, don't listen to that bullshit. He's as bad as the rest. Gimme a kiss, brother." Izzy moved Mia away from me and wrapped her arms around my body. She was tiny, so her head didn't reach my shoulders. Resting her head in my chest, she squeezed me tightly and rocked back and forth. "I'm so happy you're home."

"Are you here to stay, son?" Pop asked, still holding my ma.

"Yeah, Pop. I'm not going anywhere."

"Thank Christ," Ma mumbled, looking at the ceiling and cupping her hands in prayer—always the good

Catholic girl.

"This calls for a celebration!" Pop hollered, fist pumping the air.

"Mike, go grab the good stuff from the cellar," Ma said, shooing him with her hands.

"Why do I always have to do the shit work?" he grumbled, giving me the stink eye.

I shrugged, laughing as I looked around. Someone was missing. "Where's Anthony?"

"Yo," a voice called out from the family room.

I pushed through the crowd and entered the room his voice had come from. "Yo, douchebag. You don't even get up to say hello?" I looked down at him, my hands on my hips as I blocked his view of the television.

"I figured you'd find me when everyone else was done pawing at you."

This was exactly how my brother was and had always been. He was a cocky asshole who didn't believe in public displays of affection. Underneath, he was as gushy as the others, but he very rarely let that side show. Only when he was extremely intoxicated did he get all "I love you, man" and let his Norah Jones side show.

"You better get your lazy ass up and hug me." I kicked his feet, glaring at him.

"I'm older. I don't have to do shit." He smiled, challenging me, like the old days.

There was a time when he had been bigger and badder, but then I'd grown up and gotten more muscles. I could take him without any exertion. He still needed a reminder every once in a while, and it had been ages since I'd seen him.

"I can make you," I said, raising one eyebrow at him, unable to hide my smile.

"Fuck," he hissed as he looked me up and down. "You look like you could even take Mike. Bastard's gone soft since he met Mia. He's turned into a real pussy, but you—you look downright scary," he said with a chuckle as he stood. Sticking his tongue out at Mike, he gave me a great bro hug, maintaining his manly personality but still showing me the love I knew he was trying hard to hide.

"You're the pussy, Anth," Mike teased as he entered the room holding two bottles of champagne. He placed them on the side table next to my dad before sitting on the floor beside Mia and holding her leg in his grip.

"Sit down, Tommy. We want to hear all about your time away." Joe patted the spot next to him on the couch.

"Hey, that's my spot," Suzy whined as she walked in behind my mother.

"It was his first, sugar. Come sit on my lap." He grinned at her as he rubbed his leg.

"Okay," she whispered before padding across the carpet on quick feet, crawling into his lap, and putting her arm around his neck. Joey held her in one arm and rested his hand against her round belly, rubbing it in tiny circles.

Things had changed, yet they were still the same. Coming home after such a long absence was the strangest thing ever. I felt at home but out of place. New people added to the family, and the dynamics of the group had shifted.

Instead of the house being flooded with testosterone, the women had almost outnumbered the men. Anthony and I were the lone holdouts, but that was about to change for me. Soon, Roxy would be here with me.

I sat in my old spot, closing my eyes and reminding myself that she was Angel now and not Roxy. She'd be pissed if I slipped in front of my family. There would be a lot of questions if I did that. Gallos were quick and didn't miss a goddamn thing.

Opening my eyes, I saw everyone staring at me. No one was chatting or watching the Cubs losing—they just stared. James sat behind Izzy, pulling her back to his front before she sagged against him. He whispered in her ear, slowly stroking her stomach with his hand. She giggled, her face turning red. Even though I was the dumbass who had given the thumbs-up to the situation, I still had an urge to punch him in the face.

"First, when do you have to go back?" Ma asked as she sat in her chair next to my father, fidgeting with her apron.

"I don't."

Their mouths hung open as I sat there, leaning back and watching their shock.

"What?" I asked.

"What do you mean you don't?" Ma asked. "I don't think I quite understand."

"I quit. Plain and simple."

"Hell yeah," Joe said, slapping me on the shoulder. "You coming to work at the shop with us?"

I turned to him and blinked. I was shit at art. I certainly couldn't poke holes in people's bodies and call that art either. It wasn't my thing.

"Nah, man." I shook my head and looked at James. "Did you tell them?" I asked him.

"No, man. I didn't."

Izzy turned around and looked at him, wondering what

134

I knew and what she had been left the fuck out on. *Whoops.*

"James quit too."

Ma gasped while the rest of the family continued to gawk. "I feel like I can breathe again," she said, sighing with relief.

I chuckled at their response. I didn't think I'd ever seen the Gallos at a loss for words, especially Izzy. "I had enough of their shit. I gave them enough of my life, and they weren't getting another damn day."

"Me either," James joined in, adjusting as Izzy turned in his arms and hugged him before whispering in his ear.

Had aliens come down and abducted my sister? *Izzy* and *sweet* weren't two things that often went together. She was hardcore and could be downright scary sometimes. But with James, she melted in a puddle of goo, and I sure as fuck didn't want to know why.

"Maybe you two should go into business," Mike said, still staking his claim by holding on to Mia like someone might snatch her.

I nodded, not really having put much thought into what I'd do after leaving the DEA. Then I looked at James, who shot me a look that said maybe it wasn't a bad idea before turning his attention back to Izzy.

"We'll see. One thing at a time, Mike."

"So what the hell happened over there, son? Did you get the bad guys?" Pop asked, reaching out to hold my mother's hand.

Even after all these years, the two were like teenagers. They held hands, kissed, and hugged at every turn. They were whom we'd all gotten our love gene from, and it was something we couldn't shake—even Anthony.

"It's a long story, Pop. Bad shit happened while I was there. More than I'd like to ever discuss or care to remember. So far, they're all behind bars, and I hope they stay that way." I sighed, wishing Angel were with me. I wondered what she was doing and if she was okay. I'd left her alone in a strange house.

"Me too. You think you guys have a solid case?" He cocked an eyebrow.

"Yeah. James and I worked our asses off to make sure it would stick. I didn't want it all to be in vain." I rubbed my temples, trying to block the memories of shit I'd done that I'd never thought I'd do. Murder, disposing of bodies, drugs, and other shit I forced the fuck out as soon as it started creeping back in.

"Good," he said, nodding and giving my mother's hand a quick squeeze.

"Who's hungry?" Ma asked, standing from her chair before releasing Pop's hand. "I didn't make anything special. No one bothered to tell me my son would be home today." She turned to James and gave him the look of death. I could almost see the tiny daggers shooting out of her eye sockets.

"Uh oh," Anthony teased. "Looks like someone isn't the new favorite anymore." He tossed his head back, laughing and holding his stomach.

"We all know Thomas is the real favorite," Mike replied, rolling his eyes and making a face at me.

It dawned on me that while I'd been living in hell, they'd sat here every Sunday enjoying life and teasing each other relentlessly. I had done the work so families like mine could have these moments of peace and happiness, but knowing all I'd missed still made my heart hurt.

"Let's go, people. Sit down, and the girls and I will grab the food," Ma said, clapping her hands for us to move it.

Everyone jumped, scrambling to their feet as Ma made her way to the kitchen. Pop put his arm around me, walking next to me with a giant smile.

"It's so good to have you home. Your mother has been a wreck. I've been worried sick about you, and even your brothers and Izzy have been. It's good to finally see with my own eyes that you're okay."

"I'm alive, if that's what you mean, Pop," I replied, turning to look at him with a small smile.

"I know you've seen some shit. I can't even begin to imagine, but you're back and that's all that matters."

Everyone took their spots, and an extra chair was pulled to the table for me. I had lost my table presence, but I hadn't expected it to be left open with the two newest additions to the family.

"I'm so hungry I could eat a darn horse," Suzy said, placing her napkin across her lap before she picked up a fork.

"You're eating for two, sugar. Have as much as you want," Joe leaned over and kissed her on the cheek.

Her face turned red as she mouthed, "I love you," to him and they nuzzled. What the fuck had happened? I chuckled, trying to evoke the memory of my brother from times past. He was a badass and people were scared of him, but Suzy wasn't. They were the yin to the other's yang.

"For fuck's sake. She'd eat everything if you let her. The woman is like a machine," Anthony whined, taking a sip of the water that had been placed on the table before we'd sat down.

Izzy, Mia, and Ma walked in the room each holding giant dishes of food that let off steam. Izzy and Mia each set their bowls perfectly spaced down the table.

"I made lasagna, chicken parm, and sausage and peppers," Ma said as she placed the lasagna in front of my father.

My mouth watered from the smell. All the memories of my childhood and every Sunday dinner came flooding back. There wasn't a cook in the world who could rival her. No one. I rubbed my hands together and couldn't wait to dive in and taste all the deliciousness.

"Lasagna!" Suzy squealed, dropping her fork before she clapped her hands. "I'm eating every last drop of that, baby. It's my faaaavorite!" She practically bounced in her chair and rubbed her belly with excitement.

Ma smiled, touching Suzy's shoulder and staring down at her belly. "Sweetie, you eat as much as you want. You're feeding my grandbaby. There's plenty of food for everyone else. Would you like the first piece?"

"Yes!" Suzy yelled, her eyes and smile growing wide.

"I hate that baby," Anthony grumbled under his breath, and shook his head.

"What did you say?" Joe asked, glaring at Anthony.

"Nothing. I'm starving and it smells so damn good."

"You're always starving. Ladies and kids first! Don't be a greedy asshole," Joe barked, reaching behind Suzy and slapping Anthony in the head.

James burst out laughing. I was sure that, over the last few months, he'd been welcomed in and made to feel at home. Someday, he'd get the full Gallo treatment. I knew their asses didn't behave with him around. No one knew what that word even meant in my family.

Watching everyone chat and laugh made me feel warm, and a calm settled over me. This was where I belonged, but I didn't know what was happening in each of their lives. They spent each day with each other at work, but I was totally out of touch. I plastered a fake smile on my face, trying not to think of all the moments I'd missed, as I watched my ma dole out the food.

"When's the baby due, bro?"

"Early September." He smiled, grabbing the plate Ma had put in front of him.

"I can't believe I'm going to be an uncle and I missed it all."

"Don't be silly," Suzy said, her voice garbled by a mouthful of lasagna. "You'll be here for the birth and that's all that matters. She's going to have four cool uncles and two killer aunts."

"Four uncles?" Mike interrupted before I could ask the same damn question.

"Yes. You, Thomas, Anthony, and James."

That was interesting. Suzy had already integrated James into the family. I turned to him, seeing his face break out into a giant smile as Izzy almost fell off her chair.

"Hold up," Izzy blurted out, facing Suzy with her hand up and her palm flat. "James is not a Gallo. He's here, but not a Gallo."

"Yet," James retorted, pushing down Izzy's arm.

She turned and glared at him, her eyes growing wide and saying a million fucking things. I knew that look well, having been on the receiving end a million times when I was growing up. The girl never made shit easy. When she couldn't speak, she'd let you know exactly how she felt.

"See? Four," Suzy said with a giggle. "What baby could be so lucky?"

"Sugar, what about your sister?" Joe asked, turning in his chair and tilting his head.

"Baby, she's not a part of this family. I barely see her and she's kind of a bitch." She stabbed her lasagna and didn't look at Joe as she replied.

The entire table burst into laughter. What the hell was I missing?

"What the hell is so funny?" I asked before placing a sliver of the piping-hot lasagna in my mouth. *Fuck, it's better than I remembered.*

I let it sit on my tongue, closing my eyes while the cheese slowly oozed across my tongue. It was like heaven. There's nothing like home cooking. The food at the club had been mediocre at best. The cook wasn't a chef, but he knew how to reheat shit when we got hungry. The dive bars we'd spent our nights at didn't provide a gourmet sampling. It was shitty bar food that left a funky oil after-taste in my mouth.

"Suzy doesn't swear very much," Joe answered, because everyone else was either laughing or eating.

I still had my eyes closed, savoring the taste of my ma's cooking. Opening them slowly, I looked at him and smiled. Then I swallowed it, ready to dive into another chunk, and asked, "How the hell did she end up with you?"

We all swore. It must be genetic. I swear Izzy's first word was *fuck*. I thought having four older brothers who used it like common language didn't help. I also thought it served my ma right for having had us keep our eyes on her when we were little. Joe often had the dirtiest mouth.

"Pure luck. She swears when it's necessary." He smiled at Suzy, winking as her cheeks turned red.

"When would that be?" Anthony asked, putting his fork down and looking at Suzy, waiting for an answer.

"Eat your fuckin' food and don't worry about when that would be, jerkoff." Joe was usually easygoing, but he seemed on edge.

"You PMSing or something, man?" Anthony asked before picking up his fork and shoveling in a chunk of sausage.

"My leg has been killing me. The goddamn rain always gets me. I just wish the shit was fully healed."

"It'll go away, Joe. Give it time. Take some Naproxen and you should feel better. It won't always be like this," Mia offered.

"Yeah. It'll get worse," Mike chimed in, chuckling. "Your ass is getting old, and you're going to be chasing around a baby soon."

"I don't see you getting any younger, fluff 'n' stuff," Joe teased, laughing at his own joke. "When are you getting married and making an honest woman out of Mia?"

The veins on the side of Mike's neck bulged out. He'd never liked the terms "soft" or "fluffy." He was all about being hardcore and tough as an ox. Plus, from what I could tell, he didn't like being put on the spot about his future with Mia.

Rubbing the back of his neck, he looked down and then stared straight at Joe. "Mia and I are taking things slow."

"Bullshit," Mia coughed, hiding a smile behind her hand. "Excuse me."

"That's my girl," Izzy chimed in.

The house had shifted. It was no longer ruled by cocks and jocks, but by babes. We were all truly fucked at this point. There was no going back. Maybe it was my absence that had led everything astray. Or maybe it was bound to happen in time. The family would inevitably change once we'd decided to settle down.

"Marry the poor girl already," Ma blurted out.

"It's a huge step, people," Mike whined, his shoulders tensing as he tried to hide his discomfort with the topic.

I kept eating forkful after forkful as they discussed marriage. Joe and Suzy were happily married, along with my parents, but half of the single people at the table didn't think it was all it was cracked up to be.

"Do you ever want to get married?" Mia asked, turning to Mike and staring at him with crinkles in her forehead. "Like, ever?"

"Well, yeah. Eventually. We're young, doc. I want to enjoy life a little bit."

"Um, I'm not asking you to have a baby, you big pansy. Marriage doesn't equal a fun killer," she hissed, pushing back from the table and storming off.

Everyone was totally stunned and in shock.

"This shit happen a lot?" I asked, looking around and wondering if the estrogen was a little too much in the room.

"No," Mike answered, scratching his head. "I don't know what the hell has gotten into her lately."

"You're such a dumbass," Izzy groaned, and rolled her

eyes. "Really? She loves you and you love her. What's your issue with marriage?"

"Hey, pot. Meet kettle," James muttered before a hearty laugh burst from his lips.

I laughed, knowing that the man was going to have his balls handed to him later for that little comment.

She looked at him, moving in close enough that their noses were touching. "You watch it, Jimmy," she hissed.

Before she could continue, James's hand wrapped around the back of her neck. Then he pulled her face to his and planted an enormous kiss on her lips. She groaned, pushing him away as he gave her a deeper kiss, holding her body to his. When they separated, a popping sound filled the room. Everyone had been quiet while watching James *handle* Izzy.

"As I was saying," she said, wiping the corner of her lips like nothing had happened. "The woman wants to be your wife. We want her to be our sister. What the hell are you waiting for?"

"I don't know," Mike replied, and shrugged.

"Brother, we don't know how long we have in this world," Joey said. "My accident taught me that shit. I didn't waste another minute without making Suzy my wife. Don't fuck this up." He shook his head. "You're not good enough for her anyway. She deserves better."

"Fuck you, Joe. I'm the only man for her. I'd give my life for Mia. I quit fighting for her and the clinic. I couldn't imagine being apart from her."

"Um, again, what the hell are you waiting for?" Izzy said, throwing a piece of bread at Mike.

"Fuck," he growled, pushing back from the table and leaving to go after Mia—hopefully.

"I see that the drama around here has died down," I said, and immediately smiled as I looked around the table.

"Boobs: they're always the problem," Anthony piped in, still shoveling forkfuls of food in his mouth.

I didn't know how the guy stayed so damn thin with the amount of food he consumed. Since we'd been little, he could eat us all under the table, yet he was the thinnest of us all. I didn't even think the fucker worked out.

"I see your grumpy ass is the same. What's got your willy in knots?" I asked, glancing at Ma to make sure I wasn't overstepping my bounds.

She smiled, hiding a laugh behind her napkin.

"Women are a pain in the ass, Tommy," Anthony said. "When they aren't breaking your heart, they're mixing up your head. Nothing but trouble, in my opinion."

"What, or shall I say who, have you been hiding, Anth?" Suzy asked, touching his hand.

He quickly jerked it away like her hand was fire. "No one. I'm just saying. It's best if I just steer clear of relationships."

"You doth protest too much," Suzy said in her best British accent, which was terrible. "You're hiding something. I feel it in my bones."

"Don't start with your pregnancy ESP nonsense again, Suzy."

She smiled, making a *tsk tsk* sound with her tongue before diving back into the giant hunk of lasagna my mother had placed on her plate when she'd finished first.

"Damn, we forgot the champagne. Hand me the bottles, Izzy darling," Pop said, beckoning them down to his end.

"Let me run and grab glasses," Ma replied, hurrying

from the table and quickly returning with both hands filled with flutes.

"We should wait for Mike and Mia," I interrupted as Pop released the first cork and it bounced off the ceiling.

"They could be a while," James replied with a small grin.

While Pop handed each glass down the table as he filled them, I stared at him. He hadn't aged much in the time I'd been gone. Not as much as my mother, anyway. He still looked the same, happier than ever. This was his thing—family dinners and bullshitting. He had his boys all under one roof, but we all knew his favorite was Izzy. She'd always be daddy's little girl.

My pop stood, holding up his glass. "I'd like to propose a toast." He paused until all of our champagne glasses were high in the air. "To my family. This house is filled with more love than your ma and I could've ever imagined. You kids—"

With those words, we all blanched, hating the sound of it, and he laughed.

"You have made us proud. We hope the family expands someday. More babies and more wives would be nice. It's great to have Tommy back and in his rightful spot. To love and family. *Salute*."

"Hear, hear," we echoed, clinking glasses with the people closest to us. Then we sipped champagne, talking quietly until we couldn't eat anymore.

After putting my napkin over my plate, I leaned back and rubbed my stomach. Somehow, Suzy was still eating. I watched forkful after forkful in astonishment.

"She's growing a Gallo in there," Joe said, rubbing her belly.

"So, what about you, Thomas? Were you seeing anyone?" James asked, throwing me for a loop.

"Oh, tell us," Izzy begged, resting her head in her hand and batting her eyelashes.

Fuck. I made a mental note to punch James in the face or the junk.

I sighed, raking my hand through my hair and then dragging it down across my face. *I want to kill him with my own bare hands.* "Well, it's complicated." I turned to James and mouthed, "Fucker," to which he smiled.

"Isn't love always?" Anthony groaned before taking another sip of champagne.

"Shush it," Izzy hissed, throwing another piece of bread at him.

Ma quickly reached across the table and grabbed the remaining bread from Izzy's plate, her mouth set in a straight line. "Continue, baby."

"I did meet someone. She's amazing." I bit my lip, not sure how much of the story I should divulge.

"Where is she now?" Pop asked, placing his napkin on the table and resting on his elbows.

"She's at my place."

"Why?" Ma looked confused by my statement.

"I didn't want to scare her right away." I sighed, knowing I'd just opened a giant can of "what the fuck," Gallo-style.

"What the fuck!" Izzy yelled.

Yep, there it is. "She wanted to let me spend time with my family without her today. She's resting since we got home late last night. I didn't want to overwhelm her."

"We're not overwhelming. We're loveable," Suzy said, hiccupping as she scraped her plate clean.

146

"She's not used to a family like ours."

"What type would that be?" Pop asked, crooking an eyebrow at me.

"Pop, she has no one. No parents. No one. So yeah, we'd be overwhelming."

Ma gasped, covering her mouth with her hand. "No one?" she asked, shaking her head.

"I couldn't leave her behind. I love her too much. She kept me sane."

"She can take all the time in the world, baby."

"Thanks, Ma." I smiled, hoping it was over, but I'd thought wrong.

"What's her name?" Joe asked.

"Angel." I smiled, happy that I'd used the right name.

"Angel sounds tough. We could use another tough chick around this table."

"Bitch be trippin'," Anthony mumbled, and was quickly slapped in the back of the head by Joe. "Ma, you're going to let him treat me like that? He's hit me at least twice at the table."

"Yeah, honey. You deserved it, though." She smiled.

"What's Angel do?" Suzy asked, taking a sip of water.

"She's going to go to school," I blurted out, because for fuck's sake, we hadn't even discussed her plans.

"I can't believe they let you bring her with you, son. Isn't that risky?" Pop said, eyeing me with curiosity.

"Yeah. They declined my request to speak with her. I quit on the spot and went to her. She came with me blindly, Pop. She has no one on this earth but me. How could I not bring her with me?"

"Do you love her?" Ma asked, her devilish smile reaching her eyes.

"Yes," I replied, shocked at how easy I could spill my guts to my family.

"You can't go wrong by following your heart, Thomas. You've always been a good judge of character. If you think she's the one and worth the risk, I'll trust in your decision." Her smile grew wider. "Plus, that means more babies!"

"Jesus," I groaned. "Let's not get ahead of ourselves, Ma. One step at a time."

"Bring her next time. I really want to meet her."

I nodded, hoping that she'd be ready to face the group next weekend.

"But we'll wait."

"Wait for what?" Mike asked as he and Mia walked back in and took their seats. Their faces were flushed, like they'd just had a good workout.

"Work *things* out?" Suzy asked, giggling and shooting Mia a look.

"We've agreed to disagree," Mike answered, and cleared his throat.

"I'm sure you did." Suzy chortled, unable to control herself.

Mia just blushed, keeping her eyes downcast as she picked up her fork and began to eat again. "I'm famished," she said between bites.

"I'm sure you worked up quite an appetite," Joe responded, and as soon as the words left his mouth, Suzy hit him in the chest. He didn't budge, but he stared at her hand like it was a bothersome fly. "Sugar, hit me again and see what happens."

"That right there is sexy," she said, batting her

eyelashes before hauling off and punching him in the shoulder.

He caught her wrist, holding it in front of his body. "I warned ya."

"I'm getting tired, Joey. Will you help me lie down upstairs?" she asked, a small grin on her lips.

"I'll be right back. Let me help Suzy upstairs."

Everyone smiled at each other, knowing that was bull-shit. Those two were going to be doing the nasty in my parents' house and they didn't seem fazed.

As they walked out of the room, I looked at my ma. "You're okay with that?" I asked, motioning toward the lovebirds climbing the steps.

"I remember being pregnant quite fondly, actually. So yes, I'm okay with it." She turned to my father and smiled, grabbing his hand and giving it a squeeze.

"Bleh," Izzy said. "I swear to God, every time I come here, you two have to talk about sex. I can't get the vision out of my head."

"Baby girl, how do you think you got here?" Pop asked, staring at Izzy.

"I don't need a reminder. The mental image is disturbing. You're lucky I'm not a nun."

"They'd kick your ass out," James howled, slapping the table with his hand.

"Shut up," she hissed.

"Say it again and I'll help you lie down," he replied, the corner of his lips twitching.

"Everyone needs to stop talking about sex. Jesus," I croaked, wanting to bang my head on the table. "Dinner talk sure has changed around here."

"Yes, baby. Life changes." Ma looked at me with sadness in her eyes.

I felt her comment. Although it was innocent, it cut me deeply. She had no idea exactly how I felt, but there was so much truth to her statement. Life had changed. The Gallos had continued, grown, and evolved. I'd fucking missed it all.

CHAPTER
FIFTEEN
ANGEL

MY LIFE FELT SURREAL. One minute, I thought Blue was gone forever and I'd been left to a dead-end life with no hope for change. Then *wham!* He was back and asking me to run away with him.

My head had spun when he'd told me the truth about himself. I'd never had an idea that he was an undercover cop and not a true biker. The last thing I would've thought was that he had an entire family, a huge house, and a different life altogether.

We all hide bits of ourselves, things we don't want others to know, but I hadn't thought that this was what he'd kept hidden from me. My secret was my full name. No one knew it. I kept that shit hidden away, the only thing I could keep just for myself. They saw my body, but they didn't know all of me. I knew it was stupid, but when you take your clothes off for a living, you want to keep something from the masses. At least I did.

Besides my mom, whom I barely spoke to, and my dad, who was now deceased, no one knew the real me—no one besides Thomas. My mom didn't give a shit about me. She never had. It was all about becoming an old lady and hopping in the bed of her next victim. When the members of the MC had been arrested, she hadn't even bothered to call me. She'd vanished too, probably on to her next victim.

I sat on the couch, riffling through a magazine, as Thomas made a phone call to James. I'd had enough sitting around since I'd arrived here five days ago. I couldn't remember a day in my life when I hadn't worked. It was what I did; it was who I was. But not anymore.

Stopping on a page, I stared at an article about education. Teaching would be an amazing career, filled with rewards and children. I wanted to do something that felt like I was making a difference. My only fear was that someone would find out about my past and use it against me. How horrifying would that be if, at conferences, a father walked in and recognized me? The thought of it turned my stomach and had me flipping the page.

"Yeah, I think it's a great idea," Thomas said as he walked behind me and placed his hand on my shoulder. Giving it a light squeeze, he continued to speak. "I think we should get a business plan together as soon as possible."

I looked up, smiling at him. I was envious of their ability to pull shit together. I had a world of possibilities, but each one made me freeze up with panic. Every job and career had pitfalls, but it all came back to being recognized. It was stupid, really, because the likelihood was low, but I couldn't shake the fear.

"Come over and we can discuss it further and maybe grab a bite to eat." Sitting next to me on the couch, he pulled my magazine down and smiled at me. It was warm and genuine, and it made me feel instantly calm. He had that ability. Then he covered the phone and whispered, "Is that okay, Angel?"

I nodded, not minding a little company. Plus, I could use a little change of scenery. I had become used to a lot of people around, and this week, Tommy and I had lain low. Now I was ready to bust out of the house. Company would be fabulous, even if they were only going to talk business.

"Izzy?" Thomas asked James, his eyes darting to mine. Meeting his sister, the one I'd heard a lot about, would probably be best one on one. If she hated me, at least I'd know before having to be subjected to the entire family. "Yeah, bring Iz. The girls can get to know each other," Thomas said, leaning back in the couch and setting his hand on my foot.

Stroking the top of my foot with his thumb, he continued to talk business and plans. I tried to tune it out, silently freaking out about meeting a member of his family. *Fuck. I can't cook either.* Maybe we could order a pizza or something, because cooking for an Italian family wasn't something I felt comfortable with now—and I probably never would.

After ending the call, he tossed the phone on the loveseat, giving me his full attention. "Are you sure you're okay with this?"

Turning his body, he grabbed my feet and placed them in his lap. Continuing his light stroke, he looked at me with soft eyes. I loved the blue. I could get lost in the endless shades that changed slightly every day.

I closed the magazine, dropped it to the floor, and let myself sink down in the couch. "Yeah. I have to meet your family sometime. I figure if she hates me, the rest of the family will too, and at least we'll know ahead of time." I stared at my hands, which were resting against my abdomen.

"Angel," he said, now gripping both of my feet in his large hands. "Look at me."

I raised my eyes to him but didn't dare speak. His mouth was set in a firm line, devoid of playfulness and joy.

"They're going to love you. I told them a little about you on Sunday. My parents were overjoyed, and my siblings were curious."

"Please tell me—"

He held up his hand. "I would never. They know the basics. That I met you while undercover and that I'm in love with you. They can be overwhelming, but they're going to love you as much as I do."

His words made my insides warm. Professing his love and the future love of his parents had my body humming with excitement.

"Will Izzy like me? Fuck. Sisters can be the hardest to impress."

He laughed, brought my foot to his mouth, and touched his lips to the side. "She's going to flip when she meets you. My sister has always hated having so many brothers, so she'll look at you as a possible trump card to equalize the males in the room. She's loud and talks her mind, but I have no doubt my little sister will embrace you with open arms."

"I can't cook." I felt like I was making excuses to back out of the evening I'd just agreed to.

"We're going to order Chinese. No cooking tonight for either of us."

"But isn't that against the family rules or something?"

He held out his hand to me. "Come here, Angel."

I didn't hesitate. Sitting up, I crawled into his lap, resting my head on his shoulder. He held my body, one arm behind my back and the other clutching my legs as he stroked my knee.

"We don't have rules. The only things that are required in this family are love and devotion. My ma is the one who does the cooking, and I'm sure she'd teach you someday if you'd like that. Tonight we'll go out for Chinese. I don't want to waste the evening cleaning the kitchen and all that shit. We're going to have some fun tonight."

"Okay," I whispered, tilting my head to stare into his eyes.

Planting his lips against my forehead, he inhaled deeply, giving me a gentle kiss. "Don't ever fear anything when you're with me. I'll never do anything that will make you uncomfortable. If you don't want James and Izzy to come over, just say the word and I'll cancel it."

I didn't want him to do that. I had to get over the hump. Start meeting the family and crawling out of my safety net of this house and the cocoon we'd lived in this week.

"No, I'm really okay with it." Even if my insides were a jumbled mess of nerves, I knew it was the right time.

"Do you want to meet my family Sunday? I know my ma would be so happy to meet you."

My lips trembled, and the thought of it made my eyes water. "I don't know," I whispered, bringing my hand up to rest against his cheek. I swiped my fingers against his freshly shaven skin, enjoying the closeness.

"Let's see how tonight goes. Just promise me you'll think about it."

"I promise," I said, bringing my lips to his chin and peppering him with kisses.

"What time are they coming?" I asked, still in my pajamas even though it was almost two in the afternoon.

"Five," he replied.

When he adjusted my body, I felt his cock harden underneath my ass. Wiggling my bottom, I made him groan and make another adjustment, which resulted in his almost lifting me from his legs.

"Five? Fuck, that's early for dinner, love."

"Yeah, but we're going to talk and then go to dinner later."

My mouth formed an O. I was happy that we'd be going to a restaurant. "Well, that gives us a couple of hours to waste." I smiled up at him, giving him a sexy wink.

"Angel, when I get to feast on your body, it's never a waste." He stood, lifted me in his arms, and headed for the stairs.

"A couple of hours?" I asked, swallowing hard and feeling my insides quiver.

The man had an appetite for sex that was larger than most men I'd been with. He wasn't a selfish lover, having given me more orgasms in an evening than I'd thought was humanly possible.

"I'm going to make it impossible for you to think of anything but how I feel inside you. I'm going to eat your pussy until you beg me to stop, and then I'm going to fuck you again until you can't form a thought," he said, taking the last step and heading toward the bedroom.

"I kinda like the sound of that," I said, giggling as he carried me.

The last thing I wanted to do was worry and pace the floor for the next three hours. There was no better way to spend an afternoon than in Thomas's bed, wrapped in his arms, with his beautiful cock inside me.

***

As I stood on shaky legs, I tried to finish my eyeliner before the doorbell rang. My entire body felt like jelly after having spent the last two hours in every position imaginable. I hadn't even had time to be nervous about meeting his sister, and putting my makeup on had become a chore.

Ding, dong.

"Fuck," I muttered, taking one last look in the mirror before tossing my black eyeliner in the drawer. Running my fingers through my hair, I brought my face closer to the mirror and gave it one final look. "It'll have to do." My auburn hair was crazy. I didn't have time to straighten it, and after the last few hours in bed, it needed it.

I smoothed out the black sweater I was wearing, trying to find something to make my features stand out and not wash away my pale skin. I was wearing my favorite pair of Miss Me jeans with a fleur-de-lis on the pockets and a pair of five-inch, black, strappy high heels to match my sweater, which hung off one shoulder, showing just the right amount of skin to be sexy but not slutty.

I could hear talking coming from downstairs and a

female voice laughing and loud. Without a moment to spare, I left the bedroom and headed down the hallway. Then I stopped before hitting the steps, took a couple of deep breaths, and counted to five. *I can do this.*

Walking down the stairs, I saw a beautiful woman hugging Thomas with a giant smile on her face. Then she looked up, capturing me in her gaze.

"There she is," she said, pulling away from him before moving toward the bottom step.

Please don't let me trip. My knees still felt weak from the sexathon.

She held out her arms, waiting for me, as I took the last step on shaky legs. Smiling, I attempted to hide my inner turmoil and stood straight, showing no fear.

"It's so good to meet you," she said, wrapping her arms around me as soon as I was close enough.

I froze for a moment, locking eyes with Thomas. His face broke out into a gigantic smile—this was probably the happiest I'd ever seen him. His eyes twinkled as the corners crinkled, brilliant blue shining from them.

"You too," I whispered, finally returning her embrace.

"I promise I don't bite," she said in a soft voice. "But don't ask James. He'll say I do." She chuckled, released me, and turned toward James, giving him a quick wink.

I moved toward Thomas's side, holding my hand out to James. "It's nice to meet you."

He grabbed my hand, pulling it to his lips. "It's great to meet you finally." He gave me a tiny kiss and looked at me with a smile

"Finally?" I asked, caught off guard by his words and the kiss. Swallowing hard, I waited for the shoe to drop. I figured the family would have to find out someday, but I wasn't ready to start dealing with my past yet.

"Yeah. I knew you were his girl while he was with the MC. I was his handler, and I knew his movements and people he spent time with."

I wanted to crawl inside Thomas and escape. It must've been written on my face, the panic and fear that started in my stomach and began to spread throughout my body.

"Oh," I whispered, unable to take my eyes off him or remove my hand from his grasp.

Thomas coughed, breaking my trance. "Want a drink, Izzy?"

"Fuck yeah. I'm parched, big brother."

They left James and me alone, standing in the foyer, as they headed to the kitchen. I started to pull my hand away, but James held it tightly.

"Angel, don't worry," he said. "We all led different lives. It's in the past. I have more secrets than a diary. Shit isn't getting beyond Thomas and me."

I just stared at him, blinking, still frozen.

"We're all starting with a clean slate. Izzy doesn't know shit, and no one else will until you feel the time is right. *If* you ever feel the time is right. Don't give a second thought to the Gallos, either. They're good people. They welcomed me in like one of the family and they'll do the same for you." He squeezed my hand, trying to give me reassurance.

Family. It was a foreign word to me. I didn't even know what it would be like to be part of one.

"Thank you," I said on a shaky breath, feeling relieved

that he said that he'd keep my secret and everything would be okay.

"How about a drink, Angel?" James asked, releasing my hand to guide me toward the kitchen with his hand on the small of my back.

Usually, I'd take the gesture as a sexual one, but maybe he felt my hesitation and inability to move. "I could use one or ten." I laughed, feeling some of the pressure release from my shoulders. If Thomas trusted James, I would have to do the same.

"James, leave the girl alone," Izzy teased, pouring a glass of wine. "Don't listen to him. He acts all big bad wolf, but I know how to tame the beast." She held the glass out to me, a playful smile on her face.

"Izzy, I don't want to hear about James's beast. *Ever.*" Thomas glared at her, grabbing the bottle of wine and then filled three glasses on the counter.

"I'm just fucking happy she called it a beast," James told Thomas as he swiped a glass and wrapped an arm around Izzy's shoulder.

"No more dick talk. Let James and me talk some business, and then we can go to dinner."

I nodded, sipping the red wine and trying not to worry about being left alone with his sister. Maybe she was one of those girls who was nice when necessary and then turned into a viper when left alone. I had experienced a lot of them as a dancer. Girls could be so shitty to each other for no reason. I prayed that she wasn't like that, that her kind, playful nature was the true Izzy.

"You two go talk, and Angel and I will get to know each other better. We'll go in the living room and give you boys some private time." She stood on her tiptoes, giving James a kiss before motioning for me to follow.

I smiled at Thomas, joining Izzy in the living room. She plopped down on the couch, somehow not spilling a drop. "You didn't want to stay and listen to their boring shit, did you?"

"Nah. They're going to talk about work. I'd rather have some girl time," I replied, sitting on the other end of the couch.

"Girl talk is my favorite. I have been surrounded by dicks my entire life." She laughed. "Do you love my brother?" she asked, not beating around the fucking bush.

"Yeah, I do. He's the first person I've ever loved." My face heated; I was embarrassed for admitting it.

"Wow. James is the first man I've ever loved. So, are you going to marry him?" She smiled, bringing the glass up to her lips and staring at me over the rim.

"We haven't talked about it." I twirled the glass in my hand and wondered if he would ever ask someone like me.

"Sorry. I get a little ahead of myself. Jesus, growing up in a house with four brothers, I swear to shit that all I wanted was a sister. No house should ever be that unbalanced."

"Yeah," I said, laughing at the torture they'd probably put her through. I didn't know from my own experience, but I'd heard that brothers were usually overprotective, and no woman wants to feel outnumbered.

"You don't even know the half of it. When all I wanted to watch was *The Care Bears*, we were stuck watching *The Dukes of Hazzard* reruns because they all wanted to stare at that brunette's ass. It was horrible. Finally, the numbers are starting to balance out. Suzy, my brother Joe's wife, and then Mia, Mike's girlfriend, have helped bring the numbers closer together."

"You're into this, huh?"

"Girl, you have no idea. It's been over twenty years of their bullshit and I'm ready to break the cycle. Suzy is having a baby in a couple of months and I'm praying that it's a damn girl. I want to buy dresses and shit with lace."

I smiled at her and made the decision that I really liked Izzy Gallo.

"I hope I get to meet them all someday."

"Well, my ma is dying for you to come to dinner this weekend. Any time she sees a new girl, she immediately thinks babies. So be prepared."

I swallowed hard, trying not to focus too much on her words, but they gnawed at me. "Have there been many girls?" I asked before taking a very large sip of wine. It was more like a gulp, but I didn't polish off the glass.

"Oh, no. No one ever brings someone home unless they know they're the one."

"The one?" I asked, choking on the wine.

"Yeah. I never brought a man to Sunday dinner. Technically, I didn't bring James either. He just showed up. His ass is like a fly I can't get rid of. He made himself at home." She sighed before bursting into laughter. "I think they like him sometimes more than they like me."

I laughed too and then thought about being *the one*.

"If Tommy brought you home and wants to introduce you to everyone, then you're it for him."

"I don't know. I'm trying not to get ahead of myself here, Izzy." I took a deep breath, blowing it out on shaky lungs.

"Just let it sink in. I can see by the look in his eyes how

much he loves you. I don't think I've ever seen my brother look at a woman the way he looks at you."

A small smile spread across my face, my cheeks heating as she stared at me. "Maybe," I muttered, downing the last drop of the wine and wishing there were another bottle sitting on the coffee table.

"I'll get another," she said like she was a mind reader, patting my knee and standing.

"Great," I replied, watching her walk from the room. I slumped into the couch. "Holy fuck," I whispered, letting the knowledge that I was possibly *the one* for Thomas sink in.

Saying that you love someone and planning out a lifetime are two entirely different things. I knew he was fabulous. I'd be crazy if I didn't want to be his wife. Why would this amazing man, who was filled with love, sexy as hell, and doing well for himself, want a girl like me? I wasn't anything special. I wasn't a runway model, I didn't have money in the bank, and I sure as fuck didn't have an education. I didn't see much upside to me.

What the hell did he see?

CHAPTER
SIXTEEN
THOMAS

"I DON'T KNOW, JAMES." I looked up, seeing Izzy coming into the room. "Hey. How's it going out there?"

"Fantastic. Just needed another bottle of wine."

"Don't get drunk before dinner." I sounded a bit like my pop, but I didn't want to have them pass out on us before we ate. Wine was the worst shit to get drunk on—the hangover was nasty.

"Okay, Dad. You boys worry about you, and Angel and I will talk about you and drink. Shush it." She grabbed the spare bottle of wine on the counter and the corkscrew and stuck her tongue out before disappearing.

"I don't know how you put up with her sometimes. You must have the patience of a saint." I laughed, knowing exactly how mouthy and outspoken my sister could be.

"I have my ways, Thomas. Don't ever doubt that."

"Fuck. I don't want to know."

"Back to business. I put in a few calls, and I think it's our best option. Neither of us wants to go back into law enforcement. We're both unemployed and have more skills than half of the local sheriff's department. I think it's a killer idea."

"So, we're going to be private investigators?"

"We can be our own bosses. Hire some employees to handle the shit like computer work and phones. I think it's the best fucking idea. You have a better one?" James asked, pushing the half-empty glass of wine away.

I thought about it for a moment. I'd spent the last couple of days wondering what I'd do now that I didn't have to go back to work for the DEA. Working at Inked, the family tattoo shop, didn't hold an interest for me. I wasn't artistic and found it to be too boring. And I didn't want to sit around inside all day.

"I don't have a better one. So, we're going to be partners?" I asked, leaning back in my chair and running my hand through my hair.

"Yeah. We have to get an office and business cards and come up with a great name. There's not much competition in the area. The ones I've found are jokes with no real training. We can even reach out to local law enforcement and see if they'd let us follow up on some cold cases. Think about it, man. There's no one more qualified than we are around here for this kind of work."

"I'll talk to my lawyer this week and see what we need to do first. I want this shit on the up-and-up."

"Partners?" he asked, holding out his hand.

Sliding my palm in his, I replied, "Partners," before shaking his hand and sealing the deal.

"Let's get together next week after you talk with your lawyer and iron out all the details."

Although I knew it could be cumbersome to start a new

business—I'd been a part of Inked when it had begun—I knew it wasn't too difficult. Especially an operation with few employees and very few supplies. We could have it off the ground in a matter of weeks.

We sat for about fifteen minutes, bullshitting and talking about the DEA. Everything seemed to be going smoothly with the criminal cases for the members of the Sun Devils who had been arrested. For once, it was working out as planned.

"Let's go tell the girls the good news and celebrate," James said, pushing back from the table.

I nodded before following him into living room. The ladies were sitting on the couch, chatting and laughing, and it was the happiest I'd seen Angel.

"It's time to celebrate, ladies!" James exclaimed, slapping me on the back after I'd come to a stop next to him.

Fucker really wanted to be punched. He knew I hated that shit, and that was the main reason he did it.

Glaring at him, I spoke though gritted teeth. "Ready to eat?"

"What are we celebrating, Jimmy?" Izzy slurred, her smile sloppy and uneven.

They'd had almost an entire bottle of wine on empty stomachs. They were tipsy, giggling like high school girls, and Angel was sexy as fuck.

James's smile changed when she called him Jimmy. I knew he hated that name. A few people at the agency had tried using it on him a couple of times. James's fist had abruptly met their faces before they'd started calling him by his full legal name. Most changed to Caldo, preferring his last name to avoid any physical harm. Izzy, on the other hand, liked yanking someone's chain.

166

"Izzy, you'll pay for that later, but for now, we're going to celebrate the future. Your brother and I are going into business together."

"Oh God," she whined with glassy eyes as she threw herself backward into the couch cushions. "My brother and my boyfriend—together forever."

"Sounds like a greeting card," Angel said, bursting into laughter before Izzy followed suit.

"Maybe I should get them that little heart charm that's split in two and they can each wear one half." Izzy slapped her knees, chuckling as tears began to stream down her face.

"All right, ladies. Let's get some food into you both."

"Drinks too," Izzy told James as she wiped her face and stood.

James stroked her cheek, staring into her eyes with a grin. "Anything you want, Izzy. I'll get what I want later."

"Dude," I said, pointing my finger at him. "Don't say that shit about my sister. Especially in front of me."

"Habit."

"Get fucking new ones," I demanded, holding out my hand to help Angel stand.

A few times this week, I'd called her Roxy. Then I'd been quickly reminded not to use the name. Each time, I'd spend ten minutes chanting the name "Angel" over and over again inside my head to help make it flow naturally.

"Since she's your sister, I'll try my best."

"Ooh, baby, I love when you try your best," Izzy declared, jumping on James and wrapping her legs around his body.

"Fuck," I grumbled. This type of shit was going to happen all the time. I needed to just get used to it and ignore them or Izzy would try to push my buttons every time we were together.

She kissed his face, holding his cheeks in her hands as James held her by her ass. "I love you, Jimmy," she blurted before kissing him on the lips.

James pulled his lips away and smiled. "That's the only time I'll let you call me that."

"Ready to go, Ro—" I stopped dead as my eyes grew wide. Fuck. I knew I'd do it sometime. Watching them in my living room had me a little off-kilter. "Angel." I hated the slip-up and prayed she wasn't pissed.

"Yeah," she said with a small smile, stroking my arm. "It's okay, baby," she whispered.

"Can you two disengage long enough to leave the house and get to the restaurant?" I asked, looking over at them as they kissed.

"Uh huh," James mumbled, his lips pressed against Izzy's. "Come on, Iz. We have to go eat."

"No," she breathed. "I love how you kiss."

"Iz, babe, let's go. We can finish this in the car on the way to the restaurant." He winked at her and she instantly jumped down, marching straight for the door.

"We're taking two motherfuckin' cars," I insisted as I wrapped my arm around my girl and followed James and Izzy into the foyer.

As I grabbed my keys off the side table, they walked outside and waited until I'd turned off the lights and locked up the house. As we climbed in our cars, I thought that this might be one of the longest nights of my life.

"What's wrong, Thomas?" Angel asked as I closed the door and started the car.

"I'm so stressed tonight. I don't know what the fuck is

wrong with me." I gripped the steering wheel, feeling the leather slide underneath my palm.

"You need to relax," she said, touching my bicep and giving it a quick squeeze. "Does it bother you that much that they're a couple?"

I had to answer honestly. "Not really. I mean, it's my sister, and I don't need the shit thrown in my face. He's my best friend, and I trust him with my life, so why not with my sister's?"

"Habits die hard, baby. I'll tell you this. She loves him."

"She made that clear," I said, the mental image of her body attached to him in my living room still burned into my vision.

"Not just love. She's crazy about that man. Right before you two came in the room, she was gushing about him."

"Gushing?" I asked, looking over at Angel. "Izzy has never been a gusher."

"Head over heels in love with that man. I think they're a cute couple." She smiled, her small fingers stroking the inside of my arm.

"Yeah," I mumbled, looking over at her. Her words were true. I couldn't think of two people who deserved each other more than James and Izzy. They could spend a lifetime busting each other's balls.

"If you trust him with your life, why don't you trust him with your sister's?"

I sighed. She was right. "I do." It wasn't a lie.

"It's settled, then," she said, releasing my arm. "Now cheer the fuck up. I really like your sister, by the way."

"Either you love her or you hate her. She's one of those

people." I tried to keep my eyes off the rearview mirror. When I did glance back, I saw Izzy pawing at James, and they were both smiling.

"Well, I love her."

"Ready to meet the family yet?" I asked, hoping and praying she'd say yes.

Ma would be relentless if I didn't bring her with me. Everyone was expecting her, especially my parents. They weren't easy to disappoint without feeling an overwhelming sense of Italian Catholic guilt.

"Yeah," she squeaked, catching me by surprise.

"Yes?" I felt like a weight had been lifted off my shoulders with her agreement.

"I'll go." She pulled the visor down and checked her makeup in the mirror.

"You've made me the happiest man in the world," I declared.

"That would be James right now, but don't look," she warned, pointing at something in her mirror.

"Fuck," I muttered. Maybe going into business with James wasn't the best idea after all.

CHAPTER
SEVENTEEN

ANGEL

I GROANED as I rolled over. My eyes didn't just sting from lack of sleep—they ached as I tried to open them. How much had I fucking had to drink? My head felt like my brain was trying to push its way through my skull. My stomach churned from a simple movement. I needed to make a mental note: *Do not try and out-drink Izzy Gallo again*. The girl was little, but fuck. She was like a goddamn bottomless pit. I had never been a heavy drinker, never developed a tolerance for it, but hell. I'd try to keep up with the best of them, and she was a fucking champion.

"Baby," I mumbled, throwing my arm over my eyes to block out the light.

"You okay, Angel?" he asked in a smooth, sultry morning voice.

From what I remembered, he and James had talked business and watched as Izzy and I'd gotten shitfaced. They were so excited about the new venture, and Izzy and I were in a fit of giggles. The more we drank, the funnier shit got. They were trying to come up with names for their private investigator business, and Izzy and I came up with every funny name we could think of and almost got us kicked out of the restaurant in the process. We came up with Tricky Dicks, Private Dicks, Pick a Dick, and Quickie Dicks. If it had the word "dick" and rhymed, we said it. We thought we were hilarious, but the guys? Not so much.

"My head is about to explode," I complained, speaking slowly and quietly.

"I figured you'd feel like shit today."

"Ya think?" I asked in a snarky tone. "Fuck. How am I supposed to go to your parents' house feeling like this?"

He rolled over, the bed dipping, which almost made my stomach's contents empty on the spot. It had been a long time since I'd been this hung over. Why had I picked last night of all nights to do that shit?

"Stop moving!" I screeched, moving my hand to cover my mouth.

The bed shook from his deep laughter. "Sorry," he whispered, but continued laughing. Even though the bed was barely moving, it might as well have been an earthquake with the way my stomach was being jostled.

"Baby, you really need to stop fucking moving." I wouldn't call myself grumpy, just ill.

"I'm going to go make you a little hair of the dog."

"Ugh," I groaned, praying to pass out. It was so much better when I was asleep and oblivious to the way I'd mistreated my body last night.

"I promise it will make you feel better."

The bed dipped and sprang back to its original form, and I rolled to the side, trying to find the edge. I wanted to lie on the floor, thinking it would be a more stable surface.

"Ouch," I cried as I plopped on the hardwood floor

with nothing to break my fall. *So not a better choice.* I sprawled out, closing my eyes as I let the coolness of the floor soothe me. Everything was spinning, even the blackness behind my eyelids.

"Want me to help you into the bathroom?" he asked from the other side of the bed.

I wasn't going to open my eyes to see where he was. "No. Leave me here to die."

"I'll be right back," he said, snorting.

Then I heard his footsteps. It sounded like a bear was walking the halls. Every sound was amplified, and I couldn't imagine listening to a loud Italian family today with this type of hammering in my head.

Drool started to dribble from my lip and collect under my face on the floor. I didn't bother to wipe it away. I couldn't move. Fuck. I said a little prayer, promising to never drink again if God would only make me feel better. We all make that prayer when we're in over our head, even though we know it's a crock of shit.

His loud footsteps woke me again. "Up ya go. You have to drink this." He touched my shoulder, making my body lurch away without thought.

"Just kill me. It'll be easier," I whined, my body molded to the floor. I had to look like quite a sight. Sprawled out, naked, lying in puddle of drool, with my legs bent in an awkward way. I was too sick to even care, in all honesty.

"Nah. I love you too much to let that happen," he said, his voice closer than it had been before.

He loved me. *He* loved me. I didn't think I could ever get sick of hearing those words.

173

Peeling one eye open, I saw his knee close to my face. "I can't sit up by myself. It's impossible."

Placing his hands under my arms, he began to lift me.

"Oh, God," I grumbled. Everything started to move, and I had to seal my eyes shut to keep whatever was in my stomach down.

He propped my back against the bed and held me by the shoulders. I took three deep breaths, trying to push down the lump that had formed in my throat. Using every ounce of energy I had, I brought my knees up to my chest and rested my chin against my cool skin. Then I opened my eyes just enough to see him kneeling in front of me and looking fresh as a fucking daisy.

Removing one hand from my shoulders but still holding me steady, he grabbed the glass and held it in front of me. "I swear this will make you feel better."

In the glass was a Bloody Mary. The thought of something so salty and thick made me instantly start to gag.

"I can't," I closed my eyes.

"Come on, Angel. Just a small sip," he coaxed me, pulling my chin up in his direction.

When I opened my eyes, I was met with a look of concern and love—tilted head, soft eyes, and a small smile. He was staring down at me with the glass in his hand.

"I'll try," I agreed, knowing he was right. I needed to fight through it and somehow down the liquid.

Bringing the glass to my mouth, I grimaced when I got a whiff of liquor and tomato. I pinched my nose with my other hand. Even if I had to taste it, I didn't want to smell what I was going to guzzle. My senses were on overdrive, so blocking one out was a good thing.

"How about a hot bath?" he asked, brushing the hair away from my forehead as I tried to take bigger and bigger gulps of the salty concoction.

"Mm, hm," I grunted, feeling the thick liquid slide down my throat. If I didn't puke now, it wouldn't happen.

There's nothing worse when you want to puke than having something slide down, coat your throat, and take its fucking time to settle in your stomach.

As he walked away, I took a break from the drink. Placing the cool glass against my forehead, I closed my eyes and took a couple of shallow breaths. After the water turned on, I saw him walking back and forth, grabbing a bottle from the linen closet and some towels.

I sighed, taking a few more sips, and stared straight ahead. After drinking the last bit of the Bloody Mary, I set the glass on the floor, leaving my hand next to it. I was wiped out, physically worn, like an old shoe in need of repair.

He returned to the bedroom moments after the water turned off. "Want me to carry you?" he asked, standing in front of me.

"I can crawl," I whispered, moving forward and stopping almost immediately.

Crawling wasn't a smart idea either. My knees ached from the hard floor, my head throbbed worse from the pressure, and the Bloody Mary was starting to creep back up the way it had gone down.

"Stubborn woman," he mumbled, scooping me up in his arms and holding me against his chest.

I wouldn't say it was a better way to travel, but at least I didn't have to expel any energy and could focus on not hurling on him during the short walk to the bathtub. I slumped against him, curling into a ball as he carried me.

The water sloshed as he stepped inside the tub. Keeping me against his bare chest, he sank down into the water, holding me safely in his arms. Letting the warmth surround me, I rested my head on his shoulder as he leaned back, taking me with him.

Resting his hand on my hip, he stroked my cheek, staying silent. I snuggled against him and listened to his breathing.

"Feeling any better?" he asked, brushing his lips against my forehead.

"Yeah," I lied.

"I brought you some aspirin and water."

My body moved with his as he reached for the glass and pills he had set on the edge.

"Thanks," I whispered before placing the two capsules on my tongue and taking tiny sips of water. I didn't dare toss my head back to help them slide down. Movement, especially quick ones, made the entire situation worse.

After handing the glass back, I melted into him. I didn't know how long we lay there in that position before he started to wash my skin. Without the energy to try myself, I let him and soaked in the pampering. I couldn't even remember a time when my mother had done the simple task. I didn't have one fond memory of her taking care of me or treating me like a child. I had been a nuisance—or, at least, she treated me like one.

"Why are you so good to me?" I asked in jest. I'd do the same for him. That was what you did for someone you loved.

"I don't like when you don't feel well. I should've told

you to slow down last night, but I figured you needed to blow off some steam."

"It felt good, but I regret it today." I smashed my cheek against his pec. The water descending over my skin in tiny rivulets felt like dozens of fingertips grazing my flesh.

"I'm sure Izzy feels the same today. She won't be her normal annoying self at my parents."

"I'm sorry for last night." Even though it was fun, I was sure we had to have embarrassed him and James in the restaurant.

"Nah, don't be. You two were funny. It was nice to see you let your hair down and be yourself. I like the silly side of you. Don't ever apologize for having fun."

I smiled against his skin, letting the peacefulness of the moment sink in. Slowly, my stomach started to calm and the animal that had been trying to burrow through my brain stopped. I lost track of how long I'd been sitting in the tub. The water turned cold as I was cradled in his lap.

"Let's go back to bed for a while. We can be a little late to my parents'." He swept the tiny hairs off my shoulder, caressing my shoulder with the tips of his roughened fingers.

"I don't want your mom to get mad," I replied, even though I needed a few hours of restful sleep.

"She won't. They don't eat until later. They'll be happy we're coming even if it's a couple of hours after everyone else."

"Okay," I said, pulling myself up and finding my balance before attempting to step out of the tub. While waiting for Thomas, I swayed back and forth for a moment. Then he stood and helped me out. "Thanks."

After retrieving a towel and quickly drying us off, he

scooped me into his arms and carried me back into the bedroom. Once he'd set me down, he tucked me in and said, "I'm going to go do a few things and make some calls. I'll wake you up in a bit."

"Don't let me sleep too long. I don't want to disappoint your mom," I said through a yawn, already comfortable and ready to fall asleep.

Through half-closed eyes, I saw his beautiful smile as he nodded and kissed me on the lips. Then he grabbed a pair of workout pants and headed out the door. I didn't even stay awake long enough to hear his feet hit the first step.

***

After sleeping for a couple of hours, I felt like a member of the human race again. I no longer wished to be put out of my misery. I didn't move as quickly as I normally did, but I was able to get ready in under a half-hour, and in my state, that was a goddamn miracle.

As we pulled into his parents' driveway, I fidgeted with the bangle bracelet I was wearing. My stomach grumbled —partially from hunger, but mostly from fear. Thomas was confident that they'd love me, but I wasn't so sure. My own mother didn't love me. Why would his?

"We're here," he said with a smile on his face as he turned off the engine.

"Yeah," I replied, blowing out a quick puff of air. There was no turning back now.

"Look at me, Angel."

I dragged my gaze away from the silver bracelet and stared into his eyes.

"They're harmless. Sometimes they act like teenagers, but everyone inside will love you because I love you. Just be yourself and remember to smile. If you get over-whelmed, let me know and we can leave."

"Okay," I whispered, forcing a smile.

We climbed out of the car, and I walked next to him, my hand in his, until we stopped in front of the door. Pulling my body against him, he gave me a mind-numbing kiss. My toes curled from the passion, my mind swam with things to come, and my body instantly responded. When his lips left mine, I was left breathless and wanting more, but it would have to wait.

"I'm ready," I said, lingering on his lips.

He smiled, opened the door, and yelled, "We're here!"

People began to squeal as they gathered in the foyer. "Overwhelmed" didn't even begin to describe how I felt. I could feel their eyes on me as they hugged Thomas. Before I could say anything, his mother pulled me into a giant hug.

"I'm so happy to meet you, Angel," she whispered in my ear as she squeezed me tighter, making it hard to breathe.

"Ma, don't kill her," Thomas said, pulling her off me.

"Sorry. I kind of get carried away sometimes," she blurted as her cheeks turned pink. "My baby boy." She held her arms out, pulling Thomas into her embrace.

I giggled, knowing exactly how he felt—unable to breathe.

"Ma," he said, squeezing her back before releasing her. "This is Angel, and Angel, this is my pop."

I held out my hand, smiling at him and comparing the two men. They had the same facial features: amazing blue eyes, strong jaws, and full lips. I could see Thomas as an older man when I stared at his dad.

Without speaking, he hugged me, crushing my ribs. "Nice to meet you, love," he said, holding my shoulders and taking a good look at me. "You're stunning."

"Thank you," I replied, trying not to smile, but it was useless. I could feel the love and excitement in this house. It was abundant and easy.

"Back away," Izzy said, waving her hands and stepping in front of everyone. "She's mine next."

I laughed, reaching out and grabbing her. "How in the heck are you so damn chipper? I feel like a zombie today."

"Practice, sweet Angel. We'll get you there. Don't worry. You'll be a champ in no time."

"Oh, no, no, no. Last night was it for me," I told her as I watched everyone hugging Thomas.

"Fuck that. You're getting drunk with me again. The girls and I were just talking about a girls' night out. It's been a long time and we all need to get away from our Neanderthal men."

I chuckled, wondering how bad they could actually all be. "We'll see."

Izzy backed away, glancing over at a blonde and a brunette, and announced, "She's in, ladies. Girls' night it is!"

"Damn," I mumbled to myself, as Thomas came to stand by my side. I shrugged, plastering a smile on my face. I hadn't said yes, but Izzy, in her own special way, had sealed the deal.

"Yay!" the blonde screeched. Then the brunette echoed her.

One by one, they said hello as Thomas introduced

them to me. Joey, Anthony, and Mike were his brothers, and Izzy was the sister. They were all gorgeous, but from the looks of their parents, it wasn't surprising.

"Dinner's in five minutes," Mrs. Gallo said, clapping her hands, a giant smile on her face. "Go sit for a few minutes, but don't get too comfortable."

Everyone moved to the living room, spreading out amongst the furniture and floor. While I sat next to Tommy, he kept my hand in his, slowly stroking my palm with his thumb. It was calming in its rhythmic nature as I tried not to notice that all the eyes in the room were focused solely on me.

"How're the Cubs doing today, Pop?" Thomas asked, breaking the silence.

"Shitty, but what else is new?" Mr. Gallo said, leaning back in his chair and placing his foot across his opposite knee.

"Hey, Angel," Izzy interrupted. "Want to go help Ma with dinner? It would win you major brownie points." She jumped up from the floor, kissing James on the lips before motioning for me to follow.

I liked that idea more than feeling like a caged animal. "Sure," I replied, giving Thomas a quick peck and then joining Izzy in the kitchen.

"Ma, we've come to help you." Izzy turned, winking at me, and I couldn't help but smile. The girl was slick, and I liked her. If I could have a sister, I'd pick Izzy Gallo. "It was Angel's idea."

"Isn't that lovely. Grab the salad from the fridge, and one of you take the meatballs out of the sauce and put them in a bowl."

The smell in the kitchen was something that couldn't

181

be described. It was better than any restaurant I'd ever set foot inside. I could almost pick out the individual dishes with each inhale. My mouth watered as the dishes were placed on the counter, waiting to be brought out to the hungry crowd.

"I'll do the meatballs," I said, moving toward the stove. "In here?" I asked, grabbing a bowl.

"Yes, dear," Mrs. Gallo answered, testing a noodle over the sink.

When I pulled the lid off the giant pot, I was hit by the smell of the most divine tomato sauce ever. It was a rich red color, with specks of spices and a hint of heat. Using a slotted spoon, I took a meatball out and placed it in the bowl. One by one, I removed meatball after meatball. I didn't bother to count.

"Jesus," I muttered, digging inside, thinking there couldn't be another one, but I was wrong.

"She cooks for an army," Izzy said. "But then again, there are five hungry men and a pregnant girl who puts them all to shame."

"Oh, honey. I always make extras. Anthony usually brings some home, and lately, I've been giving some to Suzy to fill her late-night cravings," Mrs. Gallo said as she dumped the pasta into the strainer, a plume of steam collecting above the sink.

"What's left, Ma?" Izzy asked, putting the garlic bread she'd pulled out of the oven in a basket.

Mrs. Gallo started to go down the list. "Salad, pasta, bread, sauce, meatballs... Did you take out the eggplant?"

"Nope. Is it ready?" Izzy asked, placing the oven mitts on her hands.

"Yeah. It needs a moment to cool while I assemble the pasta."

This must be what it's like to have a mother who actually cares about a family. I silently watched them as they interacted with each other, feeling a pang of jealousy for all I'd missed from being the unlucky SOB to have been born to my witch of a mom. Life would've been different if my father had lived, but it never would have been like having the Gallos.

"How are you and James?" Mrs. Gallo asked as she spooned the sauce over layers of pasta.

"We're better than ever, Ma," Izzy replied, setting the tray of eggplant on the trivet.

"He's a good man, baby. I'm so happy for you."

"*Good* isn't a word I'd used to describe him." Izzy laughed, tossing the mitts on the counter before snagging a serving platter from the cabinet.

"I have a feeling he's a lot like your father—"

"Stop right there," Izzy interrupted, turning to look at her ma. "There are things a child should never hear, and that's one of them."

Mrs. Gallo laughed a big, bellowing laugh, her body shaking as her cheeks turned pink. "Child, how do you think we got five kids?"

"You're like the Virgin Mary, Ma."

"Not after your father got his hands on me. I don't think I left the confessional for a month. I had a lot of repenting to do." Her laughter grew louder as Izzy winced.

"See the shit I have to put up with in this house?" Izzy asked, throwing her hands up.

"Izzy, I don't feel sorry for you *at all.* Be thankful you have a mother to talk with like this."

Both sets of eyes looked at me, sadness written all over their faces.

"What do you need me to do next?" I asked, trying to change the subject.

"That's it," Mrs. Gallo said, walking up to me and once again giving me a hug. This time, it was gentle and brief. "Let's get my future grandbaby nourished." She placed her hand over my stomach and looked up at me with a cheerful expression. "Maybe someday I'll be feeding one inside you."

Oh shit. I couldn't imagine having a baby now—or in five years. I didn't even have my shit together. I didn't have an education or a career, and the last thing I wanted to be was barefoot and pregnant.

"Don't start that shit, Ma. You're going to scare her away. One baby at a time."

"You're next, Izzy. I can feel it."

"You better be feeling something else, because that is not happening anytime soon. I'm too young and having too much damn fun to have a baby ruin everything."

"Izzy," her mother scolded her. "Babies don't ruin anything. They bring so much joy."

"Yeah. They also bring a lot of shit and sleepless nights. I'll skip that mess for now."

"You're ridiculous. I love all my kids."

"Uh huh," Izzy muttered, grabbing the meatballs and heading into the dining room.

I picked up salad and bread, following Izzy as we made a couple of trips back and forth. We filled the glasses with drinks and made sure everything was laid out to her mother's liking before Izzy yelled, "Dinner!" from the middle of the room.

Seconds later, everyone was jockeying for a spot at the table. Thomas casually strolled in, pulling out a chair for me and waiting for me to sit before he did the same next to me.

The conversation flowed easily as the family mercilessly teased each other throughout dinner. Joe seemed like a cool dude with a hint of scary. I'd seen his type around the strip club, but he seemed utterly devoted to his wife and future child. He doted on her, refilling her plate and paying close attention to her every need. He wasn't an asshole biker, but a loving husband with that I'll-kick-your-ass-without-apologizing quality about him.

The brunette—Mia, I learned—was a doctor who ran a local health clinic for the needy population in the area. The smile on her face never left while she talked about work. I wanted that feeling. I wanted the sense of doing something good with my life.

Mike seemed like a brute. He was huge, the beefiest of all the Gallo men. He was a jokester, though, and I could tell he had a big heart. But I couldn't figure out the Mia situation. I could tell he loved her, and everyone kept hinting about marriage, but he kept changing the subject. There was more to the story, and I hoped it would come out on girls' night out.

Anthony was the oldest and the only unattached of all the siblings. He seemed pissed off about love, grumbling under his breath during dinner. Everyone gave him a lot of shit, telling him that, someday, a girl would have him by the balls. I swear I heard him say that they were already taken, but he'd spoken so low that I couldn't be sure.

Through the entire dinner, I kept glancing down at Mr. and Mrs. Gallo. Even after all the years they'd been together, they were still madly in love. It was evident by their constant touching and sideways glances. I envied them for having such a strong relationship, and wondered if that would be Thomas and me in thirty years. Allowing myself to think that way might be dangerous, but I could have a dream.

The love and acceptance in this room hit me like a ton of bricks as I took stock of those around me. No matter what they said or how they joked, behind it all was love. They accepted and loved each other.

Not once in my entire life had I sat around a table like this. I had been to huge gatherings—mostly biker parties or celebrations where members wandered about, scarfing down plates of food and bullshitting—but nothing like this.

Wondering what Christmas would be like, I imagined happy children giddy to open their presents as they sat around the tree. When I was young, I'd been lucky to get a small trinket from one of the guys my mom had been fucking at the time. I felt robbed of my childhood the more I watched this family interact. Hell, I'd been robbed of the family experience in my adulthood too—and I was pissed.

Feeling a need to be alone and wallow in my self-pity, I placed my napkin on the table and pushed my chair back. "Where's the bathroom?" I whispered in Thomas's ear.

He stopped moving, his fork touching his lips. "Are you okay?" he asked, turning toward me and looking me straight in the eyes.

"Yeah," I replied, nodding and praying that he believed my lie. "Just need to go to the bathroom, baby." I plastered a fake smile on my face, attempting to make my story more believable.

"I'll show you," he responded, setting his fork on his plate. "We'll be right back everyone," he announced, standing and tossing his napkin on the chair.

"I can go myself." I didn't want to pull him away from his family. I needed a moment to collect my thoughts.

"No, I'll take you." He smiled, brushing his fingers against my cheek.

"Don't be too long. Don't go pulling a Mike and Mia," Izzy told us before we walked out into the foyer.

"What's she talking about?"

"Long story. Don't worry about it." He stopped walking and turned to face me. "Are you really okay?" His eyes searched mine—looking for what, I didn't exactly know.

"I am," I lied again, not wanting to bring down the happy party at the dinner table. The last thing I wanted to do was ruin any moment he had with his family.

"It's a lot to take in. Remember, I know your mother really well."

"Please say you didn't—" I started before he put his index finger against my lips.

"No!" he growled, shaking his head. "I know what a shitty person she is. I wouldn't let that woman near my dick even if it would have been the only way to bring down the MC."

"Thank God." I dragged my hands down my face, trying to wash that image out of my mind. "I just needed a minute. I love your family. They're amazing. I feel like it's a crazy sitcom on television. You're one of the luckiest people I know."

"Hey," he said, lifting my chin with his fingers and forcing my eyes to meet his. "You may have gone without it for the first part of your life, but if you stay with me, they'll become your family."

Could I stay and feel like part of this family? I knew I wanted that. I wanted to be a Gallo. I wanted someone to call Mom and Dad, and a place where I felt I belonged.

"I know." I waved my hand at him, feeling my eyes fill with tears. "I need to stop focusing on what I missed and realize what can be mine."

"I'm yours," he whispered, catching a tear as it trickled down my cheek. "As long as you'll have me, I'll be yours."

His words gave me that mushy feeling as butterflies filled my stomach. I'd waited forever for those words, and the more he said it lately, the more I truly believed them.

"I'm being a stupid girl," I whined, sniffling and wiping my nose with the back of my hand in the most unladylike fashion.

"Come here, Angel." He held out his hand, waiting for me to curl into his body like I often did.

I felt at home and completely at peace in his arms. So I rested my head on his shoulder and cried softly as he rubbed my back and whispered words of reassurance in my ear.

I pulled away, leaving his shirt damp, and sniffled. After wiping my face, I was ready to face the family again, but I was sure I looked like a hot mess.

"Give me five minutes to get myself together and I'll come back in. Go eat, baby."

He grabbed my face and swiped my remaining tears away with his thumbs. "Don't take too long or I'm sending Izzy to find you." Then he smiled, pulled my face to his, and kissed me.

Wrapping my arms around him, I returned his kiss, letting my tongue wander inside his mouth for a taste.

"Sorry," I murmured against his lips as I sniffled. It hadn't been the sexiest kiss I had ever given him.

"You can make up for it when we get home," he said, a small grin playing on his lips.

"Should we go now?" I offered, rubbing my hand against his chest.

"No. You'll have to wait. Anticipation makes it better," he whispered, causing my insides to twitch.

This morning I'd prayed for death. But now I wanted him inside me. On top of me and all over my body.

"I'll let you know if it does." I winked at him before pushing away and climbing the steps.

Looking behind me, I saw him laughing and watching me sway my hips as I walked. The man was devastatingly handsome. I was the luckiest bitch alive to have him in my life. For once, the gods had picked me to hit the jackpot. Lord knows they owed me one for having given me an asshole mother.

CHAPTER
EIGHTEEN
THOMAS

WATCHING Angel through the sliding glass door as I sat on the couch, I knew the internal struggle she felt. Although this was my family, I didn't feel like a true member. Being away had altered things, and I was still trying to find my place amongst the others. I couldn't imagine her feelings about being an outsider and walking into this insanity.

She threw her head back, grabbing her stomach as she laughed. Izzy, Mia, Suzy, and Ma were sitting outside, talking out of our earshot. It was great to watch them interact from afar and study Angel's body language. She seemed at ease and more comfortable with the girls than she had when she'd walked in the door. She fit in nicely with the women my brothers had brought into their lives.

Izzy was the ringleader, which wasn't surprising, but it could be a complete disaster. She didn't put much thought into shit before she acted, which was the one thing that had scared me about her as she'd been growing up. Teenagers were already spontaneous and typically didn't think about the consequences, but Izzy had given sanity a run for its money. I'd thought she'd calm down as an adult and give the family some peace, but I had been wrong. She was the free spirit, living life by the seat of her pants.

"Nice sight, isn't it?" James asked from next to me on the couch, looking out the window with me.

"Yeah," I replied, staring at Angel and smiling. "Best fucking sight there is."

"She seems to fit in well, Thomas. You were right about her."

I glanced at him and squinted. "Did you doubt my judgment?"

"Nah, but it was some risky shit."

"I wouldn't have fallen in love with her if she weren't an amazing woman."

"Hey," Mike interrupted as he rolled over on the floor to face James and me.

"What?" I asked, happy to change the subject.

"Let's do a poker night when the girls go out. I could use a night out too."

"In the mood to lose all your money?" Joe asked Mike.

"I'm going to kick your ass, Joey," Mike responded.

"Not happening."

Mike laughed, slapping the floor. "Dude, you haven't beaten me at cards in five years."

"It's because your ass cheats," I replied, speaking up for Joe.

"Pussies," Mike muttered, sitting up and looking over at Anthony. "You in?"

Anthony glanced up from his phone, his eyebrows knitted together as he stared at Mike. "What?"

"Dipshit, pay attention. Poker this week. Are you in?"

"Maybe," he answered then diverted his attention back to his phone.

Mike shrugged and rolled his eyes. "He'll be there. What the fuck else does he have to do?"

"Don't you guys have a shop to run? How the fuck are you going to play poker?" I asked Mike.

"Wednesday, we don't have any appointments after six so far. We'll just close the shop early due to a family event."

"Doesn't really qualify as an event," James said to Mike.

"Like fuck it doesn't. A boys' night out of poker with my brothers sounds like a family event to me. It's settled. Wednesday it is. You bitches be there so I can take your money. Pop," he said, turning to face my dad, "you want to join us?"

Pop shook his head, laughing. "Son, it wouldn't be fair of me to play. I could never take my kids' money."

"That's a lot of shit-talkin', old man—" Mike replied with a giant smile on his face.

Pop held his hand up. "I may be old, but I can still kick your ass, son."

"Someone's feeling frisky." Joe laughed, standing from the couch and heading for the patio. "We gotta jet."

"Big date?" I asked, quirking an eyebrow at him.

"Yeah. With my bed and my wife."

"Dude, you still hit that when she's that big?" Anthony asked, placing his phone in his lap.

"Sexiest thing in the world is knowing a part of me is growing inside her," Joe responded, reaching for the door handle.

"My sexiest part grows inside someone too, but I sure as hell am *not* talking about a child."

"You're a sick fuck." Joe shook his head, walking outside and closing the door behind him. Then he crouched down next to Suzy, her eyes lighting up and a smile on her face as they spoke. When he helped her from her seat, he placed his hand over her belly and spoke to the rest of the table. Waving goodbye, he held her protectively against his side and led her through the sliding glass doors and into the living room.

"Bye, everyone," Suzy squeaked as she glanced around the room. "Don't get up. I'll see you next weekend."

I rose and walked up to her. "It was good to see you again, babe. You ever need anything, call me." I knew my brother was busy with the shop and couldn't always be there for her. I seemed like the obvious choice for right now. I'd do anything for Joe and, in turn, Suzy too.

"What about a Big Mac in the middle of the night?" She laughed, resting her hand on top of her stomach.

I shook my head. "That shit Joe will have to get."

"Thought so. He gets all grumpy when I get a wicked craving in the middle of the night."

"Who wants to go to McDonald's at three a.m. for a Big Mac? The smell alone turns my stomach."

"It hits the spot."

"Tonight, you can have lasagna, not a Big Mac," Joe said, looking down at her with a smile.

"You know how to talk dirty to me, baby," she snorted, placing her hand on her stomach. "I'm hungry now."

"You're always hungry," Anthony interjected without glancing up from his phone.

He'd had his face buried in that fucking thing all night.

What the fuck was so important that he couldn't put it down to spend time with the family? It was unlike him to act this way. Something was up, and he was being tight-lipped about it.

Propping her hand on her hip, Suzy glared at Anthony. "I don't know what crawled up your ass and died, Anthony, but you better get it removed…and quick."

Anthony stared back at her with wide eyes until his eyes softened, small wrinkles formed in the corners, and a huge smile spread across his face. Pop started chuckling and Joe laughed, pulling his wife closer to his side.

"Why don't you tell him how you really feel, sugar?" he asked, kissing the top of her head.

"Take me home, handsome," she replied, placing her hand on his stomach in much the same way he had done to her earlier.

Then they said goodbye, giving everyone a hug and kiss, including Anthony. When Suzy approached Anthony, she whispered something in his ear and he nodded. No one else seemed to notice, but it didn't get by me.

As they walked out, Anthony got up and headed into the kitchen. I followed him, thinking I needed to talk to him. I hadn't had a chance to get him alone and see how he was doing. Plus, I was nosy like everyone else and wanted to see what was stuck in his craw.

"Hey." I stood in the doorway, leaning against the frame with my arms folded.

"What's up, bro?"

"Just thought I'd see how you were."

"Couldn't be better," he replied, pouring himself some coffee. "Want a cup?"

"No. I'm good."

"Suit yourself."

"You doing okay?" I didn't move, keeping his escape route blocked.

One thing I knew about my older brother was that he didn't like to talk about his feelings. When we were growing up, he was the most closed off of the Gallo kids, and it hadn't changed as he'd aged.

"Yeah, why?" he asked, keeping his eyes on mine as he took a sip of his coffee.

"Something's up with you. You're grumpier than your normal pleasant self, and your face is always buried in that damn phone."

He stared at me for a beat before setting his coffee on the counter. "First, you haven't been around in ages, so what do you know about my normal self?"

Leave it to Anthony to hit below the belt. His comment was true but still shitty. I'd lost touch with everyone in my family. I didn't know them anymore. People change over time. Fuck, I was no longer the same brother I had been. I had a darkness inside me I'd never be able to shake.

I waved my hand at him. "Like that shit. You're a grouchy bastard. You were never a grumpy fucker. Crotchety, yes, but not a prick."

"It's the new me." He smiled, crossing his feet as he leaned against the counter.

"Anthony, I know I deserted you—and the entire family, for that matter—but I can tell something is up with you. Talk to me. You always used to confide in me."

"I don't know, man. It's not worth my time to even talk about this chick." He hung his head as his shoulders slumped.

"Why?"

"She fuckin' drives me crazy."

I laughed, knowing the feeling well. "It's their job, Anth."

"One minute, she's begging me to be with her, and the next, she's pushing me out the door. She has my fucking head spinning."

"Do you love her?" I asked, pushing off the doorframe and moving toward him.

He scrubbed his hand across his face, moving it into his dark hair before pulling on the short strands. "I haven't been with anyone else in months. I don't know if it's love, but I just can't be with anyone else."

"You've been a one-woman man for months?" I asked in shock.

Anthony was a hound dog. While playing in the band, he'd developed a following and loved his groupies. Sometimes loving them too much.

Nodding, he brought his eyes to mine. "Figure that shit out."

I wanted to keep him talking. Anthony was the type who spilled his guts when he was ready, and questioning him wasn't the way to go. Everyone in the family would question him, and he'd instantly shut down.

"She must be pretty special."

"I thought she was, but I don't know anymore, Tommy. I feel like I'm being led around by my balls."

"What about your balls?" Mike asked as he walked in the kitchen. Opening the refrigerator door, he paused and looked at us.

"Nothing, man." Anthony picked up his coffee and headed for the living room.

With that, the conversation was over. Mike had the

shittiest timing. It was like his greatest gift. He'd fucking ruined shit my entire life with his timing. It had started back in high school when I had Becky in my bed. That relationship had ended in a hurry.

"Way to go, numbskull."

"What?" he asked, pulling the milk carton from the shelf. Without thinking or giving a fuck, he brought it to his mouth and chugged.

"Nothing," I replied before walking out and leaving him behind.

Angel was standing in the living room, chatting with Anthony when I entered the room. "Hey," she said, touching Anthony on the arm before heading toward me.

"Ready?" I asked her, needing to get out of here and spend some time alone with her. I still had a promise from earlier to fulfill.

She nodded before walking toward my pop. Then she bent down, whispered in his ear, and kissed him on the cheek. A smile so large that his eyes crinkled at the corners spread across his face, showing the tiny wrinkles that had developed in my absence.

As we walked out the front door, I said, "Thank you."

She stopped, pulling me back toward her with her hand. "For what?" she asked, tilting her head and staring at me.

I looked into her beautiful, dark eyes. "For coming today. I know they're a lot to take in."

"I love them, Thomas. After we talked on the stairs, I let your words sink in. I needed to forget about the past and look to the future. They made me feel welcome, and that's something I've never experienced. For the first time in my life, I felt like part of a family." She smiled as pools of water collected in the corners of her eyes.

"They loved you. I knew they would. You're an amazing person, Angel. I knew that from the moment I met you. I knew I couldn't let go of you when my undercover work ended. The mere thought of it haunted me. Gnawed at my soul every time you fell asleep in my arms or professed your feelings about me. Toward the end, when you said you wanted to run away, it gave me hope that maybe, just maybe, you'd come with me when I left."

She blinked, the tears now streaming down her face. "I meant every word of it, Thomas, but only if you were by my side. Jesus, look at me. I'm a mess," she whispered, using the backs of her hands to wipe away her tears.

"No, you're not," I replied, pushing her hands away and using my fingers to catch the tiny teardrops. "You're beautiful and you're mine."

It felt good to finally say the words I'd held inside for months. Every chance I had, I said them to her, making up for lost time. I wanted to remind her how much I loved her and what she meant to me as often as possible.

"Take me home and make love to me, Thomas," she whispered, drawing the pad of my thumb into her mouth as I followed the path of tears to her lips.

I felt her tongue against my flesh. Drawing it deeper into her mouth, she sucked on it, with her mouth around it in a perfect O. My dick twitched in response, coming to life and needing relief. I couldn't wait to get her home to finish what I'd wanted to do earlier.

"If you don't stop that, we won't make it home," I growled, sucking in a quick breath as she swirled her tongue around.

Opening her mouth enough to speak, she said, "Anticipation."

"Fuck. I was never good at waiting, Angel. You should know that about me by now." After removing my digit from her mouth, I grabbed her hand and pulled her down the walkway toward the car.

"What's your hurry?" she asked, trying to keep up with my quick pace.

The feel of her lips on me had made me impatient. "You have something to take care of." I opened her door, waiting for her to get in, but she stopped in front of me with a twinkle in her eye and a smile on her face.

"I don't remember having any plans."

I swept my thumb, still damp from her mouth, against her lips. "Something came *up*." I looked down, motioning to her with my groin before capturing her lips with mine.

Tiny moans escaped her lips, the vibrations ricocheting down my chest and making my cock throb. Holding her by the neck, I devoured her mouth. My tongue mingled with hers, tasting the sweetness of the chocolate cake we'd had during dessert. Groaning softly, I knew I couldn't wait until we got home. The drive was over thirty minutes away from my parents'—way too long for my aching cock.

"Fuck," she murmured when I moved away, her eyes fluttering open.

"Get your ass in the car."

"Bossy," she whispered before doing as she'd been told.

Once I'd slammed her door closed, I jogged to the driver's side and climbed inside. Then I coasted down the street, looking for the make-out spot so many of us had used in our youth. Down the street from my parents', there was a small trail into the woods that was used for mudding. It opened to a giant field filled with tall grasses and brush. It was the perfect spot when you needed time alone and were out of cash.

As we drove down the dirt trail, branches lashed against the windows, making a screeching sound.

"I'm not going anywhere, baby. I'm a sure thing. There's no rush."

"My dick says otherwise."

She giggled, grabbing my attention and making me glance at her. She was slowly unbuttoning her top, knowing what I wanted.

"Don't," I said, adjusting my rock-hard dick as she revealed her breasts.

Her laughter grew louder as her hands fell away. Then she turned toward me, leaning over and placing her warm palm against my length. Inhaling deeply, needing more than warmth, I tried to stay calm and not just throw it into park.

When we pulled into the field, I found a spot under the only tree, trying to block out the setting sun. At times like these, I was thankful for my muscle car. It didn't have a separator between the front seats. It was the old-style seat that came in one piece and made fucking like this possible.

I put the car in park, leaving the CD player going before turning my attention to her. Lunging at her, I pushed her down onto the seat, crushing her with my weight.

Hozier's "To Be Alone" started to play. Reaching up, I pressed repeat, loving the words of this song, especially with Angel underneath me. Pushing my straining erection against her, I dry-humped her as I dug my teeth into her flesh. Then I ran my tongue over her jugular, feeling the beating of her heart as it picked up its pace.

Her fingers snarled through my hair, tugging lightly as she wrapped her legs around my back. Fighting every urge in me to rip off her clothes, I traced her pulse up her neck, across her chin, and to her mouth before sucking the air from her lungs. Grinding against her and devouring her mouth, I used one hand to undo the top button of her jeans. I slid my hands inside and groaned as I felt her wetness. Her tiny moans drove me further, and I pushed my fingers inside her. The tight space caused by her jeans didn't stop me; I needed to feel her, to taste her. As I stuck two fingers inside, my palm rested against her clit, her body twitched as I moved them in and out.

She clawed the skin on my shoulders, digging deeper with each stroke of her G-spot. "Don't stop," she moaned, pulling my mouth closer against hers. She pushed against my hand, driving my fingers in further, and rode my palm. Feeling her body begin to shake, I stilled my hand.

"No," she begged, wiggling her body underneath me. "Please," she said against my lips, nipping at my flesh.

"Not yet," I growled, removing my hand from her pants.

My dick was about ready to burst, and the feel of her slick cunt against my skin had me about to explode like a teenager.

"Taste how sweet you are." Setting my fingers between our lips, I used my tongue to lick at her juices.

She stuck her tongue out, tasting herself on my fingers. My eyes started to roll back in my head. The smell and taste of her with her tongue on my flesh was almost too much for me to bear. As I dipped my fingers inside her mouth, she sucked them clean.

Unable to contain myself any longer, I sat up and unfastened my jeans. I pulled out my cock, not bothering to pull my pants all the way down. I just needed enough to stroke her deeply. My body shook as I palmed my dick, rubbing it up and down.

Angel scurried, shimmying her jeans down her legs and panting as her eyes stayed glued to my throbbing dick. When she pushed her pants to her knees, I grabbed them from the bottom and yanked them off.

"You don't need these." I tossed them in the back seat.

My patience snapped as I reached down and ripped the lace panties off her body. She laughed, throwing her head back as I threw them on the dashboard. Those were staying inside the car as a souvenir.

When I pushed inside her, she wrapped her legs around my back. Her warmth and slickness enveloped my hard shaft as my body began to convulse with pleasure. Unable to stop, I pounded into her. While I braced my arms next to her head, she grabbed my neck and curled her body into mine. The closer she drew to me, the tighter her pussy felt. It sucked the life from my dick.

"Yes! Yes!" she wailed, fucking me back, making the impact that much greater.

This was better than any high school fucking I had done in this field as a kid. That had been amateurish, child's play. Angel was the real deal, the woman I loved, and the one I'd never get enough of—no matter how long we spent together.

My balls tightened, my spine tingled, and my dick grew harder. I was ready to burst at the seams. She rode my shaft, bouncing up and down on it over and over again, as I sat up and took her with me. Using my hips, I met her thrusts, driving myself as deep as humanly possible without tearing her in two.

"Oh, God. Almost there…" she moaned, sealing her eyes shut and tipping her head back.

Needing her to crash over the edge, I wrapped my hands around her neck and applied pressure. Angel always got off on choking, and I knew it. I knew her body better than she did. Using her neck as leverage, I pulled her down on top of me, paying careful attention to her airway. As I watched her face turn red and her eyes roll back into her head, I could barely hear her breathing. Then she let out a strangled cry as her cunt milked my cock.

The crushing force of her orgasm sent me into a mind-numbing and vision-blurring frenzy. I released her neck and pulled her hair, forcing her neck backwards as I sank my teeth into her flesh and emptied myself into her.

As I moaned against her skin, my body convulsed, riding the crest as I came. Panting, I swallowed hard, resting my forehead against her. Her pussy continued to clamp down on my cock, her body shaking in tiny after-shocks. Hozier still played on repeat as we clung to each other, trying to catch our breath.

"Fuck," I muttered, dragging my face from her neck. As I backed away, a tiny drop of blood caught my eye. I'd ripped her skin open with my teeth as I bit her. Lost in the moment, I hadn't been paying attention to how hard I had clamped down. "Shit, baby. I drew blood."

"Am I going to die?" she asked, swallowing roughly on a heavy breath.

"No," I replied, touching the wound.

"That was worth a small cut, Thomas." She sagged against me, licking the sweat off my shoulder.

"Don't start licking me again, Angel. I need a minute." Moving her off my dick and out of my lap, I set her on the seat and reached in the back for her jeans. Handing them to her, I said, "You can wear these for now, but I'm not done with you yet."

"I'm all yours, Thomas. Only yours."

About fuckin' time.

CHAPTER
NINETEEN

ANGEL

UNABLE TO SLEEP, I ventured downstairs to make myself a cup of hot tea with milk. While I was checking my phone as I waited for the water to boil, a new notification caught my eye. I had text messages from a number I didn't recognize. When I clicked on it, I froze. There were more than one, and the further I read, the sicker I felt.

Unknown: I know where u r, u little slut.

Unknown: U can't hide from me 4ever.

Unknown: If u want that boyfriend of yours to stay alive, u better find a way to get some $$$. ASAP.

Who the fuck has my phone number and how do they know about Tommy?

My hands began to shake violently as I grabbed the teapot. It jiggled in my hand, water spilling from the spout as I tried to pour a cup. The metal clattered against the ceramic mug, sounding like there was an earthquake happening.

After placing the teapot back on the stove before I hurt myself, I stared out the window. I ran down dozens of possibilities. None of them seemed right. I'd never given anyone this number. Work only had my old home phone, the only reason I'd kept a landline.

Unknown: *I know you read my messages. I'm giving u 24 hours to respond before I come for both of u.*

Sickness overcame me. I threw up in the sink, and tears began to sting my eyes. Struggling for breath, I felt as if my throat were closing, being paralyzed by fear.

This can't be fucking happening!

For once in my life, shit was going well. Life seemed to be filled with possibilities, and now someone was after me. But more importantly, they were after Thomas. He was too good of a man, and I'd brought this to his doorstep. What if they hurt him? I couldn't live with myself if something happened to him.

He had an amazing family that loved him. I had no one. Whether I lived or died was inconsequential in this world, but Thomas mattered to so many.

Feeling my legs begin to shake, I crumpled to the floor, a sob bursting from me. Tears streamed down my cheeks and I felt like I was going to be sick again.

I had known that this shit was too good to be true. Why had I let myself dream? I wanted to run upstairs and wake Thomas to let him know about the messages. He'd take care of it—or they'd kill him and come after me. I couldn't risk it. Couldn't risk him. He deserved better than that.

As I cried uncontrollably, my chest felt tight and I tried to catch my breath. Hunched over, I felt dizzy, pounding the floor with my fists. I was pissed off. How could this shit have happened? Karma sure as fuck didn't like me. She fucked with me every chance she got, and I was always the fool thinking that maybe this time it would be different.

Pushing myself up on shaky legs, I decided to do the only thing I could to keep him safe. I didn't have any fucking money, and there was no way in hell I'd ask Thomas to pay blackmail. He wouldn't do it. He'd get the cops involved, which would just make everything more dangerous. He'd gotten out alive after taking down the Sun Devils, and that shit was unheard of in my circles.

I crawled up the steps, unsure if my legs would hold me as I tried to ascend the steep incline. After pulling myself up using the banister, I slid down the hallway using the flat surface. Once I'd pushed the door open, I rested against the frame and watched him. His chest rose and fell in a rhythmic manner while he was totally oblivious to the danger that lurked so close to home. As I opened the door farther, the hinges creaked, but he didn't move. I'd learned in a short amount of time that he was a heavy sleeper—especially after the type of night we'd had after returning from dinner.

Tears dripped down my face as I sniffled and tried to pull my shit together. I didn't have any other choice. Sometimes, we have to sacrifice for the good of our partner, and I was willing to go back to my shitty existence if it meant he would be okay. He had so much to give, more than I deserved. He'd find someone in the future to make him happy and grow old with, but she wasn't me.

I crept into the closet and grabbed a bag, shoving everything I could inside. As I packed, it dawned on me that I didn't have a fucking car. How in the fuck could I leave without any way to get anywhere? They had taxis in the area. They had to. I'd grab a taxi, rent a car, and find my way back to my crappy-ass apartment and my shitty job, where men groped me for their pleasure.

"Fuck," I whispered, slamming more clothes in the bag. I didn't want to go back.

Leaning forward, I caught a glimpse of him sleeping peacefully, unaware of the hell I felt inside. Frozen, I memorized the picture before me, letting the tears of self-pity fall down my cheeks. After wiping them off, I zipped up the bag and grabbed one of his T-shirts, throwing it on with a pair of jeans. His smell surrounded me as I bent over to slip my tennis shoes on. I inhaled deeply, lingering on his scent before picking up my bag and tiptoeing to the door. Allowing myself one more look, I turned and took in the sight of his hard body with the sheet draped across his abdomen. Resisting the urge to touch him, I walked out the door, leaving it open a crack.

As I walked down the stairs, I looked around, trying to memorize his life so I could imagine him being happy when I was gone. Then, after grabbing my purse off the coat rack, I unlocked the door and headed outside.

"Shit," I mumbled, knowing I couldn't just leave. I needed to leave him a note or something to help him understand why I had to go. He couldn't wake up and find the house empty. He'd think I didn't leave on my accord, even though he'd be partially correct.

Upon finding a piece of paper on the counter, I scribbled a quick letter.

Thomas,

I realized today that I don't fit into your world. We're too different to work. You have an amazing family and deserve a woman who can be everything to you. My heart isn't in it. I'm not the right person for you. Please don't look for me. I don't want to be found. It's best if we end things now before we're both in too deep to realize what's best. Thank you for an amazing time. I'll look back on our time together with nothing but a smile. Your secret is safe with me. I'll never do anything to put you in danger.

Love always,

Roxy

I couldn't stay here and wait. He might wake and find me. I needed to get as far away from the house as possible and wait for the taxi. There was a gas station at the end of the street on the main road. I'd make my way there and call. Might as well sit around a well-lit location that was easy to find while I waited to be picked up and taken away from the one place where I felt at home.

So I left the note on the island for him to find and went to the front door.

As I walked down the driveway, I kept peeking over my shoulder, silently praying that he'd catch me and force my hand. I didn't want to go.

Stopping when I reached the street, I faced the house and whispered, "I'm sorry." I knew he'd be torn up wondering what the hell happened to me. I hoped the note would be enough to stop him from looking for me. I didn't want this all to be in vain.

Looking over my shoulder, I watched the house as it grew smaller until it faded away. The farther I walked, the more I cried. The thought that I'd never see Thomas again made me feel dead inside. What was the use of going on if he wasn't the one I'd be spending my days with?

A car approached from behind, driving slowly and following me. I wasn't a paranoid person, but they were going at almost a snail's pace. Refusing to look back, I kept my eyes forward, watching the light of the gas station grow brighter. The squeak of the brakes sent my mind into overdrive. As I turned to look back, an arm wrapped around my body as a cloth covered my mouth. I screamed, feeling a burn in my throat as I kicked and fought back. My attacker was pulling me backward toward the car as I screamed, flailed, and tried to claw at his hands but failed miserably.

My eyes grew blurry from tears, my throat started to close, and the world around me turned gray. Before I blacked out, I saw the person responsible for this—the person I'd least expected.

CHAPTER
TWENTY

THOMAS

WITHOUT OPENING MY EYES, I felt for her, needing to touch her skin. Sliding over, I searched for her in the darkness, but I found nothing. There wasn't a night that had passed where I hadn't been able to pull her against me. Startled, I sat up and looked around the room. Nothing seemed out of place, and the bathroom light was off.

"Angel!" I yelled, waiting for her to respond, but again only silence.

After climbing out of bed, I headed out the door and down the hallway. All the lights in the house were off. Hoping she was in the kitchen, I ran down the steps two at a time and then rounded the corner in the foyer. Darkness everywhere. Flipping on the light, I glanced at the kitchen and saw a scrap of paper sitting out where I hadn't left it.

As I walked up to it, I could see my name scribbled across the top. "Damn it," I said, picking up the piece of paper and reading each word carefully. I had to read it twice because there wasn't a word on the goddamn piece of paper that I believed. My heart pounded erratically in my chest as I tried to pull in breaths.

What the fuck was I missing?

Once I'd jogged into the foyer, I checked the coat rack —her purse was missing. Then I turned toward the steps and took them three at a time. When I made it to the bedroom, I ran to the closet and found half of her clothes missing.

I walked out, sat on the bed, and grabbed my phone. Hitting it against my forehead, I tried to think of my next step. First, I'd send her a message and beg her to come back. She never could say no to me. That's why she'd had to leave while I couldn't stop her.

Me: Angel, come back. We can fix whatever is going on. I love you too much to say goodbye. Give me another chance. Give us another chance.

As I stared at the screen, I held my breath, waiting for a reply. A few moments later, the message showed "read" before she started to type a response.

Thank you, Jesus. She wasn't ignoring me.

Angel: Ur Angel is busy. If you want to see her again and keep your identity to yourself, I want 1 million dollars.

I blinked, shaking my head as I looked down at the screen. Then I blinked again. I'd thought I'd read it wrong, but I hadn't. My heart, which already felt like it would burst, started to beat out of rhythm as my chest began to feel tight. Sucking in a sharp breath, I swallowed hard, trying to let the message sink in.

Me: When and where?

As I waited for a response, I paced back and forth in the kitchen like a lion in a cage. If they so much as hurt a hair on her head, I'd fucking torture them. Either way, they were dying, but it was up to them if it was quick or prolonged agony as they met their maker.

Angel: 48 hours. We'll be in touch.

Without wasting a moment, I opened up my text messages send out a mass text to my brothers, including James.

Me: Emergency! Be at my house ASAP. Joe – grab Pop.

This was a declaration of war. I couldn't go to the DEA or the cops for help. They would say, "I told you so," and just complicate the shit out of everything. I needed to keep it on the down low, and I knew my brothers would always have my back.

I ran upstairs, needing to get dressed and be ready when everyone arrived. There was a ton of work to do. Gather intel on her location and possible suspects, get as much ammo and as many weapons as possible on short notice, and come up with a plan.

In the spare bedroom, I went straight for the closet. I had boxes of weapons in there, all secured with locks. I stockpiled anything I could get my hands on. Florida didn't have stringent laws when it came to guns, so anything was possible and available at a price.

After laying each item out on the bed, I checked to make sure they were in working order and empty of any rounds. I knew James had a cache of weapons at his disposal, and I was pretty sure my brothers did as well, even if they were dusty and hadn't been used in a while.

I studied the inventory, staring at the mass of guns on the bed: Five AR-15s, three Smith & Wesson .44s, two 9mms, a sawed-off shotgun, and a brand-new Sig Sauer

P320 pistol. I pulled out the five bulletproof vests I had amassed while in training and kept on hand for future use, and added them to the collection.

The front door opened and closed before heavy foot-steps moved through the house. When I placed my hand on the pistol, I heard Mike yell, "Yo!"

Fuck, I needed to calm down. They weren't going to come back for me. They had what they wanted—whom they wanted.

"Up here!" I yelled back, shaking out my hands and rolling my neck. I needed to loosen up and get control of the situation.

Mike pushed the door opened and whistled. "Fuck, that's pretty. What the hell are you doing with all this shit?"

"Some people collect figurines. I collect guns. And for the first time, the shit is going to come in handy."

He walked up to the edge of the bed, grabbed a .44 from the collection, and checked the chamber. "What the fuck is going on? Your text had me in a panic, man."

"Angel is gone. I don't know what the fuck happened, but I got a text demanding money for her life."

"Fuck me," he muttered, pointing the unloaded gun out the window and pulling the trigger.

"Where the fuck is everyone?" I complained, glancing at my watch.

The sound of screeching tires echoed through the room. We left the guns behind, running down the stairs to meet them at the door. James, Joe, Pop, and Anthony were walking toward the door.

"Dude, what the fuck?" Anthony barked, pushing past me as he entered the house.

I rolled my eyes, not really ready to deal with his shit, but we needed the manpower.

"What the hell is going on, son?" Pop asked as he gave me a quick hug.

"Let's talk in the kitchen." I waited as they filed in one by one before I entered behind them. Then I grabbed the note off the counter and slid it in the middle of the table.

James grabbed the note, scanning over it.

"What's that?" Joe asked, sliding into a chair.

"What is this shit?" James growled, holding up the piece of paper and shaking it. "I call bullshit."

"It is. I woke to find this note," I said, snatching the paper. "Angel said she was leaving. When I texted her, I got a reply, but not one I was expecting."

"Yeah, there's no way she'd leave and go back to her shitty life." James bit his lip, knowing he'd already said too much.

I jumped in quickly, bringing everyone back to the topic at hand. "The text said they wanted one million dollars or they'd kill her and come after me."

"What the fuck!" Joe roared, slamming his hand on the table. The table jumped, falling back to the floor with a thud.

"Do you know who?" Anthony asked, sitting forward and dropping the attitude.

"No fucking clue. We need to find someone to track her phone. See if they can get a location. We need to run down a list of suspects and figure out how we're going to get her back."

"How long?" James asked, thinking like a cop and not in shock about the situation.

"Forty-eight hours." I rubbed my forehead, feeling a

headache building in my skull.

"Not enough time," Joe mumbled, pinching the bridge of his nose with his thumb and index finger.

"No, buddy. We got this shit," James said, tipping his chin to me. "We need someone who can access her phone records ASAP."

"Flash?" I offered, grimacing as I spoke. He was a sore spot for both James and me.

James winced, his eyes coming to mine with a cold stare. "Little fucker," James muttered, swiping his hand across his face to muffle his words.

"I always hated that little prick," Joe agreed, knowing full well what James had said.

"I don't trust him," Mike stated firmly with his lips set in a thin line.

Pop stood and leaned over the table, placing his knuckles flat against the surface. "Boys, it doesn't matter if you like someone. If they're useful, then you have no choice but to bury the hatchet."

Everyone quietly thought about my father's words, knowing he'd spoken the truth. For my sake—and Angel's—we had to go against our personal feelings and use any means necessary, even if that meant Flash.

"Pop's right. He's our only hope to get information from her phone and possibly find her location." I pushed back from the table, the sound of the legs scraping against the floor ringing in my ears. "James, can you call him and get him on point?" I stared at James, waiting for him to protest. I knew the Izzy-Flash situation of the past was still stuck in his craw.

"Only for you, Thomas. Only for you."

"Doesn't matter why. Just do it."

With that, he got up from the table, dialing his phone as he walked into the living room. "Flash." James's voice grew quiet as he moved out of earshot.

"What do we do first?" Mike asked, leaning forward and clasping his hands together.

I could see his muscles flex and relax as he sat there. He was pumping himself up, ready and needing a fight. He'd been out of the ring too long and missed the greatest joy of his life—besides his girl. Fighting was in his blood.

"Here's what we're going to do…" I laid out the plan, going over each step and different scenarios. A lot would depend on where, who had her, and what their true motives were.

On the surface, it seemed as if they were out for some quick cash, but it might have been a ploy. Maybe they wanted to weed me out and use me as an offering to the MC. There were more possibilities—probably dozens I couldn't even imagine.

Much of the operation lay in Flash's hands. He was our starting point, and everything would radiate and develop from his intel. As we were talking through our plans and determining the weapons at our disposal, James came back in the room and tossed his phone on the table.

"He said give him twenty." He collapsed in a chair, stretching out his legs and rolling his neck.

Not only was he tied to Flash because of Izzy, but Rebel's death was something the three of us had dealt with together. We were all culpable and guilty of that crime. I wasn't sorry that he'd died, but seeing Flash and having the three of us together would bring up old wounds of the night we'd killed a man in cold blood.

Shaking off my thoughts, I looked at James, waiting

for him to return my stare. "Good. He'll come through for us."

James nodded, crossing his arms over his chest and taking a deep breath.

"James, what about calling Bobby?"

"What about him?" he asked, looking down at his arms. His lips were almost in a frown, as if he were pouting about Flash. Maybe it was the remorse he felt about Rebel.

Even when you knew it'd been the only option you'd had, knowing that you'd killed another human being left a feeling of guilt. Rebel had been a complete piece of shit, but as a DEA agent, you vow to serve and protect. If we hadn't finished him, he would've come after Izzy and James, and I would have also been in his crosshairs. It was the only way it could have ended.

"We need him to do some digging. I need to know everything there is to know about Angel. All of her connections. And I want information on her crack-whore mother."

"Think she's involved?" James asked, bringing his eyes back to mine, a look of disbelief written on his face.

"She's a bitch who would do anything for money. She may not be responsible for her abduction, but she played a role. I'd bet my life on it."

Anger began to boil inside me. I had known she was a cunt when I'd met her. The way she'd tried to attach herself to any member with a dick who wasn't taken by an old lady... She didn't want to be a club whore. She wanted her place in the MC, but no one took her up on the chance. Roxy and I developing a relationship had to have pissed her off after she'd remained a sidepiece for years.

"Who wants coffee?" Pop asked, breaking the tension in the room.

We were on edge—James and I more than the others. But it was clear that testosterone and pissed-off male were floating in the air.

"I got it, Pop," Joe said. "Sit and relax with the guys. We know you can't make coffee worth shit anyway."

"Some things are best left to your ma." He laughed as he sat, throwing his hands in the air as an apology of sorts.

James's phone began to play "I Fucking Hate You" by Godsmack as it danced across the table. After quickly grabbing it to stop the words from continuing, he snapped, "You better have some fuckin' news."

He glared at me while he listened to Flash, tapping his fingers on the table. He needed to get over his bullshit with him. I didn't care if he'd slept with my sister or not, and neither should he. James had won; Izzy was his and his alone. Flash could never say the same.

"Got it," James said as the table quietly waited to hear the news. "What else?" He rolled his eyes, slamming his fist on the table. "Goddamn fuckin' social media. Stay by your phone, and I'll call you back if we need more."

"What did he say?" I asked before he could end the call.

Setting his phone down, he sighed. "Flash did some digging. First off, he found that she'd used her Facebook app on her phone. He found her page and she wrote a status update a couple of days ago. Thomas, her location was turned on. It has to be how they found her."

"God damn it," I said, raking my fingers through my hair and pulling at the roots. I hadn't even thought about her phone being tracked. Why had I been so fucking stupid? I should've checked her phone. "What else?" I asked, angrier with myself than with anyone else, especially Angel.

"The location was down the road from here. She must have been in the car when she updated her status. It didn't show the exact location of your house, but it was in the general vicinity. Anyway, he was able to trace her phone to a tower near Orlando. He's working on getting a more exact location, but it's going to take time."

"Just get it done. We have nothing without a location. I'd rather catch them by surprise than have to show up at a drop-off location on their terms."

"I'll call him and make sure he pushes the shit through as quickly as possible." James called Flash back. "Thomas said to get on their backs about the location. Do whatever you have to in order to get the information ASAP."

Then he stood, walked to the sink, and stared out the window. "We don't give a fuck about that. Make it happen any way you can," he barked before hanging up the phone and turning around to rest his ass against the counter. "It's done. We'll know something in the next twenty-four hours."

"Good. James and I need to call Bobby, our old boss at the DEA, and get more information." I looked around the table, taking in the angry expressions of my family. "I want each of you to think long and hard before you decide to go with us to rescue her. It's dangerous and risky. The ladies won't be happy about it. Even though I have bullet-proof vests, any of us could die."

"I'm in, brother," Mike responded quickly, nodding his head as he stroked his chin.

"Me too," Anthony chimed in, sitting back in his chair, calm and relaxed.

"Joe," I said before he could reply. "You have a baby on the way. I don't think it's a good idea for you to be there. You have the most to lose."

"Fuck that shit, Thomas. I'm there. If you're in trouble, it affects us all. You'd do the same for me. Baby or not, I'm there for my family. Suzy will understand." His stare was steely and serious. I knew that once he'd set his mind to something, there was no way in hell I'd be able to change it.

"Right." I turned toward my pop as he looked around the table. "Pop, Ma will be so pissed if you come with us. I think you should—"

He put his hand up. "If my boys are going, then I'm going. No one can stop me, especially your mother. I'm the one who taught you boys everything you know. Plus, I'd be going freaking crazy sitting at home when I knew shit was going down and you were all in danger."

"Pop—"

"Not another word, Thomas. I'm coming with you."

I sighed, dragging my hands down my face as I blew out a breath. If I didn't die in a hail of bullets, my mother might finish me off for involving him.

"I'll send a text when I have more details or when you need to come back. For now, go home and act as normal as possible. I don't want the girls in a panic."

"Uh, dude," Mike grumbled, raising his index finger.

"What?" I snapped.

"The girls already know. I mean, what the fuck did you expect? It's Monday morning and you summoned us here. They know something is up. I can't lie to Mia."

"Don't tell them that Angel's been kidnapped. Make something else up."

"Your stories better match," Anthony blurted, pushing the chair up and standing. "You know they're going to talk to each other. One slip-up and you're all history."

"Fuck," James hissed, kicking the floor with his foot. "They've probably already done a party line by now."

"Just tell them that I thought someone broke into my house and I needed help checking it out."

"You think they're going to buy that crock of shit?" Anthony asked, shaking his head.

"Why not?"

"Bro, you seriously underestimate the ladies. They're slick and smart. Nothing gets by them," he replied, picking at his nails as he smirked.

"Your lady problems get by them." I sat back and smiled, seeing his eyes shooting to mine.

Everyone around the table turned to him with a look of shock, especially my father.

"Traitor," Anthony snarled, glaring at me and looking like he wanted to lunge across the table.

Pop put his hand on Anthony's shoulder. "You have some explaining to do, son."

"Coffee?" I asked, a small smile on my face because I knew I'd thrown Anthony under the bus. I'd outed him and his dirty little secret. I didn't know exactly what it was, but I knew it involved a woman who had him by the balls.

"Nah. I better get home to Suzy. She's probably starving by now." Joe stood, squeezing Pop's shoulder before holding his hand out to me. "Call me anytime, day or night, and I'll be here."

"Thanks, Joe."

222

"I better get home and washed up," Mike said. "I have to be at the clinic in a couple of hours to help. Wait up for me, Joe. I'll walk out with you." He followed Joe into the foyer with a quick wave and a nod.

"I'm out." Anthony stood, staring down at Pop. "Ready to go, old man? I'll take you home."

The "old man" turned to Anthony, his head tilted and his eyes sharp, and stared at him. "You need to watch yourself, son."

"Sorry, Pop."

"I can't wait to get home and tell your ma that you have a girlfriend," Pop said, holding Anthony on the shoulder as they walked out the door.

"You wouldn't."

"Ain't so old anymore, am I?" Pop asked, closing the door.

"Want a cup?" I asked James, knowing he wasn't a morning person, much like myself.

"Please. I'll call Bobby and have him do a background check and dig into Angel's past. We need to isolate any potential problems and determine which ones are credible threats."

"I'll pour, you call." Standing by the coffee pot, I stared outside and wondered where she was.

Had they hurt her? Was she in pain? Had they killed her? The thought of that made me want to hurl, my stomach clenching tightly in a knot from thinking I'd never touch her again.

"Bobby," James said, pulling me from my thoughts as I grabbed the pot and poured him a cup. "I'm putting you on speakerphone." I placed the coffee in front of him as he said, "Bobby, we have a problem."

CHAPTER
TWENTY-ONE

THOMAS

IT HAD BEEN twenty-four hours since she'd disappeared. Fear gripped me at times, but the anger kept me going, driving me forward to find her. During the day, my family had been there for me. One by one, they had come over to sit with me and attempt to calm my fears. My brothers and James hadn't been able to keep the information to themselves and had to bring the girls over with them. I couldn't be angry that they hadn't kept their promise to not tell the ladies.

I'd racked my brains for hours, trying to figure out why someone would do this to her...and to me. Was it one of my enemies, or were they truly after Angel?

There were so many people who would want to bring us harm. It boggled my mind.

My family was putting their lives on the line for Angel, someone they barely knew, because I'd asked. Without their saying it, I knew they were watching me, worried I'd go Rambo and try to rescue her myself. Although it did pop in my mind from time to time, I knew it wasn't wise.

There were several things we knew for certain:

Sarah Roxanne Parker had created a post late Sunday afternoon, about seven hours before her disappearance. The post was about being happy and how quickly life had changed. Her location had been turned on, and anyone in the world could have tracked her because the post was set to public. It was a mistake many people made, not knowing they were giving their location to every stranger who bothered to look.

Besides Facebook, online connections were minimal. We were unable to check her messages without risking tipping off the people responsible for her disappearance.

She had very few enemies or people who could be classified as a threat, but I had too many to count. The suspect on the top of the list was her mother. There were no other people Bobby could identify as possible assailants.

After hours of trying to track her cell phone, he had been able to determine that they were located in the northern part of Orlando. They would have a better idea after I received another message.

Although she'd had a sketchy career, she was a decent person. The people she'd worked with were sleazeballs and scumbags, and any of them could have played a role in her disappearance.

We didn't have much to go on, but I assembled the guys. They were ready to roll at any moment. The waiting was driving me fucking crazy.

A few hours ago, I'd received a text with instructions for the drop. I'd receive a text tomorrow at noon with details.

Sitting at the kitchen table, I sipped on whiskey and

dragged on a cigarette as I plotted my revenge. Bobby was working on an exact location and a possible cast of characters as Flash kept tabs on her social media and any other possible information that could be leaked from her account. My job: just hang tight.

Who the fuck could hang tight in this situation? I couldn't sleep. I couldn't relax. The only thing I could do was smoke and stare at the second hand of the clock while it moved as if it were in slow motion. Tick. Drag. Tick. Drag. Tick. Sip. Tick.

Getting drunk wasn't the answer. If something happened, I couldn't take the chance of being shitfaced and wallowing in self-pity. It would put her life at risk as well as my family.

As I stubbed out my cigarette, my phone moved against the table like a Mexican jumping bean. I checked my text messages.

Anthony: You up?
Me: What the hell else would I be doing?
Anthony: I'm coming over
Me: You don't have to. I don't need a babysitter.
Anthony: STFU. I'll be there in 10.

I poured another half glass of whiskey, needing an extra dose to deal with Anthony's grumpy ass at a time like this. After a few sips and about six hundred ticks later, there was a knock at the door.

"Yo!" I yelled out, too exhausted to even get up and answer the damn door.

Anthony walked in, stopped in the doorway to the kitchen, and stared at me. "Dude, what the fuck is wrong with you?"

"I don't know what the hell you're talking about." I

swirled the whiskey in my glass, watching the liquid hug the edges.

"You leave your door wide open, you're drinking in the dark, and you don't even get your lazy ass up to answer the door. It's not like you to be so careless, Thomas."

I tore my eyes from the glass and glared at him. "You don't even fucking know me anymore, Anthony. I'm not the same person that I was when we were growing up."

He glanced at me for a moment before heading for the cabinet to get a glass. He sat down, pulled the bottle across the table, and poured.

"Here's what I know," he began, and took a swig. "At your core, you are the same man. I can't imagine what you went through while working for the DEA. I know it was some hardcore shit. But you need to listen to me, little brother."

I sighed, rubbing my eyebrows to relieve some of the tension that had settled there. "You'll never understand," I muttered, digging my fingers into the inside corners of my eyeballs as I pinched the bridge of my nose.

"I don't say much. I watch everyone. I take it all in. Store that shit away for a later date. I'm not the chatty one like Mike or the aggressive one like Joe, but I know everything that happens in this family. It doesn't matter what went down while you were with the Sun Devils. It doesn't matter what heavy shit happened. It does not define you."

"Some sins are unforgivable, Anthony." I shook my head, feeling the weight of my actions on my soul.

"There's nothing that's unforgivable in the eyes of your family. You're still the same man you were when you left for training." He sloshed the whiskey in his cup before taking a swig, his eyes not moving from mine.

"I'm not. I have blood on my hands, Anthony. I'm no better than the criminals in the MC." I closed my eyes, breathing in slowly.

"We've all done shit we regret. You're a victim of your circumstances. Stop beating yourself up for what happened while you were doing your job. They put you in that position. You needed to stay alive and did what you needed to make that happen."

I opened my eyes, looking up at him. I knew his words were true. What had happened wasn't my fault. Protecting my family, surviving, and getting out alive were the reasons behind everything I had done during the time I'd been a member of the Sun Devils MC. Even though my mind knew it, the guilt ate at my heart.

"Anth, I feel that what happened to Angel is God's way of punishing me." I felt the anxiety clawing at my insides. "There are things I can never tell you. Things that happened that only James knows about, and we both live with the guilt each day. I'm not the same happy guy who walked out the door over a year ago. Some of my joy has been replaced by darkness, the sins of my past unable to be extinguished by my deeds of the future."

He wrinkled his nose and snarled. "That's such a crock of shit. No one defines you but yourself. Your deeds of the past do not weigh on who you are as a man. Fuck what other people think of you. The only people who matter in your life are your family and friends. I know you'd jump in front of a bullet for any of us, and we'd do the same for you. That's the measure of a man, not the shit they did to stay alive."

I stared at my brother as he reached for the whiskey

bottle and topped off his drink. "When did you get so wise?"

"I'm just old. Fuck. I'm older than I care to admit. Forty is creepin' up on my ass, and it scares the hell out of me." He blew out a breath and pulled the glass to his lips before taking a slow sip.

"You still have years until you hit forty," I scoffed.

"Whatever. I know who you are, Thomas, and so does the rest of the family. You're a good man. Case closed."

I sighed, knowing I wasn't going to be able to make him understand.

No one ever would.

The only people who knew my dirty deeds were James and Flash, and in many ways, they were just as culpable as I was. James put the bullet in Rebel's head, but we buried the body and covered up the crime.

I'd helped the Sun Devils take out members of rival clubs.

I'd helped secure drug shipments and create distribution channels.

I'd been there for every shady deal and criminal act.

I wasn't innocent.

I'd spend the rest of my life repenting for my sins and trying to reverse the bad I had done.

"What's the plan for tomorrow?" he asked, setting the glass on the table and resting his head against the wall.

"I'll know more around ten. I'll get details at noon, and we'll move from there."

"You want us here at ten?"

"You can stay here if you want. I probably won't sleep, but the guest room is yours." I rolled my glass between my fingers, watching the liquid move inside.

"I'll stay here in case you need me, Thomas." He crossed his arms over his chest as he yawned.

"Thanks, Anth. I know you have your own shit going on."

"Family first," he replied, his mouth set in a firm line.

"Yeah," I mumbled, reaching for the whiskey.

He placed his hand on mine. "No more for tonight. You need your head clear tomorrow."

I glared at him. "Fine," I blurted, a little irritated, even though he was right.

I couldn't allow my momentary panic to risk the lives of Angel and the rest of my family tomorrow. That would be something I'd never be able to live with—the darkness would swallow me whole.

"What's been on your mind? What's going on with that woman you're so hung up on?" I needed to change the subject, even if only for a moment.

"Fuck," he groaned, a heavy sigh escaping him. "I don't even know where to start."

"We have time to kill." I gave him a small smile, trying to give my mind a break from the possibilities that kept creeping inside. I couldn't get the image of Angel suffering to stop playing through my brain.

"She hides me," he said, closing his eyes as he spoke. "Her family hates me, and for that, she keeps me in the shadows."

"Why would she do that?" I asked, gawking at him.

He slowly opened his eyes and stared at me. "It's complicated. We come from very different worlds. I'm not accepted by her brothers and her parents."

"I take it Ma and Pop haven't met her?"

He shook his head and reached for his glass, wincing

as he swallowed. "Nope. I'm not bringing her around the family unless there's a future with her."

"So, you're not sold on her?"

"That's the fucking problem. I am. I've never wanted anyone the way I want her. I've never given myself so completely to someone like I have with her. I've never been faithful, but it's only her. I fuckin' can't win. She shuts me out and disappears. Just when I think I'm over her and ready to move on, she comes back and my walls come crashing down."

"She has you by the balls, Anth."

"I refuse to let it continue. Either she fights for us and moves beyond what her family thinks or I need to put an end to it. Women like her are the reason I've sworn off love."

"Brother, you've sworn off love because of the plethora of pussy falling at your feet," I said, forgetting my panic for just a second before I sobered.

"That too," he replied, a laugh rising from his chest as his body began to shake. "It still falls at my feet, but I step over it now and steer clear."

"Yeah. I find that hard to believe."

"I swear it's some fuckin' sick cosmic joke, Thomas. The first woman I want to be with treats me like shit. She yanks me around by my dick, pulling me in and then tossing me out. She fuckin' makes my head spin."

"Sounds like you're in love."

"Um, no." He wrinkled his nose and shook his head. "I'm in lust."

"You keep telling yourself that, Anth."

"Women are impossible."

"It never gets any easier."

"You love her, yeah?" he asked, as a smile spread across his face.

I'd sworn off love besides my family, but she'd crept inside and become part of me. Being without her was like floating through life missing an anchor. She was my tether to a world that was filled with the possibility of happiness.

"Yes," I confessed with a shaky voice. "I've never loved any woman the way I love her."

He scrubbed his hands across his face and pulled in a breath. "Fuck women. Nothing but trouble, I tell you."

"Yeah, you're fucked," I replied, laughing at the look of sickness on his face. He couldn't deny any longer that he loved the one woman who'd tried pushing him away. "You need to decide if she's worth the fight."

"One thing at a time. Let's focus on getting your woman back and then I'll figure out how to get control of my balls again."

I laughed, standing from my chair and slapping him on the shoulder. "You never get it back."

"Fuck," he hissed, grabbing his glass and finishing off the last drop of whiskey in his cup.

"I'm going to jump in the shower and try to get some sleep." The clock said two, and I knew the crew would be here in eight hours and ready for action.

"I'm going to just crash on the couch and watch a movie until I fall asleep."

Walking to the sink, I saw Angel's cup still sitting next to the teakettle. I'd been unable to move it, to wipe away the last trace of her from before she'd disappeared. Placing my cup in the sink, I stared outside and thought about her.

Let her be okay.

This wasn't the time for us to end.

She deserved better than to go out this way.

I had to step up to the plate and rescue the girl I'd dragged into this life. If I had left her behind, her life would have been shitty, but she wouldn't have been in danger.

"Okay," I said to Anthony, my eyes starting to sting from the tears I refused to let win. I wouldn't cry and wallow in pity. I needed to ready myself for an assault on whoever was responsible for her abduction. I'd make sure they wouldn't come out alive. "Night," I said, waving as I walked out of the kitchen and climbed the steps to my bedroom.

***

I tossed and turned all night. My mind was a clouded and tangled mess of emotions. Sitting on the edge of the bed, I rested my elbows on my knees.

I needed to get my head on straight.

Angel deserved a clear mind and me at my best.

I couldn't let her down. I wouldn't let her down.

I cracked my neck, rolling it from side to side to ease some of the tension before I stood. Then I grabbed a pair of jeans and a T-shirt, put them on, and headed to the bathroom. Not bothering to shave, I stared in the mirror as I scrubbed the night from my mouth.

The circles I had under my eyes had grown darker in the last twenty-four hours. The scruff on my face matched what I felt inside—wild and raw, and I sure as fuck looked it. Spitting the toothpaste into the sink, I washed away any self-doubt I had and decided I'd face the day with a new outlook. Today, I'd get my fuckin' woman back.

Anthony and I spent the morning carrying the weapons we'd need downstairs and placing them on the dining room table. We checked each one to make sure they were in working order. By the time we were finished, the guys had started to show up.

Joe and Mike arrived first, guns in hand and ready to kick ass. Pop showed up, cool as a cucumber, just before James strolled in the door looking like his badass self. Around the table, we devised our plan and bullshitted until the information started to roll in.

Just past ten, Bobby began texting me. He had been able to determine a location based on Angel's phone because it had been left on and in use during her capture. Cell towers weren't as easy to pin down as television crime shows liked to make the public believe, but with time and resources, it was possible.

She was being kept in a tiny ranch outside of Orlando.

We were able to pull up the location on Google Maps, so we studied the surrounding area. With a clear plan of attack, we loaded the guns and climbed in Pop's Escalade. The back was loaded with some of the most kickass weaponry available to the public—along with some that might have the tracking numbers scratched off, courtesy of me.

The one thing we had going for us was the element of surprise. I watched the minutes tick by as James drove. The car remained silent, each man staring in the distance, fidgeting, or watching the world go by as we came closer to our destination. Everyone was on edge, even if they didn't admit it.

We all had something to lose. My something was Angel, but theirs were their lives. Even with their ultimate demise possible, they had still agreed and willingly gone into battle for me. No matter what happened, they had my back. This was how a true family should operate. We were a unit.

If someone fucked with one Gallo, they fucked with us all.

CHAPTER
TWENTY-TWO

THOMAS

AS WE PULLED down a side street near the location we had been told Angel was being held, the tension inside the SUV had grown to a fever pitch. The air was electrified to the point where the sparks were almost visible. Everyone was humming with anticipation and fear, ready to face whatever lay inside.

The fear I felt wasn't for me, but for the ones I loved—including Angel. If something happened to any one of them, it would be my fault. I'd never be able to forgive myself. The only person to blame for the entire situation was myself. I'd brought Angel back with me. I'd introduced her to my family.

Listening to their chatter, I noticed a man watching us through tinted windows in a car nearby. I studied his build, trying to figure out if I knew him. Only a select few knew we were coming here. Slowly, the car door opened and the man climbed out. My heart was racing as I waited to see who the mystery man was—until I saw his face.

Flash.

"Fuck," James yelled from the front, noticing Flash as he walked toward the Escalade.

"What?" Joe barked, looking around before homing in on Flash. "I fucking hate him."

"Cut him some slack," I responded as I opened the door and stepped out.

"Thomas," Flash said, giving me a quick chin lift.

"Flash," I replied, holding out my hand to him. No matter how the other guys felt, Flash had been there in the end and helped bring down the Sun Devils. He'd kept his mouth shut about what happened with Rebel.

"I thought you could use a little more help." He shook my hand, looking over my shoulder and into the vehicle.

"I appreciate it."

"I couldn't just sit there and wait to hear what happened. I needed to help out. You got everything ready?"

"Yep," I said as the others piled out of the SUV and James popped the back.

Without another word, everyone grabbed weapons, jamming them in the waists of their pants and filling their pockets with ammunition.

"What's the plan of attack?" Flash asked, standing behind us as we finished grabbing everything we could possibly carry.

"First, I'm going to go ahead and check everything out while everyone waits here. I don't want us going in totally blind. You stay with the guys and make sure there's no one watching us."

Before he and the others could respond, I took off in the direction of the house where she was being held. I studied my surroundings as I walked, looking for anything that was out of the ordinary, but there was nothing. If this were a professional kidnapping and extortion plot, they would have had guards outside. Plus, they probably would've known better than to leave her phone on during her captivity.

It took everything I had in me not to charge the door and find her. My heart was beating faster than it ever had, pounding against my ribcage. Sweat dotted my brow as one drop trickled down my face. My palms began to feel clammy as my stomach filled with butterflies—but not the good kind. Within the next ten minutes, I'd either be happy or... I couldn't even think about it. I wouldn't let myself.

Peeking through the windows on the side of the house, I was able to see through tiny openings in the sheer drapes. The first two bedrooms I checked were empty. The third bedroom had the drapes drawn, so I couldn't tell who was inside. Leaning against the glass, I placed my ear on the exterior, listening for any movement...but there was nothing.

Walking on light feet, I made my way to the front of the house and the large bay window. I stood off to the side, staying out of sight, and tried to get a visual. Inside were three people, but I couldn't tell much else. The window coverings hid their identities. Listening for a few seconds, I couldn't make out what the muffled voices were saying. Needing to make a plan, I headed back toward the guys and prepared for battle.

As I rounded the back of the house, making my way to the car, I saw everyone coming my way.

"What the fuck, man? You can't just go off all Rambo and bullshit," Mike said, hitting me in the chest with his flattened palm.

I bounced off his hands and maintained my stance. "Chill the fuck out. I needed to get my eyes on the house. I wanted to see who was inside."

"What did you see?" James asked, pushing Mike out of the way.

"Three people in the front room. I couldn't see in all the rooms. I don't know if she's in there or not." I scratched my head, wondering if we had this all wrong.

What if she wasn't in there? Maybe she was being held in another location or the information we had was fucked up. This could turn into a crazy-ass clusterfuck in a hurry and we'd be left with nothing. I'd have no Angel and we'd be in a world of legal trouble for bursting into a house. A little breaking and entering wasn't how I wanted to start my life as a civilian.

"She's in there," Flash interrupted, coming to stand next to James.

"You sure?" James asked, turning to look down at Flash.

"I have no doubt. If she isn't, the people who took her are. Either way, it's win-win." Flash crossed his arms, puffing out his chest.

"It's a win if we get her back."

"It's settled. Let's get our asses in there and get her," Joe said, ready to kick some ass. He had a gun in his hand and one tucked in his jeans.

All the important men in my life and Flash were there with me, standing by my side and willing to put their existences on the line. If I ever doubted the love we felt for one another, today answered that question.

We took a few minutes deciding who would stay in the

back of the house, dividing up the exits to make sure there was no escape.

"Let's do this shit," Anthony said when we finished planning, shifting from foot to foot. I'd never thought of him as aggressive, but in this moment, he was ready.

"Boys," Pop interrupted, holding his hands up to catch our attention. "Please be careful. I love you all dearly, and I want you all in one piece."

We nodded, silently agreeing with him.

"That includes you too, Flash and James. Keep yourselves safe. I love you boys."

"Love you too, Pop. We'll be safe," I said, with a quick nod. "Let's hit it."

We scattered, surrounding the house to take our positions. I stood by the front entrance with James. Flash was stationed at the back door with Pop, and Anthony, Mike, and Joe stood at the side of the house to make sure no one crawled out a window.

Every one was to wait for us to enter through the front door. They were to stand down and be prepared for anyone who tried to escape. James and I would handle the situation inside, whatever that may be. If gunshots were heard, Flash was to enter the house through the back entrance and leave Pop outside to stand guard.

James and I stood on either side of the front door and stared at each other as we listened to the people inside. To say that my heart was ready to burst with the ferocity with which it beat would be a major understatement. I'd been in situations that had been just as deadly, but when it was more than just your own life on the line, the risk and fear were heightened.

Squeezing the handle of my gun, I could feel the moisture of my palm against the warm, slick metal. Closing my eyes, I inhaled, drawing in a long breath as I tried to steady my nerves. I counted to three, opened my eyes, looked at James, and then nodded. It was go time.

James moved in, kicking the door in with his right foot. The wood easily gave way, the door flying open and smashing into the wall. A female screamed, which was followed by yelling.

"Put down the gun, motherfucker," James barked, holding his gun out in front of him, his eyes trained straight ahead.

Moving out from his shadow, I stood at his side and trained my gun on the other man.

"Two of us and two of you. Put down the fucking gun." James didn't move, keeping his arm straight in front, his aim right at the man's head.

"You're outnumbered. We have the house surrounded. We can do this the easy way or the hard way!" I yelled, unable to control the anger in my voice. "Put. The. Fucking. Gun. Down." I put slight pressure on the trigger—not enough to cause it to fire, but I was fucking ready.

The guy to the right was the scumbag I had given a beating to in the strip club—the man who'd stalked Angel, creeped her out, and followed her around. The second guy was from a rival MC. I couldn't place which one, but I knew we'd crossed paths before.

The female sat there and stared at us with wide eyes. I didn't need to be told who she was. I knew it the moment I saw her. It was Angel's fucking cunt of a mother. She'd sold out her own daughter for money. It wasn't surprising, but the lengths she would go to were astonishing to me.

How could someone as sweet as Angel have come from such trash?

"You have this all wrong," Angel's mom said as she started to stand, trying to smooth out her tattered denim miniskirt and death metal tank top. Her face was pocked, most likely caused by meth. She was a fucking mess.

"Sit the fuck down!" I barked at her, not moving my gun from the man I had it trained on.

Sitting slowly, she kept talking. "There's no need for weapons, boys. It's not what you think."

"Shut the fuck up," James said. "Put down your fucking guns or you go out in a body bag."

"Treena," the biker guy said, "what the fuck?" He didn't look at her, keeping his gun and his eyes locked on me.

"A misunderstanding, sweetheart. Don't worry. I'll clear it up." She cleared her throat, leaning over to grab a cigarette off the table.

"Stop fucking moving, bitch," James said, ready to blow his fucking gasket. The vein in the side of his neck looked like it was about the burst. I could see the fucking thing pulsing out of the corner of my eye.

She dropped the cigarette and looked me straight in the eye. "Roxy asked me to help her get your money, Blue. She's in on it." She smiled, leaning back against the couch and rubbing her legs together suggestively.

"You're fucking lying." My blood pressure doubled, the sound of my blood as it coursed through my body filling my ears.

"I'm not, handsome. She told me all about you. She's a gold-digging whore. Like mother, like daughter." She licked her lips, yellow showing behind her lips.

"I don't believe you." I shook my head. I knew Angel, and she wasn't her mother's daughter. This woman might have given Angel life, but wasn't responsible for the woman she was today.

"Believe what you want, Blue, but you'll learn the truth in time."

The sound of the back door opening caused the biker dude to turn toward the noise.

As Flash entered the room with his gun extended and ready to fire, I saw the panic flash in the bastard's eyes—the man who'd already felt my fury once before. Without warning, shots began to ring out.

I emptied my gun, trying to avoid hitting Flash and whoever else had entered the house against orders. James did the same, the echo inside the house ear-shattering.

When the gunfire ended, two men lay on the ground, bleeding. They were surrounded by blood and riddled with bullets. I didn't have to check their pulses; they were dead as fucking dead could be.

"Fuck!" I yelled, realizing this wasn't going to be easy to explain.

"Jesus Christ, Flash. You were supposed to wait outside. What the fuck, man?" James asked, waving his gun.

"Fuck you. Mr. Gallo told me to get my ass inside and I did what I was told." He held his arm, covering a patch on his sleeve that was turning red.

"You've been hit," I mumbled as I scrubbed my hand across my face.

"It's nothing. Just grazed." Flash moved his hand, staring down at the wound. "I'll fucking survive."

James stalked toward the couch. "Where the fuck are

you going?" he asked as he dragged Treena by her feet from the sitting area. "Where the fuck is she, you lying whore?"

"In the back bedroom! Please don't kill me!" she wailed, kicking her feet at James.

"Don't fucking move!" James commanded, pinning her to the floor with his foot on her thigh.

Without wasting time, I headed to the back of the house, leaving the others to deal with Treena. The tiny hallway had a couple of closed doors. As I threw them open one by one, each empty room made my stomach sink further and the feeling of helplessness grow. Finally, I found her in the last bedroom curled into a ball, crying.

"Angel, baby," I whispered, kneeling at her side. After removing the blindfold and rope from her wrists, I grabbed her body and pulled her into my arms. "I got ya," I said, holding her tightly.

Her face was tear-stained and splotchy, her hair matted against her face and dried.

"Shhh," I whispered, stroking her cheek as she sobbed. Her body shook, her crying so intense that she shuddered in my arms. "You're safe."

She clawed at my shirt, digging her face into my chest. "I didn't think you'd come," she sobbed, the words hard to understand through her tears.

"Angel, I'd never leave you behind." I rocked back and forth, stroking her cheek and wiping the tears away as they flowed down her face. "You're safe now."

She didn't speak as she continued to cry. I let her, holding her and trying to comfort her through the realization that it was over. Then her body grew slack in my arms, relaxing against my chest with heavy breaths.

"Are they all d-dead?" she stuttered, looking up into my eyes.

"No, Angel. Your mom is alive." I smiled at her, moving the hair out of her eyes.

"That bitch. She did this." She sucked in a breath, new tears forming in her eyes. "Who does that shit to their kid?"

"A nasty woman, babe."

"Thomas, I'm so sorry for all this. It's my fault." She stared at me with wide eyes that conveyed a world of sadness and hurt, and it gutted me.

"It's not your fault. You didn't ask for this to happen, Angel."

"It is, though," she whispered. "I know I fucked up. She found me because I posted on Facebook. I fucked up."

"It happens, love. We may want to rethink social media for a while, though," I said, trying to hold in a laugh.

"It's not funny," she said, slapping my chest. "I brought this to you. I led them to you."

"Do you know who they were?"

She nodded, swallowing hard before speaking. "I saw them in the club a couple of times. They were from the Kings, I think. I'm sure she was the ringleader."

"It doesn't matter anymore. It's over, Angel. You're safe and I'm taking you home." I held my lips against her forehead, feeling the warmth as I said a prayer of thanks.

I had more to be thankful for than most men. My family had my back, and everyone had come out safely after the gun battle. The woman I loved had survived. Life was about to change. That's the beauty of it all. Nothing stayed the same for long. Whether good or bad, things could change in the blink of an eye. I had to hold on to the good and push out the bad, letting it fade away into the past. I needed to let go of my sins, atone for my behavior, and do good in the future. I'd make amends with society through deeds worthy of forgiveness.

"Son." My pop's voice pulled me from my thoughts.

Looking over my shoulder, I saw him staring at me from the doorway. "Yeah, Pop?"

"You okay in here? How's Angel?" he asked, his face soft and his eyes riddled with concern.

"She's fine, Pop."

"We'll be waiting for you outside. The cops just pulled up and we have some explaining to do." He shrugged, giving me a quick smile before leaving us alone.

"You ready for this, Angel?" I asked, holding her in my arms as I stood.

"I can do it, Thomas." She nuzzled her face into my neck, holding my cheek in her hand. "I'll do anything you ask."

"Just tell the truth." I carried her down the hallway, stepping over the bodies as the police entered the house.

They moved around the living room, taking in the crime scene and talking with Joe, Anthony, Pop, Flash, Mike, and James. Treena was sitting on the couch, sobbing into her hands, a cigarette dangling from her fingertips.

"I'm taking her outside," I said, making my way to the front door before she caught a glimpse of the blood. It wasn't something she needed to see.

Outside, there was an ambulance parked at the curb with the back doors open. Once I'd carried her to the open bay, I set her in the back and called over the paramedic.

"She was being held captive. She needs to be checked for injuries and dehydration."

"Yes, sir." He hurried inside, grabbing a few machines and quickly hooking her up to check her pulse and blood pressure.

"Don't leave me," she wailed, tears beginning to slide down her face.

"Angel," I said, touching her cheek. "I have to go inside and talk to the cops. Let them take care of you so I can take you home. Please do this for me."

She nodded, choking back the tears. "Okay."

"Promise?"

"I promise, Thomas. Don't be gone too long."

I gave her a quick kiss on the lips. "I'll be back in a few minutes to check on you."

As I started to walk away, she grabbed my hand, stopping me in my tracks. "Thomas, I love you."

I turned around, smiling at her. Even in her state, she still radiated beauty and grace. This was the woman I loved. The one with a complicated, fucked-up childhood that didn't dull her luster.

"I love you too, Angel." Then I let our fingertips drift apart as I moved away. Before I disappeared inside the house to explain the clusterfuck of bodies and blood, I looked over my shoulder, taking one last look at her.

After being questioned for hours by the local authorities, we were finally free to go. The sheriff told us to be available when necessary and not leave the state until we'd been cleared of any wrongdoing. Since James and I were ex–law enforcement and Flash was still with the FBI, we were given more leeway than many would have been given in a situation such as that. Her mother was taken into custody and would be prosecuted for extortion and kidnapping. I'd rather her be dead, but I couldn't kill Angel's only living relative.

I sat in the back of the SUV on the way home. James drove, Pop rode shotgun, and Mike, Joe, and Anthony sat in the middle row, smashed together to give me privacy in the back with Angel.

The paramedics said that she was in good shape—slightly dehydrated with a couple of bumps and bruises but otherwise healthy. She might have been physically okay, but I knew it would take a while before she mentally felt at peace. I'd do everything in my power to bring the brightness back to her eyes.

The guys talked during the drive, retelling what had happened when Flash had burst through the door. Keeping my eyes focused on Angel as she fell asleep against my chest, tucked in my arms, I listened to their laughter, soaked in the love that filled the SUV, and sucked it all in, putting it away for a time when the darkness would start to take hold. I'd remember the love I felt for my family, the sense of belonging I had, to push off the sadness and stay grounded in the truth. I was loved. No matter my sins of the past, my family and Angel would always be my future. Forgiveness wasn't something I needed to seek from them; it was granted without hesitation.

I was the luckiest man in the world. I had everything I ever wanted—love, family, and a purpose. The greatest purpose I had now was lying in my arms, and I'd make her forget the past and revel in the future.

As we drove down my street, I could see the distant figures of the Gallo women. They formed a semicircle as they stood in my front yard, waiting for us to arrive. Those women were our other half, the thing that made us what we were—an amazing family that was stronger and more loving than most.

"Angel, wake up. We're home," I whispered in her ear, stroking her cheek.

Her eyes, still red from crying, fluttered open before a small smile crept across her lips. "Hey," she whispered.

"Looks like we have company, boys," Pop called out, pointing through the windshield to the Gallo women.

"Yep. This might get hairier than the gun battle back there," Anthony replied, laughing as he flipped through his phone.

"Not a chance. They're going to be happy to see us," Joe said, reaching for the door handle before the car even stopped moving.

After hopping out and leaving the door ajar, he ran to Suzy and collected her in his arms. Her feet dangled from the ground as he hugged her.

"Barf," Anthony blurted, watching intently out the window.

Mike nudged him with his shoulder. "Shut the fuck up, dude. I know all about your piece of ass. You're just pissed she isn't here."

Anthony shrugged before I heard him sigh. "Fuck off, bro."

One by one, they piled out of the car, going to the loves of their lives and repeating the actions Joe had done with Suzy. Anthony looked like the odd fish. No one hugged him first, kissed his face, or gushed over him for returning safely. When my father released my mother, she was the one to wrap Anthony in her arms and kiss his cheeks. Someday, he'd have his—sooner rather than later, if my gut was right.

"Can you walk or do you want me to carry you?" I asked Angel, looking down at her as she started to sit up in my lap.

"I can walk, Thomas." She pushed off my lap and climbed out of the car while holding on to steady herself. Then she covered her eyes, the sunshine blinding today, and waited for me to stand behind her.

Ma was the first person to break rank and head straight for Angel. As she approached, she gave me a quick nod and a smile before holding out her arms.

"Baby girl, I'm so happy you're safe," Ma said, staring at me as she hugged Angel.

Angel broke down into tears, melting into my ma's comforting arms, and rested her head against her shoulder. "I'm so sorry, Mrs. Gallo," Angel cried, her body shaking as she spoke.

Ma rubbed her back. "There's nothing to be sorry about, Angel. Everyone is safe and you're back." Ma was trying to keep it together and pretend like it was no big deal, but I knew her better than that. "I've been through crazier shit with this family."

Next to me, James was holding Izzy, kissing her deeply—probably a little too deeply in front of the family. Either my parents didn't mind or they were pretending they didn't see. Fortunately, Izzy broke the kiss, holding his face in her hands.

"I love you, James. I've never been so worried about someone before. I didn't fucking like it. Don't do that type of shit anymore. I couldn't take it."

"I'm fine, babe. Don't ever worry about me. I love you too, Iz."

"All I do is worry about you and your macho 'I have

something to prove' bullshit. You are not indestructible. Remember that, please, next time you go off trying to pretend you're Jason Statham."

"I'll take that. He's pretty badass, babe." James laughed, earning him a small slap to the cheek. "Watch it. I may just show you how badass I really am, love. Don't start something you can't finish." He smiled, winking at her as a giant smile slid across her face.

Jesus, they made me ill.

Love changes a person. It doesn't make us inferior, but it lets us be the person we were truly meant to be. It completes us, brings out our true nature, and helps us become a better version of ourselves.

Looking around James, Izzy locked eyes with me. "Tommy!" she screeched, moving quickly and jumping in my arms.

"Hey, baby girl. It's good to see you," I whispered, squeezing her tightly.

"You too. Don't do this shit again either," she mumbled into my shoulder before she sighed.

Ma released Angel as Mia and Suzy each took turns hugging her and welcoming her home. All the girls were in tears. It was like a watching a Lifetime movie playing out before my eyes. Tears, smiles, laughter, and—most of all—love.

"Who's up for a cup of coffee?" Ma asked, wiping the tears from her cheek. "If that's okay with Tommy and Angel."

"It's fine, Mrs. Gallo. I need a shower, though. I can't imagine how I smell." Angel winced, sniffing her shirt. "Yeah, shower first."

251

"You shower, baby girl, and I'll make you something to eat too."

Angel nodded, a giant smile on her face as Ma wrapped one arm around her shoulder and walked with her to the house.

"I'm proud of you, brother," Izzy said before we followed the crowd inside.

"For what?"

"You're a good man. She was broken. I've known enough broken girls in my time, but you saved her."

"I couldn't leave her in the hands of the kidnappers, Izzy."

She shook her head, gripping my side tighter as we walked. "Not what I meant, Tommy."

I felt my face heat as color rushed to my cheeks. "I love her. Nothing else matters."

"I always knew you were a big softie like the others." She smiled up at me, reminding me of when she was a little girl.

She always looked at me like I was a superhero. She'd had me wrapped around her little finger since the day she was born. I would've walked through fire if she'd asked me, and I'd do anything to protect her. Knowing that she was with James, someone so much like myself, I felt that I could finally let go of my overprotectiveness of her. James would willingly give his life to save hers.

I had someone new to protect, a woman who needed to feel part of something bigger. Belonging is important to everyone, and she'd lacked that her entire life. I'd spend eternity trying to bring her joy and making her never regret her decision to come with me.

It was my sole mission to make her feel loved.

CHAPTER
TWENTY-THREE

ANGEL

FOR A WEEK, Thomas treated me like I was ready to break. He tried to do everything for me. It was sweet, but there's a point when enough is enough.

"Thomas," I said, watching him hover as he straightened up the living room. "Come here and sit with me." I patted the cushion next to me.

"I was about to start dinner," he stalked in my direction before collapsing on the couch.

I turned to face him, pulling one leg under my body. "Dinner can wait. We need to talk."

"What's wrong?" He repeated my motion, tucking his leg under his body.

"Nothing, baby. I'm perfect. Maybe better than perfect, actually. I need you to stop treating me like I'm fragile. I'm not."

He placed his hands over mine, stroking the top with his thumb. "You went through something very traumatic, Angel."

"I know, but I survived. I want to stop living in the

253

past and start our future. I can't sit in this house any longer and watch you clean. It's not who you are. I'm not a sitter either. There's only so much television and reading I can do before I start to go a little crazy." I gave him a small smile, hoping I hadn't hurt his feelings. I just wanted us to go back to normal—whatever the hell that was for us.

"You should've said something sooner. I didn't want to push you and didn't feel right doing it until you said something." He smiled back, his cheeks turning pink as he spoke.

"I didn't want to make you feel bad, baby. Every day, I would pray you'd touch me like you used to and that we'd move forward."

"I just wanted to give you time," he said, holding the side of my face in his hand, sweeping his thumb across my cheekbone.

"It's been long enough. You and James need to work on your business, I need to find a job, and you need to make me feel like your woman again." I tilted my head, melting into his touch, and closed my eyes. "I've missed the feel of you against my skin."

Cupping my face in both of his hands, he pressed his mouth against mine. "Like this?" he whispered, hovering over my lips.

"Yes," I moaned, feeling the hairs on my arms standing up as he spoke.

"And this?" He kissed down my jaw and licked my neck, biting gently near my collarbone.

"Just like that," I pleaded, pushing my body forward.

I had very little on, having selected a black babydoll nighty when I'd dressed this morning. The soft silk against my skin, especially my nipples, as I walked around the house had about driven me over the edge.

He slid his hands down my shoulders, the heat of his palms scorching my cool skin before they settled on my forearms. He backed away and looked at me. His eyes were hungry, the need and burning he felt for me evident in his stare.

"I want you so damn badly. I could barely control myself any longer."

"I love when you lose control, Thomas. Show me how badly you want me." Jutting my chest out, I offered him my body, wanting to feel him inside me for the first time in too long.

A small growl escaped from deep in his throat as he pushed me down into the cushions, moving his body on top of mine. Capturing my mouth in a commanding kiss, he gripped my waist, digging his rock-hard cock against my aching core.

His jeans did nothing to hide his want as I pushed against him, trying to create friction. Every time his hand moved, my body would break out into' goose bumps, leaving a wake in his path. My nipples hardened, throbbing to be touched, as his hands moved farther up my sides.

My tongue captured his, dancing together, as our hands touched each other everywhere.

"Thomas," I moaned.

"Mmm." He slid his thumb against my nipple, sending a jolt of electricity through my system.

As he rubbed back and forth, I felt breathless and kissed him back, letting him caress my breast. His rough fingers plucked at my hardened nipple, pulling on it through the soft material. I arched my back, melting into his touch. I wanted more.

When his lips left mine, my breathing was heavy and uneven. After kissing a path down my neck, he stopped over my pulse, running his tongue over the spot. Then he ground his dick against me while he teased my breast.

Tipping my head back, I offered my neck and chest to him, spreading my legs farther to give him better access. As he sucked my breast into his mouth through the silk, his hand moved to my core and dampness pooled between my legs.

He groaned as he slid his fingers across my pussy. I was soaked, the need I felt for him overwhelming after not having been touched sexually in so long. As his fingers swirled around my entrance, I closed my eyes, pushing my head into the cushion.

One finger entered me, stroking me deeply as he rubbed my clit with his thumb, tenderly circling around it. I needed to hold something, ground myself in the moment, so I clutched the cushions in my hand.

His hot breath mixing with the tug of his teeth sent shivers straight to my core. My pussy gripped his fingers, pulling him deeper and wanting more. When a second finger stretched me, a dull and luscious ache took over, and he pushed them deeper.

"Oh God," I moaned, my eyes rolling back in my head.

"So fuckin' good," he growled against my breast, causing vibrations through my skin.

"I want you, Thomas," I said, moving my bottom to drive his fingers in deeper.

He didn't respond with words, instead moving his mouth to my other breast and curling his fingers inside me.

Adjusting his body, he moved to the side, increasing the thrust as he kept his fingers turned up, working my insides. Feeling the pressure building, I shuddered in his arms.

"You like this, don't you?" he asked with my nipple between his teeth.

"I want more," I whined, riding his hand as his fingers hooked inside me and stilled. "Thomas," I said, pushing against his palm.

He chuckled, rubbing his hand against my clit as he kept his fingers buried inside. Whimpering, I tried to get him to move his fingers, but his body vibrated from laughter. He bit down harder on my nipple, shocking my system as I clenched around him. His fingers moved, thrusting inside at fevered pace. Letting my leg fall off the couch, I opened to him fully, offering everything I had to give.

Digging my toes into the carpet, I lifted my bottom, thrusting myself against his hand. As I felt him stroke my G-spot, I gulped for air. My nipple was trapped, as my body shook in his arms. The orgasm to end all orgasms was building inside me. Before I could brace myself, it broke loose, tearing through my system and stunning me.

Frozen in place, I screamed. My body grew rigid against his. I sucked in air, trying to pull it into my lungs. Riding his hand, I bucked against his palm. His fingers slowed, stroking me deeper as I experienced the last shock waves in my system. Shivering in his arms, I saw stars as I sucked in a ragged breath.

My eyes drifted open, taking a moment to focus before I locked eyes with Tommy. He looked proud.

"That was so damn sexy," he said softly, his fingers buried deep inside me.

"Yeah," I replied, still unable to form thoughts. My

body was coming down from the unbelievable orgasm that had almost decimated me.

"I'm not done with you yet." He smiled, pushing his weight off me as he sat up.

When he held his hand out, I slid my palm against his. Still struggling to catch my breath, as he helped me sit up. He pressed his mouth to mine as I breathed him in, using his air as a means of survival. He nibbled on my lips, drawing them into his mouth. I grabbed his shoulders, digging my nails into his flesh before running them down his back. Pulling me closer as I crawled into his lap, he smashed his chest against mine. Holding my ass roughly in his hands sent tingles up my spine. I loved when he possessed me, making me feel owned. He released my mouth and grabbed me by the hips, draping my body over the back of the couch.

"Thomas!" I squeaked, wanting to face him when he entered me.

"Shhh, Angel," he whispered, putting his mouth next to my ear, his hot breath cascading across my skin.

The couch dipped and bounced back before the sound of his zipper echoed through the living room. Looking over my shoulder, I watched as he removed his jeans and tossed them to the floor. His body was rock hard, his penis red and solid. He flexed his muscles, giving me a show. My face heated. My cheeks growing more flushed than they already were when he climbed back on the couch. Squeezing my eyes shut, I held my breath as he rubbed the head of his dick against my opening.

"You're so wet," he hissed, stroking the tip through my folds as he captured my wetness.

When he pushed down on my back with one hand, I

melted into the couch, relaxing my body against the pillows. My breasts stuck out over the top, my ass was in the air. I felt exposed and ready.

Then he pushed his cock inside, filling me to the point of pain. I let my head fall forward and took what he wanted to give. As my body fused with his, he gripped my shoulder and hip, holding me in place as he pounded into me. Crying out, the pleasure heightened from my orgasm. I bit my lip to control the scream I felt bubbling from within.

I needed this. I wanted him. A week without him touching me as if he needed me to survive had left me feeling empty inside. With that feeling erased, I let myself get lost in the feel of him inside me. While he surrounded me with his touch, I pushed against him, tipping my head back and keeping my eyes open.

With one hand still on my hip, he dug his fingers into my hair and fisted the strands. Pulling my head back farther, I felt captured. My ass bounced off him while he jammed his dick inside me. I didn't get a moment's reprieve. Held to his body by my mane, I felt the tug each time he thrust my body against him to drive himself deeper. His hand gripped my hip more roughly, and he dug his fingernails into my flesh. The slight bite of pain kept my attention. My scalp ached, my pussy throbbed, and my body responded to the battering he was giving me. This is what I had been looking forward to since my rescue. He was touching me the way he used to.

I cried out, feeling another orgasm building inside me. Wanting to close my legs, I started to inch them together. Before I did, he stopped them. Releasing my hair, he brought his hand down hard on my ass.

"Hold still," he growled, running his palm against the spot he'd just smacked.

Then his hand left my hip for a moment, pushing between my shoulder blades. Forcing my upper body farther over the couch and my ass higher in the air. His cock slipped out before the couch moved under my feet. Tapping at my heels made me inch my feet farther apart until I couldn't open them anymore. Using my hands to keep my balance, I placed my feet flat on the floor.

His fingers raked through my wetness before rubbing against my asshole. Sucking in a breath, I felt the rough texture of his thumb against my opening. When he slammed his rock-hard shaft into me, his thumb slipped inside, sending a shock through my system.

"Oh!" I yelped, the quickness of his action catching me off guard.

"Jesus, I missed being inside you," he bit out, hooking his thumb fully inside me.

"Fuck me, Thomas!" I cried out, the orgasm simmering under the surface.

"You're mine, Angel. Only mine," he said, driving deeper inside me with increasing force, battering my pussy.

With his thumb buried in my ass, I felt fuller than I had ever before. Maybe it was the week of his having been near but not touching me in a sexual way.

"Only yours," I whispered, my face tingling with the blood pooling in my head.

While my body was tipped forward, I had the sensation of being choked without his fingers wrapped around my neck. It heightened my sensitivity as my vision began to blur.

My body lurched forward with each pound against my ass. His body began to shake, his breath ragged against my back, as his thrusts became erratic. Calling out my name, he squeezed my hip as he gave me three last thrusts before I fell over the edge with him. My pussy milked his cock, taking everything he had to give. My arms felt weak, quivering as I tried to hold up my weight and not tumble off the back of the couch.

As his body collapsed against mine, he wrapped his arms around my waist, stopping me from falling. Then he pressed his cheek against my spine, drawing in heavy breaths as his heartbeat reverberated through my back.

Adjusting himself on the couch, he pulled me into his lap, resting his chin on my shoulder. My back rested against his front, our hearts beating in rhythm as if speaking to one another.

"I love you, Angel," he whispered, drawing in a shaky breath and splaying his hands across my stomach.

"Love you too, Thomas." I smiled, looking over my shoulder at him.

"Give me a minute. I don't think I can walk yet," he said, his body twitching as an aftershock shot through him.

I giggled, tipping my head back and resting it against his face. "My entire body feels like jelly. I'm perfect right where I am." Then I snuggled against him, wiggling my ass in his lap.

"Stop that or you're going to make me hard again," he said, sinking his teeth into my shoulder.

Warm in his arms, spent from the two orgasms, I melted into him and drifted to sleep.

CHAPTER
TWENTY-FOUR

THOMAS

WATCHING Angel through the sliding glass doors, I smiled, knowing that she felt at ease in my parents' house. She had easily become a member of the family, been welcomed into the fold, and seemed relaxed around everyone. Izzy had taken her under her wing, whether I liked the idea or not, and talked with Angel every day. They shared secrets, told stories, and giggled like high school girls, gossiping about everyone and everything.

Izzy had offered her a job at the tattoo shop as a receptionist, needing to give Mike a break from the paperwork. I thought it was a great idea, even though I wouldn't be able to keep an eye on her. She assured me that she'd be fine, that she needed to be out amongst the people, and that Izzy would watch out for her.

I knew Angel could take care of herself. I felt overprotective of her, and it wasn't out of jealousy, but worry for her safety. I'd almost lost her once, and I wasn't looking to go through that experience anytime soon.

She was going to start working on Tuesday by learning

the ropes, and then she'd slowly take over the day-to-day operations, including the books. I told Angel that, ultimately, I wanted her to work with James and me in our new business, but the choice would be hers.

Izzy and the others at Inked were way more fun than James and I could ever be, but I wanted her near me as much as possible. I wanted to be able to take a break each day and steal a kiss or taste her at every opportunity. Hopefully, once we were ready to start the business and had an office, the luster of Inked would be gone.

"Yo! You there?" James asked, drawing my attention away from Angel.

"Sorry. I spaced out for a second." I rubbed my face, pulling at the corner of my eyes.

"As I was saying, we should be able to get everything off the ground in the next couple of weeks. We just need to find an office space in a central location." James sipped his coffee, shaking his foot as he propped it on his knee. "Have any thoughts on where?"

I shook my head, still thinking about Angel and the free time I'd have in the coming weeks. It had felt like forever since I'd had absolutely nothing to do. It was good that we were starting this venture now, giving me something to focus my attention on instead of the void that would have been there.

"Closer to Tampa or a place near the beach. We could have the offices in Clearwater."

"That would be close to us both, but it needs to be easily accessible for our clients." He placed his coffee cup on the table and rubbed his chin between his fingers. "I'll tell the real estate broker to focus on Clearwater and see what she comes up with."

"We need to figure out a name so the accountant can get started on the incorporation paperwork as soon as possible," I said, standing from the table and grabbing a cup from the cabinet.

"Hey, guys. How's it going in here?" Pop asked as he entered the kitchen.

"Good, Pop. We're trying to get shit ironed out for the business. We can't figure out a good name."

"Let me think. A name is crucial in the success of any business."

"We know," I replied, reaching for a second cup and filling them both.

"I'm partial to Caldo Investigations," James chimed in from the table.

"I don't want to use our names," I said, glancing at my pop as he clutched the coffee in his hands and walked toward the table.

"Are you using 'PI' or 'investigations'?" Pop sat down across from James.

"Either. We're more concerned about the first half of the name." I sat next to him. Sliding the cup against the table, I watched as the cream swirled, mixing into the dark coffee.

"Hmm," Pop said, tapping the ceramic mug with his wedding ring.

"Torrid PI," James blurted out, giving us both a huge smile.

"Nah," I said, shaking my head and sighing.

"Confidentially Yours," James said, his eyebrows moving toward his hairline as his smile grew wider.

"That sounds like a male escort service."

"Yeah, not good," Pop said, laughing. "But you'd

probably get a lot of business."

"Undercover Liaisons," James tried again, his smile not as big this time.

"It's a good play on words, but still seems like you're male escorts."

"I like that it sounds kinky. You're such a killjoy, Thomas," James said with a laugh.

"How about ICE PI?"

"Ice?" James asked, his eyebrows knitting together in confusion.

"Yeah. It stands for Investigate, Catch, and Enforce," I replied, feeling proud of my name.

"That's shitty," James barked, breaking out into laughter and slapping the table.

"Yeah, 'cause Confidentially Yours was so fucking fantastic." I glared at him, watching his laughter fade.

"You two give me a headache," Pop interrupted, shaking his head. "All the names are good. Just pick one."

"We should ask the girls," James said, tipping his chin toward the sliding glass door and all the Gallo women.

"Did you forget the night Angel and Izzy started coming up with names? Let's just figure the shit out without their input."

"ALFA PI," I said with a shrug.

"I like it." Pop said, standing from the table as he grabbed his mug.

"It could work." James nodded slowly.

"What's going on in here?" Joe asked as he walked in the room with his arm around Suzy.

"We're just talking business," I said, giving Suzy a smile as she rubbed her stomach.

"I'm so hungry. Oh my God." She looked around the

room, her eyes catching the pie on the counter. "Ooh, pie. I want a piece, baby."

"I don't know where you put it all," James said, stretching out his legs and putting his hands behind his head.

"I swear to God this baby is going to be fifteen pounds. I've never been so hungry in my life."

"I can vouch for that." Joe laughed, kissing the top of her head.

"You eat as much as you want to, dear girl," Pop said, grabbing a knife from the drawer.

Just as Pop stuck the knife in the pie, the sliding glass door opened.

"Are you touching the pie?" Ma asked, looking over at my pop.

"Suzy wanted a slice," he declared. Apple pie was his kryptonite, and my mother had known it when she'd set it out to torture him.

"I'll cut the pie before you turn it into a fruit bake with crumb topping." She laid her hand over his, stopping him from finishing the job.

"Anything you want, love." Pop smiled at her, moving his hand away from the knife.

"Who wants pie?" Ma yelled out, waiting for a response. She didn't really need to ask; everyone wanted her apple pie. No one ever turned down her baking.

The family slowly filed into the kitchen, waiting their turn for a slice. Suzy was given the first piece—and the biggest, which didn't escape Anthony's notice.

"Why does she always get the biggest piece, Ma?" he asked, staring down at his sliver. "Shit is so unfair."

"She has a human being growing inside her."

"I'll never be able to use that excuse," he mumbled, stabbing at his pie as if trying to kill it.

Angel grabbed two plates and brought me a slice before she sat on my leg. "I brought you some, baby," she said, holding out the plate for me.

"Thanks, Angel. I'd rather taste a different piece," I whispered in her ear, watching her face turn red.

"Thomas," she said, her eyes sliding toward my family without moving her head.

"They didn't hear me," I said, setting my plate on the table and pulling her into my lap. I nibbled on her ear, listening to her breathing change. "You want pie or cock, Angel?"

"You really need to ask me that?" she whispered as she looked at me over her shoulder.

"Eat quick. I want to bury my dick inside you. I'm aching to touch you."

"Reel it back, tiger. You went a week without it." She laughed, cutting the pie and placed a slice on her tongue.

Watching her mouth as she slid her tongue against her fork made my dick twitch. I wanted to feel her lips wrapped around my shaft and her soft tongue slide against my hardness.

"I need to make up for lost time. Eat quick."

"What are you two whispering about over there?" Ma asked, pouring herself a cup of coffee.

"Nothing, Mrs. G.," Angel replied, staring at her plate.

"I could use more grandbabies," she said as she took a seat at the table.

Everyone choked, mumbling under their breath as they tried to ignore Ma.

"I know you all heard me. I want babies. Suzy is going

267

to give me one, but that's not enough. I expected to have more little ones running around this house by now," she whined, cutting into her slice of apple pie.

"We aren't even married, Ma. Only Suzy and Joe are husband and wife. Isn't there some sin against sex before marriage we'd be breaking in the eyes of God?" Mike asked, a small grin on his face.

I rolled my eyes. There wasn't a virgin at this table. I knew it. They knew it. And my parents knew it.

My ma smiled, looking at Mike with a mischievous glint in her eye. "Michael, don't you bullshit me. I remember the time I caught you with Emma in your—"

"Ma," Mike interrupted, holding up his hand. "That's not proper table conversation."

"All I'm saying," she said, trying to contain her laughter, "is that I know I taught you about birth control. But damn, can't someone have an accident?"

"Don't listen to her," Pop said, standing behind my ma. "You'll do it when you're ready."

"We weren't ready when we had Anthony," she confessed, glancing at Anthony standing in the doorway.

"I'm the mistake that started it all," he grumbled, his mouth full of pie, crumbs falling from his lips.

"You were the furthest thing from an accident, Anth. I was so happy when I found out we were having a baby. The day you were born was the first time I ever saw your father cry."

"Probably tears of sadness at how ugly he was," Joe threw in, bursting into laughter.

"Asshole," Anthony hissed, sticking out his tongue at Joe.

"He couldn't help how he looked, Joe," Izzy added.

"Stop! Your mother graced me with a baby boy to carry on the Gallo name. Who knew we'd end up with three more before my princess was born?" Pop said, squeezing my ma's shoulder.

Izzy beamed, her smile so wide that I thought her lips would crack.

"We know. We know. Izzy was the most beautiful baby ever," Mike said, rolling his eyes and gagging.

"Michael, since Mia is at work, when are you going to grow a pair and ask her to marry you?" Anthony asked, changing the subject.

Mike sighed, pinching the bridge of his nose. "I have it all planned. It'll be soon."

"You're such a pussy," Joe teased. "Just ask her already."

"Michael, the girl loves you. If you don't ask her soon, she may not wait around for you to ask," Ma said, reaching across the table and touching his hand. "Sometimes, you have to have faith in your love and stop being a pussy." Ma burst into laughter and slapped the back of his hand.

"I will. I have it planned out."

"Jesus, you and your plans. Whatever happened to spontaneity?" I asked, squeezing Angel and pulling her against my chest.

"I want it to be romantic. Something she'll remember for a lifetime."

"At this point, she'll remember it forever since she thinks it's never going to happen," Izzy said, smacking him on the back of the head. "Just ask her already. She's getting pissed."

"She is?" Mike asked, his mouth hanging open.

269

"She is, brother. What's the plan?" Izzy asked, taking a seat in James's lap.

"I want to recreate our first date. Take her to the beach and ask her where we began."

"That's so romantic," Angel said, sagging against me.

"See?" Mike said, motioning toward Angel. "I want her to be surprised. A romantic dinner under the stars, waves crashing around us as I ask her and she says yes. It's the only place that makes sense to me." Mike stared at Izzy, pausing as he waited for their eyes to connect. "When are *you* getting married, Izzy?" he asked.

"I'm not ready for that yet," she said, biting her lip as she avoided James's gaze.

"One step at a time," James replied, moving the hair off her shoulders before kissing her skin.

"I'm taking my girl home to start on this baby problem," I said, moving Angel off my lap and standing.

"Thomas!" she yelled, slapping me on the chest as she stood.

Everyone burst into laughter as I swung her over my shoulder, waved goodbye, and headed for the door.

Things had seemed easier the last week since I'd brought Angel home. I felt like a member of the family again. Maybe it was everyone coming together to help me find her, or just the time that had passed since I'd left the MC.

"Thomas!" Angel screeched, kicking her feet as I carried her out the front door.

"Shut it, woman," I said, slapping her on the ass as I descended the first step. "Ma wants babies, and by God, we're going to give it a shot." I laughed, feeling her body sag against my shoulder.

"I'm all about practice, but motherhood…"

"Baby," I said, stopping and pulling her down my chest. Capturing her face in my hands, I looked into her eyes. "You're not your mother. You have so much love to give, Angel. You're going to be an amazing mother someday."

"You think?" she asked, her eyebrows shooting up as she held her breath.

"I know," I replied, rubbing my nose against hers. "But for now, we're going to just practice. I need to be alone with you before we have little ones running around the house."

"Thank God," she whispered, drawing air into her lungs and closing her eyes.

"Now get that beautiful ass of yours in the car, Angel. I have plans for you tonight."

She screeched, running toward the car and sliding into the front seat.

The woman made me laugh, which was something I hadn't done in years. While I'd been with the MC, there hadn't been much laughter. She'd brought it back into my life, filling it with so much joy that I couldn't fathom how I'd been so damn lucky.

For the first time in a long time, I could honestly say that the future looked bright. I was ready for whatever might come my way, as long as Angel was by my side.

CHAPTER
TWENTY-FIVE
ANGEL

THOMAS HAD RESCUED me from my mother and a life of despair.

I had very few happy memories from when I'd been growing up. I didn't have visions of laughter and hugs. Nothing had filled my childhood but bitterness and resentment. My mother blamed me for everything: her fucked-up life, not being wanted by men, her addictions, even losing my father. I was the bane of her existence, and she had no qualms with telling me exactly how she felt.

The Gallo family had taken me in, made me feel welcome, and loved me. Never in my life had I felt part of anything, let alone a family, but the Gallos made me feel at home. I'd grown attached to Ma Gallo over the last two months. She took time out of her day to call and check in on me, she invited me to lunch, and she even gave me cooking lessons. She did motherly things with me that I hadn't had as a child.

If I had grown up differently, I wouldn't be with

Thomas, living an amazing life, and calling the Gallos my family. I looked to the future, shutting out the past to move forward into a new chapter in my life.

Looking around the table, I couldn't help but smile. My cheeks hurt from the perpetual grin that had been on my face since the day my new life had begun and my mother had been placed behind bars. Tonight, all the Gallo women, those born into the family and the rest like me—taken in and made to feel like a family member—surrounded me.

Before my abduction, we'd talked about having a girls' night out, but it hadn't happened. Afterward, the guys had been too paranoid to let us out alone. Sometimes they got a little carried away with their macho authority. But finally, after two months, we had been granted a reprieve. Mainly because Suzy had finally given birth and she'd demanded a night out.

Joe, being the man he was, had said yes and made sure to make it happen. He'd wanted to give Suzy a night to "let loose." The men were having their poker night at Joe's, but I imagined it wasn't like the games in the past. All the Gallo men would pitch in and take care of one tiny human being for a night. It had been tempting to stay behind and watch five grown men babysit one small baby girl, but I had given it up to spend a night laughing with my sisters.

Suzy sat across from me, her face glowing from a mix of motherhood and the alcohol Izzy had insisted she drink. Her cheeks were losing the roundness that had been caused by the weight gain of pregnancy.

I had been there the night she'd given birth to

Giovanna Bianca Gallo three weeks ago. Big, bad Joe had cried tears of joy and gushed over his daughter. I'd never seen a father prouder because he had a daughter. Izzy had fallen to her knees, thanking God for making the baby a girl. The numbers were finally tipping in favor of "vadge," as she'd put it. Ma Gallo had instantly nicknamed the baby Gigi, and it had spiraled from there.

"So, how did you get him to say yes?" Izzy asked Suzy.

Suzy swirled her daiquiri, holding it between her fingers. "I just said please," she replied, her cheeks turning pink as she giggled.

"That's bullshit," Mia blurted out, tossing her head back with a hearty laugh.

"Joe doesn't give in that easily, Suzy. How did you really do it?" Izzy asked, looking at Suzy with a raised eyebrow.

She bit her lip, a smile slowly spreading across her face as her cheeks grew almost rosy. "I told him if he ever wanted to have sex with me again, I wanted a night out with my girls."

"You floozy. You know that was a crock of shit," Izzy spat out, shaking her head.

"I know, but it freaking worked. I wanted to see you girls, so I had to pull out the big guns and pumped enough breast milk to feed a small army."

"Well, thank shit for small miracles," Mia said, bringing her martini to her lips and taking a tiny sip.

"What's more amazing is that the guys agreed to go over and help him with the baby," I added, laughing as I pictured them again staring at the baby like a foreign object. "Do they even know what to do with a baby girl?"

The table erupted in giggles before Izzy spoke. "They helped raise me, so I'm sure they have some idea."

"Yeah," Suzy said, putting the straw in her mouth as she talked around it. "He's so protective of her. He's not afraid of taking care of her, but damn, he's so crazy about Gigi. I never thought I'd see the man amount to a pile of gushy love like I have seen him over our daughter."

Mia coughed, choking on her martini. "Are you jealous, Suz?" The diamond on her finger momentarily blinded me as it sparkled in the light.

"Nah. It makes me happy. I needed out of babyland for a night. I've missed you girls."

"Babe, we've been over, like, every other day to see you and the baby," Izzy said, holding up her hand and calling over the waitress.

"It's not the same. I needed one-on-one time with you ladies. No baby, no Joe—just us."

Izzy pointed to the table, looking up at the waitress. "Another round, please."

The waitress nodded and headed off toward the bar.

"I'm going to be drunk if I have another," Suzy whined, sucking down the last bit of her drink until she was slurping air.

"You can use a drunken night. I'm sure Joe will thank me." Izzy winked at Suzy.

"He didn't last time." Suzy laughed, slapping the table and snorting. Then she sobered, turning her attention toward me. "So, Angel, how's it over there at Casa Badass?"

I almost spat out my drink as I sipped the last of my martini. Then I set down my glass, wiped the vodka off my face, and smiled. "It's going really well."

"Tommy is so damn sexy," Suzy said before hiccupping.

"All right, tiger. You're cut off," Mia said, pulling the glass away from her as soon as the waitress set down the drinks.

"My hormones are a hot mess. I can appreciate the beauty of man. There's no one like my Joe, though. He's it for me."

"Good answer," Izzy said, giggling as she pushed the drink back in front of Suzy. "Keep drinking."

"When's the date, Mia?" I asked, changing the subject.

"We haven't set one yet. I waited forever for him to ask. I'm happy knowing it'll happen."

"You know Ma isn't going to let you two be engaged forever," Izzy interrupted, a giant smile on her face.

"She's lost in Gigi world for now. Speaking of which, when is your ass going to get engaged, Izzy?"

"I'm not ready for all that. Let me just enjoy the man for now, Mia. I don't need a ring to know he's mine." Izzy toyed with the gold choker around her neck, rubbing the dangling heart locket.

"Did James buy you that beautiful necklace?" I asked, noticing that she'd played with it many times this evening. Stroking it, she caressed the cool metal.

"He did." She nodded, releasing the locket from her fingers and grabbing her drink.

"Is that a collar?" Suzy blurted, moving her face closer to inspect it.

"What the fuck are you talking about, Suzy?" Mia asked, her eyebrows knitting together as she looked at her.

Suzy turned to Mia and smiled. "I read a lot. I'm into

erotic books. It reminds me of some of the BDSM books I read during my pregnancy." Turning her attention back toward Izzy, she asked again, "So, is it a collar?"

Izzy's face flushed as she bit her lip. "I never knew you were such a kinky bitch, Suzy," she replied.

"By the look on your face, I'd say she nailed it," I added, knowing that Izzy was usually truthful. That response had been evasive.

"Like a dog?" Mia asked, rubbing her forehead. "I'm shocked."

Izzy rolled her eyes, blowing out a hard breath. "It's not like a dog, Mia. Jesus. Get out more, woman."

"Then 'splain it to me, sister." Mia lifted her drink, tipping it toward Izzy and taking a sip while waiting for her response.

We stared at Izzy, watching her turn ten shades of pink, before she cleared her throat. She straightened her shoulders, slammed back her drink, and then began to speak.

"James is into the lifestyle."

"I fuckin' knew it. I knew I loved that kinky bastard," Suzy said, her body shaking as she giggled.

"Does Joe know you're into this shit, Suzy?" Izzy asked, still avoiding the topic.

"He does." She nodded, a giant smile spreading across her face. "He reaps all the benefits of my reading. We may not live in the 'lifestyle'"—she used air quotes—"but we do like to role-play."

"Oh, Jesus. Way too much information," Izzy said, blanching and making a gagging gesture.

"You asked." Suzy smiled, taking a sip from her daiquiri.

"I'm waiting," Mia said, tapping the table with her fingernails.

"The necklace," Izzy said, rubbing it again with her fingers, "just means that I'm his. We're committed to each other. No one else can touch me."

"Usually, if there's a collar, then there's a leash somewhere in there too, no?" Mia asked, cocking an eyebrow at Izzy.

"God, this isn't what I wanted to talk about tonight," Izzy groaned.

"There's nothing better to talk about. I don't want to talk about shitty diapers. Spill the goods, Izzy. We want the dirt," Mia demanded, leaning forward and waiting for the details.

I laughed, throwing my head back as they spoke. This was the sisterhood I'd always wanted as a child. I would've been happy with just one, but now, I had three. They were kickass, obnoxious, funny as hell, and loyal to the core. The girls helped make me feel like I was meant to be a part of the family.

There wasn't a day that went by that I didn't thank my lucky stars that I'd caught the eye of Thomas, that I hadn't gone insane during my time with him while he was working in the MC. I'd almost ended things with him, my feelings too much to bear at times as he'd kept me at a distance.

My life wouldn't be the same if I'd let my head lead instead of following my heart. Thomas was the most amazing thing to have happened to me in my life. For once, I felt like I had a home. I had a purpose. I had a reason to live. Life no longer was just about surviving—it was about enjoying the little things. The kisses, the laughs, the family dinners, and the love of a good man were all I needed to make it through each day.

I was thankful for the future and grateful for my past, knowing that, without it, I wouldn't have been sitting there in that moment, enjoying an evening with my girls and then going back home to my man.

…Continue the Gallo Family Saga with Without Me, Anthony Gallo's story. Please visit *menofinked.com/without-me* for more information or *menofinked.com/inked-se* to grab the next special edition paperback.

Want a signed copy for your bookshelf?
Visit *chelleblissromance.com* to learn more.

ABOUT THE AUTHOR

I'm a full-time writer, time-waster extraordinaire, social media addict, coffee fiend, and ex-history teacher. *To learn more about my books, please visit menofinked.com.*

Want to stay up-to-date on the newest Men of Inked release and more? Join my newsletter.

Join over 10,000 readers on Facebook in Chelle Bliss Books private reader group and talk books and all things reading. Come be part of the family!

See the Gallo Family Tree

Where to Follow Me:

facebook.com/authorchellebliss1

instagram.com/authorchellebliss

bookbub.com/authors/chelle-bliss

goodreads.com/chellebliss

amazon.com/author/chellebliss

x.com/ChelleBliss1

pinterest.com/chellebliss10

MENOFINKED.COM

MEN OF INKED SERIES

"One of the sexiest series of all-time" -Bookbub Reviewers
Download book 1 for FREE!

- Book 1 - Throttle Me (Joe aka City)
- Book 2 - Hook Me (Mike)
- Book 3 - Resist Me (Izzy)
- Book 4 - Uncover Me (Thomas)
- Book 5 - Without Me (Anthony)
- Book 6 - Honor Me (City)
- Book 7 - Worship Me (Izzy)

MEN OF INKED: SOUTHSIDE SERIES

Join the Chicago Gallo Family with their strong alphas, sassy
women, and tons of fun.

- Book 1 - Maneuver (Lucio)
- Book 2 - Flow (Daphne)
- Book 3 - Hook (Angelo)
- Book 4 - Hustle (Vinnie)
- Book 5 - Love (Angelo)

MEN OF INKED: HEATWAVE SERIES

Same Family. New Generation.

- Book 1 - Flame (Gigi)
- Book 2 - Burn (Gigi)
- Book 3 - Wildfire (Tamara)
- Book 4 - Blaze (Lily)
- Book 5 - Ignite (Tamara)
- Book 6 - Spark (Nick)
- Book 7 - Ember (Rocco)
- Book 8 - Singe - (Carmello)
- Book 9 - Ashes - (Rosie)
- Book 10 - Scorch - (Luna)

THE OPEN ROAD SERIES

Wickedly hot alphas with tons of heart pounding suspense!

- Book 1 - Broken Sparrow (Morris)
- Book 2 - Broken Dove (Leo)
- Book 3 - Broken Wings (Crow)

ALFA INVESTIGATIONS SERIES

Wickedly hot alphas with tons of heart pounding suspense!

- Book 1 - Sinful Intent (Morgan)
- Book 2 - Unlawful Desire (Frisco)
- Book 3 - Wicked Impulse (Bear)
- Book 4 - Guilty Sin (Ret)

SINGLE READS

- Mend
- Enshrine
- Misadventures of a City Girl

- Misadventures with a Speed Demon
- Rebound (Flash aka Sam)
- Top Bottom Switch (Ret)
- Santa Baby
- Fearless - (Austin Moore)

View Chelle's entire collection of books at menofinked.com/books

To learn more about Chelle's books visit *menofinked.com* or *chellebliss.com*